The Cure of Silver Cañon

Center Point
Large Print

Also by Max Brand® and available from
Center Point Large Print:

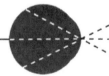

**This Large Print Book carries the
Seal of Approval of N.A.V.H.**

The Cure of
Silver Cañon

MAX BRAND®

CENTER POINT LARGE PRINT
THORNDIKE, MAINE

A Circle Ⓥ Western published by
Center Point Large Print in the year 2016 in
co-operation with Golden West Literary Agency.

February 2016
First Edition

The name Max Brand® is a registered trademark with the United States Patent and Trademark Office and cannot be used for any purpose without express written permission.

The text of this Large Print edition is unabridged.
In other aspects, this book may vary
from the original edition.
Printed in the United States of America on permanent paper.
Set in 16-point Times New Roman type.

ISBN: 978-1-62899-874-0

Library of Congress Cataloging-in-Publication Data

Brand, Max, 1892-1944.
  [Short stories. Selections]
  The cure of silver cañon : a Circle V western / Max Brand. -- First edition.
      pages cm
  Summary: "In three western stories, men risk their hero status in the community in order for truth to prevail"-- Provided by publisher.
  ISBN 978-1-62899-874-0 (hardcover : alk. paper) 1. Large type books.
   I. Brand, Max, 1892-1944. Señor Coyote.
   II. Brand, Max, 1892-1944. Power of Prayer.
   III. Brand, Max, 1892-1944. Cure of Silver Cañon. IV. Title.
PS3511.A87A6 2016
813'.52--dc23
                                                      2015029633

Acknowledgments

"*Señor* Coyote" by Max Brand first appeared as a two-part serial in *Argosy* (6/18/38–6/25/38). Copyright © 1938 by Frank Munsey Company. Copyright © renewed 1966 by Jane Faust Easton, John Frederick Faust, and Judith Faust. Copyright © 1996 under the title "Slip Liddell" by Jane Faust Easton and Adriana Faust Bianchi. Copyright © 2016 by Golden West Literary Agency for restored material.

"The Power of Prayer" by John Frederick first appeared in Street & Smith's *Western Story Magazine* (12/23/22). Copyright © 1922 by Street & Smith Publications, Inc. Copyright © renewed 1950 by Dorothy Faust. Copyright © 1996 under the title "The Power of Prayer" by Jane Faust Easton and Adriana Faust Bianchi. Copyright © 2016 by Golden West Literary Agency for restored material. Acknowledgment is made to Condé Nast Publications, Inc., for their co-operation.

"The Cure of Silver Cañon" by John Frederick first appeared in Street & Smith's *Western Story Magazine* (1/15/21). Copyright © 1920 by Street & Smith Publications, Inc. Copyright © renewed 1948 by Dorothy Faust. Acknowledgment is

Table of Contents

Señor Coyote

"*Señor* Coyote" was first published under Frederick Faust's pen name John Frederick in two installments in *Argosy* (6/18/38–6/25/38). It was the last Western short novel Faust wrote. It was fitting that the story was published in *Argosy* since Faust's earliest Western fiction had been sold to *All-Story Weekly* and *The Argosy* owned by The Frank A. Munsey Company, which merged the two magazines in 7/24/20. In this story, Frank Pollard, a small-time rancher down on his luck and owing the bank $500, looks to his legendary friend, Slip Liddell, to give him the money before the banker, Foster, forecloses on his ranch. Liddell refuses to pay Foster even for his friend. Pollard threatens to do something about it, and then the bank is robbed and Foster shot. Will Liddell help when his friend is accused of the crime?

I

At noon Pollard owed the bank of Henry P. Foster $500, but he owed it with a smile. That night Pollard had lost his smile, the bank had lost a lot of money, and Henry P. Foster had lost his life.

In the beginning, it was that confident smile of Pollard's that surprised his friends. They sat in with him at the Royal Saloon and drank the beers he bought for them with his last dollars. The Royal is a comfortable place with ponderous old adobe walls that shut out the heat. The shadows that gather inside it are so thick that even the swing-door cannot let in shafts of light that penetrate to the heart of the place.

It is one huge room, with a bar that runs most of the length of one wall. To the rear are tables covered with green baize for the poker games. Other, smaller tables string along through the room, leaving plenty of open space for the standees at the bar. Behind the bar stands Chuck Sladin, with a signed photograph of Robert Fitzimmons hanging above the mirror, and his revolver, as everyone knows, lying on the shelf before him.

Age has turned Sladin the color of stone and gathered the sunburn of his youth into a few blotchy freckles, but he still looks alert and aloof.

He gave most of his attention now to the table where Pollard sat with Soapy Jones, Mark Heath, and Pudge McArthur. Soapy and Pudge had blunt, rubbery faces that would have been useful in a prize ring, but Mark Heath was young and straight and big and handsome enough to be any girl's hero.

Pudge McArthur kept saying, between drinks: "What's the main idea? Five hundred isn't much, but it's enough to let old Foster squeeze you out of your place. It's not the biggest place in the world, but you'll be damned lonely without that corral to stir up dust in. So what's the idea of that big grin?"

"I told old Foster to come up here and get his money at noon," said Pollard. He stopped smiling and laughed a little. "The money'll be here, all right. Listen to that banjo going by. I'll bet that's Tom Patchen. He's the banjo-pingingest feller I ever heard. Push the door open and see is it Tom?"

Somebody pushed the door open, but the banjo player was out of sight. All they could see were the colored streamers that fluttered across the street, because San Jacinto was having a fiesta and when San Jacinto has a fiesta it dolls up right to the guards, because the people down there are fond of their town and they like to dress it up. Any other town that far west would have called the show a rodeo, but San Jacinto called it a fiesta.

That town felt different and it acted different

because it felt that it *was* different. As a matter of fact the waterlily pads down there in the San Jacinto River are as big as the top of your table, and the flowers are bigger than your head, and the cypresses along the banks go slamming up into the air like thunderheads in the sky. San Jacinto is mostly adobe, weakening at the knees but looking patient enough to stand there a couple more centuries. It has a big plaza with palm trees in the center and a white-faced church with a bell tower, and you can't tell whether you're in Old Mexico or New. There are eight and a half Mexicans for every American and eight of the Mexicans go around in sandals and home-made straw hats unraveling at the brim, with cornhusks stuck inside the band for cigarette papers and a twist of tobacco for the makings.

San Jacinto *is* different, and the men inside the saloon enjoyed that difference while the door was open because, although the fiesta did not open up for a day or two, the people of the town already were tuning up for the show and you could hear guitars and banjoes thwanging and mandolins trembling all over the place.

When the door closed, Soapy Jones, who was helping to spend Pollard's last dollars, said: "Loosen up, Frank, and tell us where that money is going to walk in from?"

Mark Heath said: "*We* ought to find that money for Frank."

"Easy, easy," cautioned Pollard. "No good guy ever has any money in his pocket."

This Pollard had a funny, good-natured face with a big Adam's apple pushed out in front of his throat and a kink in the back of his neck to match it. You could trail him for a year and never see him take a quick step—or hear him speak a quick word, or a mean one.

"The whole of San Jacinto is gonna feel sick if you get frozen out o' your place," Heath went on. "How much would I get for that Jasper of mine, that old cutting horse? How much you think, Pudge?"

"That Jasper looks kind of bad in the knees," answered Pudge.

"He can stand up to the whole branding season with any man's bronco."

"Yeah, but looks is looks."

"There ain't anybody going to sell his horse for me," put in Pollard, "because there ain't nobody needs to."

The others looked at him with affectionate concern. He took a drink and licked the beer froth off the edge of his lip. Then he said: "Is Slip Liddell good for five hundred bucks?"

"Hey! You know Slip Liddell?" exclaimed Heath. Because he was younger than the others this news was more exciting to him.

"Kind of," said Pollard. He rubbed his red chin-stubble with the back of his hand and chuckled a bit self-consciously. "I kind of know him, all right," he admitted.

"Is Slip Liddell coming here?" asked Heath.

"Right at noon, *pronto*," answered Pollard.

"That'll raise a crowd," Heath remarked, and pushed back his chair.

"You sit right still and keep it to yourself," cautioned Pollard. "Liddell sure hates a crowd."

"That's how he got his name, the way he can slip through a crowd," suggested Soapy Jones.

"No, no. He got that name from the way he can slip the cards when he's dealing blackjack," objected Pudge McArthur.

"That's wrong," said Mark Heath. "When he was a kid, he wasn't as big as he grew afterward and they called him a slip of a kid."

"A slip of dynamite, you mean," Soapy commented, and with his fat lips he sneered enormously and pushed his sombrero back on his head and scratched his bald spot.

"How come you and Slip are such friends?" asked Heath.

"Well, it was back there when he wasn't known so good, when he was doing a tramp royal around the world and driving the shacks crazy on every railroad from Mexico City to Juneau. He'd just begun to play cards and work out systems for roulette and faro and all that, and I saw him in that joint over there in Tucson . . . Matty White's place. This kid Slip . . . he wasn't any more than a kid, then . . . he steps up and cracks the roulette and he gets rolled for about fifteen hundred bucks and looks sort of bewildered. Then he kicks the croupier in the shins and turns over a couple of tables and breaks off the roulette wheel right at the floor. When he did that, you could see the apparatus under the boards. There was a brake, all right.

"A ruction started. Slip Liddell reached into the cash box and took a handful of money, but when he started to leave, there was a lot of trouble. Some of the *hombres* hanging around Matty's place were hot stuff in those days. So I made a noise and a bit of trouble by the front entrance and I drew a bit of attention from the strong-arm boys, and the result was that Slip and me both got away. Without more than a few bumps we got away."

"I know Matty's place," observed Soapy Jones. "Lucky you both didn't die young."

"If I knew Slip that good," said Pudge dreamily, "I wouldn't trade it for five thousand in spot cash."

"Sure," agreed Pollard, "and I've never touched him before today."

"Here's your banker," said Soapy.

Banker Henry P. Foster walked through the swing-door and stood at the bar, resting an important hand on the edge of it. He filled a whiskey glass right to the brim, raised it with a sure hand, tasted it to make sure what he was getting, and poured it down his throat. After that he lit a cigar, gathered it back in a big pucker in the corner of his mouth, and looked around the room. When he saw the men at the table, he gave one nod to all of them. He said in his sharp, clear voice: "Well, Pollard?"

"It ain't noon yet," said Pollard. He added, under his breath: "The old beagle."

He had no particular hatred for beagles. He hardly knew what they were. The word simply came to him.

"Suppose that Slip Liddell didn't come?" suggested Pudge McArthur.

"He never disappoints you," Pollard answered, growing nervous.

"Suppose he comes but don't have that much money?" said Mark Heath.

"Yeah, and whoever heard of him not having that much?" asked Pollard.

"There was the time he was down in Mexico and they slammed him into the hoosegow," began young Mark Heath.

"Yeah, that was a lot of baloney," said Soapy Jones.

Then a tall young man pushed open the door with his left hand and stepped inside. He stepped quickly out of the brilliance of the doorway and into the shadow of the wall.

"By Satan . . . it *is* Slip," whispered Mark Heath.

17

II

The cut of him was like the cut of fifty thousand other cowhands and yet there was a difference that stopped the eye. Mark Heath put it in a second whisper as he stared, saying: "Look at how he's set up like nobody's business."

He was not as big and as strong as he appeared to the excited eye of young Mark Heath, but there was plenty of him at that. You've seen his like in the picture of a football team. He was what is called a good-looking mug. There was nothing beautiful about him. He was just a mug. But if he came into your house, your wife and daughter would begin being foolish right away. He always wore a faint smile as though he had seen something pleasant and was still enjoying it.

As he came on across the room, it was plain that he had ridden those chaps through a lot of scratchy brush but somehow he didn't look as though he had wrangled many horses or roped many cows recently. And as a matter of fact he had not. Except when he changed location, the toughest work he did was wrangling a pack of cards. The reason he wore that single mark of deep thought between the eyes was that he never played suckers. He preferred professionals, perhaps because he had scruples about taking the money of the innocents, but even more because the professionals carried more hard cash in their wallets and would put it on the line.

Pollard was so glad to see him that he strode across the room and grasped his hand and started steering him toward the bar. Jimmy Liddell would not have that. He said: "But I want to meet your friends, Frank."

That pleased the men at the table. It pleased Mark Heath particularly. He gave Liddell's hand a tremendous grasp when it came his turn. Afterward, Liddell moved the fingers of his right hand one by one and made a pretended face of pain. "Your friends are too strong, Frank," he said, but he smiled at Heath and wrinkled his nose in a most friendly way. Then he ordered drinks. He was not loud about it, but suddenly it became almost rude for anyone else to order a drink.

Pollard could hold in no longer. He broke out: "Slip, I've got to have five hundred dollars."

"Now?" asked Jimmy Liddell.

"Yeah. Right this minute," said Pollard.

"All right." Liddell nodded, and reached into the inside pocket of his coat. Pollard lay back in his chair and looked around him triumphantly.

The other men wore constrained smiles. They were wishing that they could have a chance to do a thing like that but they were wondering if they could be so free.

Pollard stood up as Liddell, under the shelter of his expert hands, counted out bills.

"I'm gonna lay it on the bar right under his nose and then I'm gonna tell him to go to blazes and how to get there," said Pollard. "The blasted old shark-skin, I'm gonna tell him what I think."

"Tell who?" asked Liddell, lifting his head.

"That square-faced old son-of-a-bitch at the bar. Look at him," said Pollard.

"I saw him when I came in," answered Liddell, without turning, and put the money back in his billfold, and the leather fold back in his pocket.

"What's the matter?" asked Pollard.

"I have five hundred for you, not for your chum over there," answered Liddell.

"Yeah, but listen . . . Slip, I owe him the money . . . he'll foreclose on me," explained Pollard.

He was a big, bony man as he bent over, arguing with both hands. Making everything clear with the flat of his palms, he seemed to have an extra joint in the middle of his back. Liddell studied him with clear, undisturbed eyes.

Pollard broke out into a sweat. "It's my house and my land, Slip!" he pleaded suddenly. "It's . . . it's everything. I got a hundred acres. I got a mule I harness up with my horse and plow the bottom land by the creek. I got some cows. I got a white man's chance the first time in my life."

"I told you a year ago that you were a cow-puncher, not a rancher," said Liddell. "You've lost five hundred in a year. You'd lose five hundred more the next year."

The other men leaned forward in their chairs, shifting their glances from face to face, hungry. This was news. This was a story for anybody. Their sympathy was for Pollard, and with angry bewilderment they eyed Slip Liddell.

Pollard said: "I had a flock of bad luck. You don't understand. I had three of the fattest steers you ever saw, and when that blizzard came in January, they drifted against the fence line and there they were in the morning. You don't understand, Slip."

His voice was hoarse.

"Yeah, I understand," answered Liddell. "Sit down and have a drink."

Pollard sat down, and just then big Henry P. Foster said loudly: "Well, Pollard? It's past noon, you know."

He was smiling a little as he spoke. There was even a sort of smile in his voice and you could tell how glad he was. Pollard only stared at him and then tossed off his drink.

"I'll send my men up in the morning," said Foster. "Just see that nothing is removed."

Pollard jumped up. He shouted out: "You're worse than a coyote! You're worse than a buzzard! You eat rottener meat!"

Foster turned a varnished crimson. He turned from the bar and came at Pollard like a real

21

fighting man, but then his eyes fell on Liddell and he stopped. He kept looking at Liddell as he made a backward step or two, and then went suddenly out of the swing-door into the street.

"It's fun for him," said Pollard. "Putting me out of my house is fun for him. I hope he burns and the money in his pockets. I hope he dies and is damned. I'd like to have the finishing of him."

Liddell said: "You mean some of that for me, don't you?"

Pollard fell wearily into his chair. His head dropped back and he looked sick.

"It was a swell sort of a little dump," he said. "I had a lot of swell times in it. I'd rather hear its windmill clanking and the water going plump into the tank than any other music that I ever heard. I'd rather be buried under those cotton-woods than in a churchyard."

Mark Heath remarked: "There oughta be something done about a buzzard like Henry P. Foster. Somebody oughta take him up in a big way."

That was when Pollard said what everybody remembered afterward. He said: "Yeah, I'm a poor sap. I only talk. I don't *do* anything about it. But I gotta mind. . . ."

Up to about 3:30 p.m. you always can get a check cashed in the First National at San Jacinto. The closing hour is 3:00 but there is half an hour of leeway and a lot of people are sure to come in at

22

the last minute. It makes them feel that they are being favored. As a matter of fact there were four clients near the cash window at 3:20 that afternoon when a tall man, masked to the eyes, came in with a pair of Colt revolvers and held up the place.

The cashier was a fellow named Clement Stevenson with a big reputation. He was in that Perrytown bank in 1927 when Sam Candy and his gang stuck up the place. Clem Stevenson pulled a gun and fought it out with them. They shot the legs out from under him and he still fought from the floor until Candy and his men had enough and lammed. With a hero like that inside the cage of Foster's bank, you would have thought that no robber could do a thing, single-handed, but as a matter of fact poor Stevenson simply put up his hands and begged the hold-up man not to shoot. Perhaps all the red had run out of his blood back there in Perrytown.

He was not a very experienced robber, or else he was a bit nervous. He could have had what was in the safe, which ran up to more than $18,000, but, instead, he took only what was in the cashier's cash drawer. Afterward, rumor fixed the loss at only $2,700. He took this with the heel of his left hand, without putting up his second gun, and pushed it down into a coat pocket just as Henry P. Foster came out of his office with a double-barreled riot-gun in his hands. The robber beat him to it with a comfortable fifth of a second. He put one bullet under Foster's collarbone and a second one right between his eyes.

Then he ran out and swung onto the back of a gray horse at the curb and galloped away around the first corner. People wandered around in confusion. They talked a considerable bit about outrages and the dilatory law. After a couple of hours somebody remembered the gray mustang that belonged to Frank Pollard, whose place was off on the edge of town.

That was enough to start them off. The sheriff didn't need to ask for volunteers. As a matter of fact the whole town wanted to be in on the show; fifty of the boys went out with Sheriff Chris Tolliver.

Pollard's shack stood on the edge of a deep gully, a big draw where the water ran with a rush in the spring flood time. The boys surrounded the other three sides of the cabin while the sheriff and a couple more went up to the front door. Perhaps Chris Tolliver made a mistake in saying why he had come. At any rate the first thing they knew there was a crash down the side of the gorge through the bushes.

They got there too late.

Frank Pollard had jumped right out through a window. He should have broken his neck, but the bushes broke his fall. He legged it down the windings of the draw into the dusk, and, while the posse scattered and pursued and shouted and fired a lot of shots at shadows, only a few of them saw Pollard gallop away on a gray horse into the willows down by the creek.

They spent two days searching the willows but they never found Frank Pollard. It made a good-size bit of talking. A lot of people were glad that the banker was no longer with them but on the whole it was considered a slap at the reputation of San Jacinto and a black eye for the old town at the very moment when the fiesta was about to begin.

The bank itself offered $1,000 as a reward, and then some of the heartier merchants and ranchers around San Jacinto got together in town and built that reward clear up to $5,000.

About three hundred of the lads went right out on the man trail. But along came a sandstorm the very next evening and swept the entire crowd back into town with red eyes. And when the next morning came, there was the opening of the fiesta and all that to think about so that hardly a single manhunter remained on the trail that afternoon. Nearly everybody was out on the fiesta grounds when Liddell rode into town with Pollard's gray mustang on a lead and went to the sheriff's office.

That office is in one of the few San Jacinto buildings that is not of adobe. It is a small frame shack that started out as a school, turned into a grocery store, and wound up in the hands of the sheriff.

Liddell went up the steps and walked into the big, echoing, single room. It offered merely the imaginary privacy of corners for the clerk and the two deputies. Only the clerk was there with the sheriff on this day, and the sheriff was standing at the window looking out at the street.

This fellow, Sheriff Chris Tolliver, had that winey, sallow, sour Italian look about him, with plenty of end to his nose, bulge to his eyes, and pout to his lips. He had one of the biggest mouths you ever saw and the middle of the lower lip was always cracking to the raw so that it was a painful thing to see him smoke a cigar.

He turned now and said: "I see you found Pollard's horse."

Liddell nodded. He went over to the sheriff's desk. The clerk was standing up, looking rather frightened.

Liddell took out a pair of spurs and laid them on the desk. They were expensive spurs, gold-plated except for the rowel that stood out at the end of a long spoon-handle curve.

"Kind of pretty," remarked the sheriff.

"Pollard thought so," stated the clerk.

"Did those belong to Pollard?" asked Sheriff Tolliver.

The clerk answered again, saying: "They sure did. I remember them fine."

Liddell laid an old-fashioned single-action Colt on the desk, and then he paused to wink his eyes and dab at them with a fingertip. He must have been through the thick of the sandstorm. The whites of his eyes were pink and he could not see very well.

"Here's the initials carved into the butt," observed the sheriff. "Did this belong to Pollard, too? I thought you were his friend."

"Did you?" asked Liddell.

Some heavy footfalls came up the steps and across the porch where Liddell was squinting the water out of his eyes. The door was nudged open.

"Hey, look!" shouted the clerk.

The golden-bay head of a horse was looking in through the doorway.

"Is that your mare?" asked the sheriff. "Tell her to come on in."

"She's just a young fool," Liddell said with disgust. "Come on in, Sis, while you're about it."

She came in. The floor was old and had a slant to it. Sis did not trust the creaking of the boards. She studied them with a lowered head, sniffing. She picked her hoofs up and put them down with intelligent care, like a good mountain horse.

"And shut the door behind you," said Liddell, still with a face of disgust. "Where were you raised, anyway? In a barn?"

She turned, taking delicate care of her footing, and with a swing of her head she shut the door.

Then she came to Liddell. When she reached him, she uttered a little whinny, no louder than a man's chuckle.

"She's spoiled," said Liddell. "No mare has as much sense as a horse, and this is just a young fool that's been spoiled."

"I can see that," said the sheriff.

His clerk made a step or two away from his desk, grinning enormously with joy.

"Back up!" commanded Liddell.

The mare backed up half a step. She stretched out her neck and nibbled at the rim of Liddell's hat.

"Quit it," said Liddell.

She quit it and tossed her head high in the air as though he had struck at her with his hand.

"She's spoiled a hat or two for me already," said Liddell. "I'm trying to get rid of her but nobody wants her."

"Maybe not," agreed the sheriff. "Not at your price, maybe they don't. If there was an inch more on her legs, she'd be a thoroughbred."

"She has the inch more on her legs," answered Liddell.

He took a wallet out of his inside coat pocket and laid it on the desk. There was a thick wad of bills in it and through the lower part of the wallet and the bills drove a half-inch hole, or nearly half an inch.

The clerk swore.

He had the seen the blood on one side of the wallet that glued the greenbacks together. There was plenty of the dark stain on the yellow of the pigskin. The sheriff picked up the wallet.

"You aim to say that this is Pollard's wallet?"

Liddell said nothing. The sheriff opened the flap of the wallet and began to count the money inside, flipping the corners of the bills without withdrawing them. "There's twenty-seven hundred and fifteen dollars in here."

"That's what Pollard stole from the bank, isn't it?" asked Liddell.

"That's what the bank was saying yesterday," agreed the sheriff. He took out a cigar and bit the end off it. He stuck out his tongue and moistened the ragged end of the cigar. Then he lit his smoke while Liddell watched the crack in the middle of the lower lip.

"Where's the body?"

"In the San Jacinto," said Liddell.

"How come?" asked Tolliver, looking at Liddell with his tired, bulging, sour-wine eyes.

"I came up with him at the mouth of the cañon," answered Liddell. "After he dropped, I thought it was too bad to leave him out there for the coyotes . . . and the flies. The river was jumping and yelling its head off. I just rolled him down the slope."

"It was a fool thing to do."

"Why? He used to be a friend of mine."

The clerk made a face like he had swallowed acid.

"A friend of yours . . . an old friend, wasn't he?" asked the sheriff, studying Liddell. He licked the crack in his lip and waited.

"There's a five thousand dollar reward offered for Pollard," remarked Liddell without the slightest emotion. "I'll take that along with me."

"Maybe you will"—Tolliver nodded—"but just wait till I look the thing over, will you? The people that are putting up the cash will want to be sure that Pollard is dead. The bank will want to be sure, too."

"The bank won't care, so long as it gets its money back," stated Liddell, "and the rest of the people will take your word. Are you going to give it?"

The sheriff said: "Don't get tough with me, Slip."

Liddell answered, smiling: "I never get tough with anybody."

The sheriff said: "All right. Only don't ever think that you can get tough with me. You can't get away with it."

Liddell was smoking a cigarette. He took a puff of the smoke in his hand and threw it gently toward the sheriff, still smiling. The smoke made a dim streak in the air to mark the gesture.

"Old Tolliver," said the mild voice of Liddell. Then he walked out of the office. The mare followed him. She went down the front steps gingerly and on the street below she cut a caper or two as though she were glad to be out of there.

The sheriff shut the door. He took out a handkerchief and scrubbed a sudden sweat from his face. He said to his clerk: "I thought for a minute the hellion was going to be tough with me."

The clerk, who was watching with a sick smile, answered: "Yeah, so did I."

III

Out there in the street, staring at Pollard's gray mustang and looking white around the gills, was young Mark Heath. He looked at Liddell with eyes that kept on seeing trouble.

"Has he come in and given himself up?" asked Heath. "Is he in there?"

"Who, Pollard? He's dead," answered Liddell.

"Dead?" Heath gasped.

He caught hold of a stirrup leather and leaned against the gray old mustang, and the mustang leaned back a little.

"Did you like him a lot?" Liddell wanted to know.

"He was swell to me," said Heath. "He was swell to everybody, but he was fine to me. Did he have the bank's money on him?"

"Yeah. Twenty-seven hundred dollars."

"Twenty-seven hundred. . . ."

"That's just what the bank missed."

"Sure. Sure. That's right," agreed Heath. "Only it seemed like a pile of cash for poor old Frank Pollard to get all at once. He was a kind old boy, all right." He half closed his eyes and took a couple of deep breaths.

Liddell said: "You're a good fellow, Heath. I like you. I believe in you. That's why I'm sorry to tell you that I was the one who killed Frank Pollard."

He went off down the street and left Heath stunned behind him.

The mare followed Liddell. Now and then she pretended to be afraid of the flapping of the pennants and streamers that decorated the street, and, breaking into a gallop, she went a jump or two beyond her master and then turned and waited for his comments. He said: "You're silly. You're silly, is all you are." But she did not seem to mind these remarks.

From the far side of the town automobile horns honked and there was a rapid muttering of hoof beats as the people came back from the races. The thirsty ones were traveling the fastest, but everybody was pretty thirsty. And there were ten horses to one automobile.

The way San Jacinto lies with only a bit of flat laid down in a junk heap of mountains, not much of 1938 can leak into the atmosphere. The only direction you can use an automobile is right up and down the river windings but, if you travel toward any other points to the compass, a horse is better and a mule is best. That is why San Jacinto keeps its flavor like an old story that children love.

When there are two thousand more added to its population one of the big airlines intends to make it a stopping point so that air tourists can get a glimpse of the old color, but probably San Jacinto never will add the needed two thousand. It goes on living on sheep and goats and cattle and mules and burros and that sort of thing, although the Mexicans raise some good crops on the irrigated flats below the town. So when the population came in from the races at the fairgrounds, most of it was aboard mustangs; they were what made the rapid drumming to which Liddell listened as he passed on through the town.

It was hard for him to believe that he was escaping all notice, and now, in fact, he discovered a pair of people on saddle mules, following behind him, kicking their short-stepping animals into a trot to keep up with him. One of the two was an old man with a humped-over back and a gray spade of a beard and a long face, pulled out far in front. The other was a raggle-taggle youngster in blue jeans and a cap. It seemed apparent that they had recognized him but he turned out of the main avenue before they could overtake him.

The streets of San Jacinto wind about as though they were laid out by the maundering leisure of grazing cows. They are narrow streets. In some of them two riders hardly can pass without touching stirrups. Liddell turned down one of the darkest of these alleys until he came to the shop of a silver-smith that had a window full of silver wheelwork and other intricate spider webs of metal. There was even cloth of silver and gold woven by the wife of the smith.

Liddell went into the shop and saw in a corner among the shadows the immobile figure of the silversmith's wife. She was a pyramidal creature, declining upward from large hips to narrower shoulders that supported a head without the column of a visible neck. She wore a mustache of formidable black hairs. Her complexion was that of an old chamois that has been used for years to polish automobiles. Everything about her was gross, heavy, and static except her hands that seemed to have been kept delicate by the nature of her work. Her fingers were aflash with rings and she gestured a great deal when she talked.

Liddell said: "Juanita, I am very tired. Show me where I may sleep."

"Armando!" called Juanita. No emotion could struggle through the fat of her face, but her voice went up a half octave with each word and her shoulders hunched as she repeated: "Armando! Armando!"

Armando Pinelli rushed out of the inner shop. He wore a leather apron and glasses. He was no bigger than a wasp, a dingy wasp that tunnels in the earth. When he saw Liddell, he threw up both hands and cried out: "Saint Anne . . . Saint Mary of God . . . it is the *señor*!"

Juanita said: "Take him to the rear room where he can sleep. His eyes are sick, so call Dolores to put something on them. He is very tired, so hurry."

Armando Pinelli was all voice and hands as he led Liddell out of the shop through the cramped little courtyard where the paving stones were always as damp as winter, and so into the shed where a mule stood in a dark stall. They put Cicely, the bay mare, in the adjoining stall, and Pinelli took his guest across the court and into the house again. He was about to climb the stairs, but Liddell said: "A downstairs room, Armando. Any place will do. But the idiot mare gets lonely and has to have a look at me from time to time. Otherwise she grows nervous."

Armando was distressed. There was no place on the first floor worthy of a dog's kennel, he said. He had no choice but to show Liddell into a little room whose low, unshaded window opened on the court. There was a washstand in a corner and a ledgeless box spring laid on the floor against the inner wall. Liddell groaned at the sight of it and fell flat. The springs creaked up and down under his weight.

Armando, at the door, shouted: "Dolores! Dolores!" When he had no answer, he named two or three saints with a good deal of violence and shouted again. But it was not until three or four outbursts followed by the bringing in the name of St. Christopher, the patron of travelers, that a casual step came down the stairs. Her hands were raised to her hair, and at the same time, with a girl's multiplicity of mind, she was arranging a lovely mantilla of black lace.

"Idiot," said her father. "I haven't asked you to go out on the promenade. Why have you loitered to make yourself fine?"

"Do you think I want to look like an Indian squaw when I see *him?*" she demanded, without being in the least degree perturbed.

"How do you know it is he?" demanded her father with an instant suspicion.

"I heard his voice in the court," she answered. "Besides, for what other person in the world would you be rushing about and shouting?"

"Ha?" said Armando. "Nevertheless, run instantly and get something to wash and comfort his eyes."

"*Dios,*" said Dolores. "Do you mean to say that he can't see me, after all?" But she ran up the stairs again as lightly as a dancer, and when she came down again, she was carrying a bowl of warmed water and cloths. Even with that to bear, she made an important entrance, holding the basin on her fingertips as though it were a precious vase, and crying out: "*Señor* Jimmy! Welcome to San Jacinto!"

He folded back one arm to lift his head and look at her. "I thought that I came here to sleep, but the fact is that all I needed was to see Dolores."

"The poor eyes . . . the poor eyes," murmured Dolores. "Can you see me at all?"

"I can," said Liddell, "from your slippers to the beautiful shawl."

"Mother of heaven!" cried Dolores. "It is a mantilla of the sheerest lace . . . you are blind. My poor little old one."

She sat down beside him on the box spring and began to wash his eyes with a small daub of cloth, uttering tender murmurings.

Armando Pinelli, who was a man of an intensely practical nature, appeared for an instant at the door to say: "That is good, my sweet. Be kind to him, but not *too* kind."

A moment later, Dolores was explaining to Liddell: "My little father has no brains except in his hands and he uses all their wits on his silver. But what a day for me. To see you again when you are more than half blind and when I have on my new fiesta dress!"

"Tell me about it," suggested Liddell. "It's red, isn't it?"

"It is red," she agreed, "with little workings of gold through the pattern so that it shines and shadows in folds as the light runs over it."

"Dolores, it must be as lovely as an altar cloth."

"No, if you are going to open your eyes and stare, stare at me and not at a worthless dress. Now close your poor eyes again, and tell me what you saw. No, don't tell me."

"Why not?" he asked.

"Because you will tell me the truth. And the truth is a terrible thing for a girl. I don't even dare to look into my mirror without smiling and fixing my eyes a certain way and tipping my silly head to one side or the other."

"I'll sing you a song," said Liddell.

"I'll get the mandolin, then," Dolores said.

"No. Give me your hand instead."

"So," murmured the girl. "Ah, my crazy heart. It's doing a dance, *Señor* Jimmy."

He sang one of those old Mexican songs that are hard to translate because there is so many idioms in them. He sang it softly, and the words made a sense somehow like this:

> The waterfall sings night and day
> It throws up its white hands, rejoicing;
> The currents are like wild horses
> But after running a little way they stand
>   still;
> Their windy manes fall down;
> The waters grow as quiet as ice
> Because they wish to take, deeply, an
>   image

Of a tree whose feet are close to the pool.
They take the whole of that slender image
   to the top
And show also the stars toward which it
   is pointing.

When he had ended, the girl still swayed a little with the rhythm of the music. At last she began to bathe the closed eyes once more.

"When you sing . . . ," she said.

"Well?"

"When you sing, it is not a very good voice."

"No. I'm only a campfire howler."

"It is not a very good voice, but it is as though you took my heart in your hands, *Señor* Jimmy."

"Dolores?"

"If my mother were not so big and fat, would you marry me?"

"Dolores!"

"If it were not for that black, horrible mustache, would you marry me?"

"Sweetheart . . . ," said Liddell.

"No," said the girl. "Don't answer. But you can feel with the tips of your fingers that *my* lip is smooth."

She leaned so close that he did not need to use the tips of his fingers.

"Dolores," he said, "you are more to me than . . ."

"Hush," she broke in. "Everything is so beautiful inside me, just now, that one lie would break my heart. Now . . . let the big yawn come . . . and now you are comforted and ready for sleep. Ah, you men . . . there is not much priest in you." She put small wet pads over his eyes and arranged a bandage around them. "When will you be hungry?" she asked.

"When I wake up," answered Liddell.

"When will you wake up?"

"When you leave me," said Liddell.

But as a matter of fact he slept on through the end of the day, through the twilight and the night, and into the crisp chill of the dawn.

IV

At the end of the day there is a change in the Royal Saloon of San Jacinto. During the sunlight hours there rarely are any in the place except Americans, but in the evening Mexicans of the upper classes and even a few *vaqueros* come into the Royal to sit down to a poker game or play the roulette wheel. For the first time during the day, wine appears. Chuck Sladin keeps good French wine in his cellar and he always has a supply of California, red and white; he even can produce champagne for great celebrations. With his grim, tired old eyes, like the eyes of an ancient eagle, he discourages arm waving and loud noises so that the games at the rear of the saloon will not be too annoyed.

In the evening, also, the bar service is enlarged by Mexican waiters in clean whites who go softly about among the tables. An oddity is the way the Mexicans and the Americans keep apart and aloof even when they are rubbing elbows. The Spanish and the English language gather in separate pools; Spanish and English eyes forget one another and seek only faces of the same blood.

The Royal did a good business on this night, with Mark Heath at a table against the wall talking with Pudge McArthur and Soapy Jones. It was 3:00 a.m., the hour when the tongue begins to stumble and repeat itself as alcohol commences to anesthetize the brain. It was the time when maudlin good will enlarges the hearts of the drinkers, unbuttons pocketbooks and mouths, and pours mist into every eye. An inward, spiritual struggle was troubling the soul of Heath. At last he had his chin resting in both hands, his face almost covered by the fingers as he said: "This is what eats me . . . he makes poor old Frank love him, and then he shoots him in the back."

"How do you know he shot Pollard in the back?" asked Pudge, opening his eyes and his mouth to express his astonishment.

"Why else would he have rolled the body down into the river?"

"I don't foller that," Pudge said, shaking his head.

"Listen, dummy," broke in Soapy Jones, who

was the brains of the pair, "if he hadn't shot him through the back, why didn't he leave the body lie and let the sheriff go out and identify his dead man?"

"He says it was because he didn't want the coyotes and the buzzards to get at the body," protested Pudge.

"Sure he says," sneered Heath. "Go on, Soapy, and make it straight for Pudge."

"Look, flathead," pursued Soapy. "He comes up to Frank out there by the San Jacinto and he shakes hands and talks to him, and tells Frank about things, and pretty soon Frank turns his back, and then this Liddell, this Slip Liddell, he sinks a bullet through the back of Frank's head."

"What a skunk this Liddell turned out to be. And me looking up to him all this time like he was something extra," complained Pudge. "Sure, if he shot Frank through the back, he wouldn't want people to see it. He'd have that much shame."

"Yeah, he'd have that much," sighed Heath. "But will I ever have shame enough to do anything about it? Frank was swell to me. He took me in. He loaned me money. He set me up when I was flat. But I let him be murdered, and then I let the murderer walk around and collect blood money for the dirty job."

"It ain't your job to butt in," advised Soapy. "Me and Pudge have known Frank three times as long as you. The question is . . . what should we do about it?"

"Pull a gun and shoot Liddell," suggested Pudge. The violent idea shocked him, and he showed the shock in his eyes. Their chance to develop this theme was interrupted, however.

The same couple who had followed Liddell down the street—the old fellow with the long, pulled-out face and the ragged youngster who accompanied him—had entered the saloon and gone up to the bar. The old fellow carried an accordion under one arm.

"We don't want no free music in here," Chuck Sladin announced sternly. "And how old are you, kid? I don't serve anyone under eighteen."

This brown-faced youngster, obscured by a cap that looked much too big for his head, turned to the old man and said quietly: "Well, Pop?"

"Go ahead. Show 'em how old you are," directed Pop.

In a moment, coat and trousers of blue denim were tossed to Pop. The heavy shoes were kicked off the feet and replaced with dancing slippers. Finally the big cap followed the rest of the outfit, and let a bright bob of hair tumble out around her ears. She had on loose blue trousers and a blue silk shirt and around her middle she wore a red sash that took all the boy out of her and left only woman.

"Yeah, and what is it? A circus turn?"

Old Pop unlimbered the accordion at the same moment. He rocked it into a rippling, crazy, swinging jig time and the girl began a tap dance.

Chuck Sladin leaned over the bar to watch her feet with critical eyes. He was not fool enough to turn a real attraction out of doors, but he wanted no cheap panhandling in his place. It took him a long moment to decide, then he leaned back and began to clap his hands softly together to keep the beat of the music.

She really was good. She had no great weight to shift about and she was as supple as a blacksnake. Besides, she had imagination in her feet.

In the bar that night there were a couple of lads from the Truxton Ranch up in the hills. A radio gave them music on the long winter nights and when the range didn't leave them too tired, they used to knock the frost out of their toes by tap-dancing, and when they heard the clatter of the girl's slippers it was too much for them. They came out with a couple of Indian yells and raised a good rattling thunder on each side of her.

"Go it, Skeeter!" yelled Pop. "Hop onto a table where they can see your feet!"

Instead of that, the Truxton lads pitched her up onto the bar and she began to sway and skip and ripple her feet up and down the bar, her slippers seeing their own way among the glasses and the bottles. Chuck Sladin only made sure that that those light slippers failed to scar his varnish, and then he let the show go on. A thing like that was good for business. The Truxton boys got out of breath, but Skeeter was as tireless as a hawk on the wing.

She was not beautiful. When her face was still, she looked as grim as any boy, but she took care to be smiling and she knew how to let her teeth and her eyes flash. She knew how to put in the old appeal, too, and a hermit would have come right out of his cave to see Skeeter weaving into some of her warmer numbers. And all the while the cool little devil was taking stock of the men in the place and reading the minds of their pocketbooks.

She wound up with a bit that old Pop announced as "Saturday Night". The music for it was only a soft humpty-thumpty on the accordion, but the feet of Skeeter brought a galloping horse right into town, walked a cowpuncher into a drunken party, staggered him through a fight, gave a couple of pistol-shot stamps for his death, and finally followed his body to church the next morning with a demure piety that made even the Mexicans laugh till they cried.

After that, she hopped off the bar and went around with Pop while he passed the hat. When they came to Mark Heath, he put in a $10 bill. The brown claw of Pop tried to close over that tidbit, but the girl's hand flashed in and got the money away. She stuffed it back in Mark's pocket and said: "Thanks, but I don't know you that well."

In spite of that they made a good haul of almost $15 because the men in the place were heeled for fiesta spending. They then went over to a corner table with a couple of tall beers and Pop undid a package of lunch while Skeeter slid back into blue jeans and tucked the brightness of her hair under the big cap again. Nobody bothered her, either, because she had a way of taking an admiring glance out of the air and handing it back well frosted.

Only Mark Heath came over and tried to sit at her table. Old Pop was thinking of that $10 bill and he pulled back a chair, but the girl said to Mark: "Don't you go and try to get yourself dizzy about me, handsome, because *I* am not getting dizzy about anybody these days."

"Will you have a drink on me, then?"

"I won't have that, either," answered Skeeter. "You can't give me anything but love, baby, and I don't want that today."

So Heath went back to his table and people laughed at his lack of success, but the clumsy blue jeans and the cap swallowed her up so completely that she was almost forgotten, as she sat with her back to the crowd, digging her small, white teeth into a tough slice of yesterday's bread with a slab of bologna laid over it. She took big bites and chewed hard, and helped mastication along with a good swallow of beer from time to time.

She was the hardy one for you. She could turn

her hand into a fist that meant something. She looked as light and strong as a jockey, and she was still stronger than her looks. Ten minutes before, half the men in that room were giddy and grinning about her, but now she was nobody's business except her own.

Old Pop had his yellow fangs in a sandwich and said through the bread: "Ten dollars. Ten dollars. . . . You keep us in the gutter. You keep us in the dirt."

"Listen, Pop," she answered, "I'd rather heist the dough than glom it off a kid like that when he's dizzy about me."

"Let them be dizzy, you fool!" directed Pop. "God made you . . . and you make men dizzy . . . and that's that. Use the gifts that God gave you, Skeeter." And he frowned at her.

"If I had a drop of your blood in me," said Skeeter, "I'd cut my throat and hang myself up by the heels to get rid of it. But shut up and listen to the talk that's going around. They're all talking about Slip Liddell. That *was* Slip that we followed today, then."

"Yeah," agreed Pop. "He shot a pal out in the hills and came back to town to grab the blood money. That's what your hero done, and the boys don't seem to like it."

"I don't believe it," said the girl.

"Who cares what you believe?" demanded Pop. "I'm talking about the facts."

"You can't talk facts, Poison Face," answered Skeeter. "You hate everything too much to tell the truth about it. Slip Liddell . . ."

"He shot his partner in the back. The whole town knows about it."

"He never shot a man in the back in his life."

"Yeah. You ought to know. You were raised in the same house with him," sneered Pop.

"I know what I've heard of him," she said. "I've seen the faces of some shacks that he'd worked on. I've heard the line they pull about him all the way from 'Frisco to the Big Noise. Listen, Poison, he won't even play a sucker. He saves himself for the professional crooks and beats them at their own stuff."

"He shot Frank Pollard in the back for five grand," said Pop, and grinned till his teeth showed and his eyes disappeared. "What made him Galahad to you, anyway?"

She replied: "Who do they still talk about up and down the line? He lived where he wanted to and never hit the stem . . . he never battered privates. He was tramp royal when he wanted to travel. His hand was heavier than the other guy's blackjack. The cops and the shacks had chills and fever when they turned him up. He always had a limit and he always had it while the day was young. He never pulled a job . . . he never gave a pal the red lights . . . he shelled out to every sucker that was on the fritz . . . he never passed up a gal that was on the street without giving her a hand-out. And now you try to cross him up with me by saying that he shot somebody in the back? Listen, Pop, one of these days when you try to pull the poison on me like this, I'm going to take it on the lam, and then you can try to walk the cash out of the pockets without Skeeter."

"You're dopey about a guy you never saw," commented Pop, totally undisturbed by this outburst.

"I *have* seen him," said the girl. "I saw him today. I knew him by his picture."

"When did you ever see a picture of him?"

"Four, five years back I saw it in a daily rag, somewhere. But I wouldn't've had to see his picture. I would have known him by the way he walked."

"How did he walk?" Pop asked.

"Like he was going somewhere," said Skeeter.

"You're nuts," said Pop.

The voice of Pudge McArthur suddenly dominated the saloon. He was standing on a chair at the bar, ordering a round of drinks and making a speech as the liquor went down.

"We're not gonna take it!" roared Pudge. "We're not gonna lie down and take it!"

"We ain't gonna lie down and take it!" shouted an answering voice from the crowd.

That was Soapy Jones. The girl spotted him at once. Then she glanced over at the wall and saw Mark Heath still at his table with his chin on his fist and his eyes bright with calculation. She studied him with a bright curiosity for an instant.

"Nobody is gonna bamboozle San Jacinto!" bellowed Pudge. "Not even if his name is a big name. Nobody is gonna shoot a friend through the back and come in to get blood money. They can't put it over in San Jacinto. Not while we got so many good ropes in this town!"

"We got trees to hang the ropes on, too!" shouted Soapy Jones.

"Who you talking about?" demanded old Chuck Sladin.

"You know who I'm talking about," answered Pudge. "And I wanna tell you that the dead man was a friend of mine. He was the kind of a man that would give you his last ten cents, and he smiled when he done it. He was the kind of a man that he couldn't say no to a friend. He was more'n a brother to me. He was more'n a brother to the rat that shot him through the back."

"Name him! Name him!" called two or three voices. The others waited with faces prepared for anger and outrage, and Pudge McArthur roared mightily: "Slip Liddell . . . the crook . . . the gambler . . . the murderer! It's Liddell that I'm talking about. And there ain't guts enough to San Jacinto and there ain't ropes enough and there ain't hands to pull 'em, to take care of a skunk like Liddell! There ain't . . ."

His voice grew dim in the rising outcry of the mob.

Skeeter said: "Unlimber that accordion, Pop. Play something jolly. Play something that'll get into my feet. We've got to change the mind of these boys." She was whipping out of the blue jeans as she spoke and tucking her feet into the slippers.

"Leave them be," answered Pop, grinning. "If he's as much man as you think, they'll do nothing but bend their teeth when they bite him. If he's as much man as you think, he'll blow 'em down faster than they can come up."

She said: "Get that accordion off the strap and hop lively or I'll never shake a foot for you again."

He obeyed gloomily and muttered: "It's a wrong gag to play twice in the same joint. They get tired of handing out the cash."

"They're not handing out the cash. *We* are," she answered.

And a moment later she was at the bar rapping money on the edge of it, and calling for a drink all around. She hardly could make herself heard, for the anger and the resolution of Pudge McArthur had spread to nearly everyone in the room and they were beginning to mill like cattle before a stampede. Once they started spilling through the door into the street, nothing but more men and more guns could stop them.

There was no harm in having another free drink, however, and there was no harm in watching the girl clattering up and down the bar. To see her laughing made you think of every good time you ever had in your life. It made your own toe start tapping and started your head nodding. And it was plain that there was nothing but good nature and merriment in her, for now she was buying another round. When she jumped to the floor, Pop got her by the shoulder and shook her.

"Are you gone clean crazy?" gasped Pop. "Are *you* spendin' money when it's your job to make others spend on *you?*"

"Shut up and make an accompaniment for those two over there who've started singing," directed Skeeter. "Keep on playing. Liven it up. Put a smile on that old leather mug of yours."

"Wait . . . ," Pop began, but she was gone through the side door of the saloon before the others could notice her swift way in a crowd.

V

It was not the cold of the morning that wakened Liddell, but a young voice that said: "Hi, Slip! Hi! You're overdue. Wake up!"

He pulled away the bandage and found his eyes almost healed from the effects of the sand-storm. Still a haze remained across them, slowly clearing, and through that haze he saw a slim figure seated in his window. A big cap sloped down over the head. The jacket and trousers were faded jeans. He saw a brown face weathered right into the grain of the skin. It was a sleek, slim youngster, almost too handsome, almost too effeminately light of wrist and hand.

"Who are you, brother?" asked Liddell.

"Skeet they call me. Or Skeeter, sometimes. You better be up and vamoose, Slip."

"Yeah?" drawled Liddell, making his head comfortable on the fold of his arm.

"Some old pals of yours are around smoking up trouble."

"What pals?"

"Those two fat-faced hams . . . Soapy Jones and Pudge McArthur. And who's that smooth guy, called Heath?"

"Mark Heath? He's one of the best fellows in the world," answered Liddell. "He's a straight-shooter and he's worth having for a friend."

"Is he *your* friend?"

"He'll never be my friend, I'm afraid," said Liddell.

"He's making trouble for you now," she told him.

"What trouble?"

"Talk," said Skeeter.

"Where?"

"Up at the Royal all night. They're still there."

"What were *you* doing at the Royal all night?" demanded Liddell.

"I helped the barman wash up and snitched a few beers. I'm not talking about me. I'm talking about you."

"I hear you."

"D'you want to know what they're saying?"

"I can't keep you from telling me."

"You won't be so upstage when I tell you. They're saying that you double-crossed your old partner. They're saying that you did in Frank Pollard. They're saying that you killed him when he wasn't looking . . . for the blood money."

"Did I shoot him in the back?"

"You did."

"Was somebody looking from behind a rock?"

"No. But that's why you rolled the body down into the San Jacinto, so that nobody could see where the bullet went in through the head and came out through the face."

"If I murdered a friend like that . . . they ought to raise a mob and lynch me," commented Liddell.

"That's what Soapy and Pudge are talking up. They almost got a crowd started before I left and came to tell you. They ought to be along in ten minutes. Maybe less."

Liddell yawned. "I'd better be getting along, maybe."

"You better be," declared Skeeter. "There's a

bay mare walking loose in the court here. You borrow her and light out. She looks as fast as a hawk."

"Sis!" called Liddell. "Hi, Cicely!"

The bay mare put her head in through the window. She seemed to be resting her chin on Skeeter's knees.

"Ready for another trip?" asked Liddell.

The mare shook her head.

"Couldn't you take me on just a little, tiny trip?" asked Liddell.

Cicely shook her head with an angry decision.

"Get out of my sight, then!" exclaimed Liddell. "Fine gratitude you've got for all the oats and barley I've poured into you!"

The mare backed away into the courtyard again.

"How'd you do it?" asked Skeeter. "How'd you make her shake her head like that?"

"Why, I asked her a question, and she answered it, that's all," said Liddell. "She's like all women. There's no gratitude in her."

"You're a funny sort of a guy, all right," observed Skeeter. "But maybe you'll feel less funny when they use you to stretch out forty feet of new rope."

"Maybe I will," agreed Liddell. He began to make a cigarette. His hands, using separate intelligences, found the brown wheat-straw papers and the little sack of tobacco with the big revenue stamp stuck on it. The fingers turned the paper into a trough, sifted in the tobacco, smoothed it, leveled it off, turned it hard, then engaged one lip under the other and rolled up the smoke. He glued it with the tip of his tongue, turned one end over, and lit his smoke. But not for an instant did he give this bit of work his attention. He was saying: "How did you know I was down here?"

"There's a good beam end sticking out the stable window," remarked Skeeter, pointing. "That'll be better than the limb of a tree when they come to string you up. Wait a minute! You hear them now?"

In fact there seemed to be a swarming hum from higher up the street.

"They don't know where to find me, brother," Liddell pointed out.

"Everybody in town knows where you are and why you're here," answered Skeeter.

"Why am I here?" asked Liddell

"Because there's a gal in the house with hips and eyes that work together. Even the kids in the street laugh at her when she goes by . . . but everybody knows that when it comes to the gals, you're a swell horse trainer."

"You little pint of dishwater," Liddell said, sitting up. "I've got a mind to take you by the nape of the neck and pour you down the sink."

"You big, four-flushing ham," said Skeeter, "I've a mind to come down in there and knock the dust out of you."

Liddell leaned back on his bed with a sigh. "Breeze along, kid," he said. "Thanks for bringing me the news. Breeze along back where you came from. By the way, where *did* you come from?"

"That's my business," answered Skeeter. "You hear 'em coming now? Slip, get up and out of here. There's thirty, forty of those bums and they're mean."

Liddell rubbed at the dimness of his eyes, but they wouldn't clear. There was something about Skeeter that was very unlike other people.

"How old are you, Skeet?" he asked.

"To hell with me!" snapped Skeeter. "Are you going to lie right there and let 'em grab you?"

"Fourteen . . . fifteen . . . ?" said Liddell. "Where you live?"

"Wherever I find the living good."

"Are you on the bum?"

"Are you gonna be sorry for me?" asked Skeeter, with head tipped to one side.

"I'd as soon be sorry for a wasp or a butcher bird, or any other thing that's small and full of teeth and claws. How long you been on the bum?"

"Listen, mug," said Skeeter, "I'm not one of the punks that batter the back doors and get the dog or a cold hand-out. I come in the front way and sit down to my ham and . . ."

"You play a sob story and get the women mothering you, eh?" asked Liddell.

"Leave me out," said Skeeter. "There's a mob in this town that's going to have the hanging of you and like it."

"It's after five," answered Liddell. "If whiskey started them, the booze will be stale and cold in 'em. If a man-size dog barked at 'em, that whole gang would turn and run."

"You don't think you're taking a big chance?" asked Skeeter.

"No," answered Liddell. "A mob is like a mob of town dogs. They only chase the things that'll run from 'em."

"It knocks me for a loop," murmured Skeeter.

"Thanks for bringing me word," he said. "Wait a minute . . . are you broke?"

"I don't want your coin," answered Skeeter.

"Why not?" asked Liddell.

"I ought to be doing the paying. You're putting on the show," said Skeeter.

"You're a queer little mug," Liddell said, and yawned.

"I'll tell you something a lot queerer than me. Some of those thugs in the saloon are going to think you over when they're dirt dry and stone sober. And then maybe they'll oil up their guns and come for you. Maybe they're coming now."

"They won't come now," said Liddell.

"That fellow Soapy Jones, has he always hated you?"

"No. Soapy used to be a friend."

"He'd chew poison if he could spit it in your face now. He hates your heart, Slip."

"Why shouldn't he?" asked Liddell.

"You mean, it don't bother you?"

"It bothers me, all right. Soapy is a bulldog, and he'll hold on."

"But you don't hate him for it?"

"Listen, kid. I killed the guy he loved."

"Everybody seems to've loved this Frank Pollard," remarked Skeeter.

"He was one of the kind that was always trying to help others and the poor sucker couldn't help himself," answered Liddell.

"How come you slipped the lead into him?" asked Skeeter.

"Don't you go through life being surprised by things. I'll give you some advice."

"Shoot," said Skeeter.

"Get off the road . . . settle down. You'll never be more than half a man. You couldn't take care of yourself in a pinch."

"The hell I couldn't," said Skeeter.

"What do you use? A knife or a blackjack?"

There was a silence.

"You settle down. You're going to be one of those slim sizes all your life. Learn stenography. Get off the road."

"I'll be darned if I sharpen pencils all my life," declared Skeeter.

"You're a fresh sort of a kid," Liddell said

sleepily. "I don't know why I like you. But you get off the road and settle down. I'm telling you."

"It's OK. It's OK," muttered Skeeter. "But leave me out of this. The point is there's a gang in this town that'll never rest easy till they shoot the wishbone right out of you. Why don't you get out?"

"Maybe I will. Right now, I'm sleeping," answered Liddell. "So long, kid. Thanks for coming."

"OK." Skeeter nodded. "I've just tried to get some sense into you. When you wake up and find things have happened, remember me. I tried to make you move with common sense."

"I'll remember. Good night," said Liddell, and turned his face to the wall.

VI

After that interruption, Liddell slept on into the warmth of the morning. Then he took a bath and sat down to a breakfast of toast and Mexican chocolate, frothed by Dolores herself, with Dolores to look at as he ate and drank. Her beauty had an extra edge because she was frightened, and she was frightened because she had heard ugly rumors from the street. She followed him to the door, afterward, begging him not to go out through the curious crowd that was gathered in front of the silversmith's.

But Liddell went out. All voices stopped when he appeared. Then murmurs began. They were pointing him out. They were saying that he was the man who had done it. A woman with a broad face and a red nose leaned out of a window and yelled: "He shot his partner in the back! Put the dogs on him! He shot him in the back!"

It was plain that the town of San Jacinto had been hearing plenty about Slip Liddell during the night. When he walked into the sheriff's office, Chris Tolliver was running the tip of his tongue, with a painful slowness, over the crack in his lip. He looked at Liddell as though at a bodiless image of the night before.

"What about that five thousand?" asked Liddell.

"I've forwarded your claim and proofs," said the sheriff shortly. "I sent it up to the attorney general. Maybe we'll be hearing in a couple of days." He smiled all on one side of his mouth, as though in that way he would less endanger that splitting lower lip.

"It's funny, is it?" asked Liddell.

"Kind of," agreed the sheriff. He rubbed his bulging eyes, always tired, always reddened.

"A five thousand dollar joke, eh?" asked Liddell.

"Kind of," repeated Chris Tolliver.

The secretary pretended to be busy, but he had stopped typing and shuffled many papers softly together, searching for something that he obviously would not find.

"Tell me where the point is. I could use a good joke," observed Liddell.

"The point is . . . will you be here in San Jacinto when the money comes through?" asked Tolliver.

"Why not?" answered Liddell.

"Some of the boys were ready to pay a call on you this morning."

"They'd've found me in, too. What about it?"

"When they come to call, will you be there?"

"They won't be calling."

"Won't they?"

"No," said Liddell.

"Maybe not. Maybe I don't know my town," remarked Tolliver.

Liddell went back to the silversmith's. The air was full of noise like the 4th of July. For the custom in San Jacinto during the fiesta season was to keep the day and the night alive. Hurdy-gurdies pushed through the streets; mandolin players strolled and serenaded favored windows; snatches of band music always were growing and disappearing out of the distances; and the children of the town suddenly multiplied by ten and poured, chattering and yelling, into every crevice of quiet.

In spite of himself, he did not wish to pass down the street in front of Pinelli's. He did not want that fat-faced woman to lean out of the window with her denunciation as she had done before. So he took another way home, though it meant climbing a wall. When he reached the courtyard, he stepped into the stable. The mule stood there with dreaming eyes and a cruelly puckered mouth but Cicely was gone.

When he asked in the house, no one could tell what had happened. Armando rushed off upstairs to Dolores and that left Liddell for a moment alone in the shop with Juanita. She softened her voice in a half audible whisper.

She looked up at Liddell with the friendliest of smiles so that if her husband returned down the inner hall he would observe only that expression on her face, but what she was saying was: "Why don't you go, *Señor* Jimmy? Why don't you go before you have the house pulled down over our heads? The whole town hates you. And Saint Mary of God knows that I've hated you these years." She was still smiling.

"It's good for your complexion to do a little hating," answered Liddell. "It takes ten years off that pretty face, Juanita."

Her smile stretched and froze in place, and then both her husband and her daughter came with clattering feet and a double outcry down the stairs and into the hall.

Liddell did not wait for them. He knew by the exclamations of dismay that they had no news of how the mare had gone, so he stepped into the street and ran the gantlet this time of silent eyes, which looked at him as at something monstrous.

He went neither north or south through the town with his inquiries because in those directions ran the river roads, where automobiles could overtake even the swiftest of horses. But he went east with inquiry first and then west, and it was near the western rim of the little town that he found a peddler leading a mule that carried two great hampers and the peddler had, in fact, seen just such a golden bay mare ridden toward the hills by a ragged young lad. He described the rider.

"Skeeter," said Liddell softly to himself, and stood still, looking west toward the ragged sides of the range so ineptly named Monte Verde. No horse in San Jacinto could overtake that wise-footed Cicely with such a featherweight as Skeeter on her back, and an automobile might as well try to run down a shark's throat as through those rocks. He stood there for a moment with anger overtaking him from behind, as it were, until the weight of it turned his face crimson.

After a while he went down to the station, taking empty byways because he had no wish to be recognized again, but most of the people were away at the fairgrounds and the streets were clear enough. He had been looking at his mental map of the country all the way, and he was quite clear as to what he would do. He found out at the station that no passenger train went east for some time but while he was asking questions a long freight came around the bend like thunder out of the west.

It came closer, the empties in the string rattling like snare drums.

Liddell walked away from the station platform until some stacked piles shut him away from the view of San Jacinto. The big engine passed him at that moment, struggling powerfully against the grade, and a moment later he spotted a brakeman, a big man with arms akimbo and a deep-visored cap.

To him Liddell signaled a high sign that every tramp and every brakeman understands. The answer was a favorable wave of the hand and Liddell decided on the next empty flat car. The train was not doing more than thirty miles an hour. When he sprinted, the procession of cars slowed up perceptibly. Then he turned and jumped for the steel ladder with arms and legs stretched out before him, as a cat jumps when it goes into a fight. Feet and hands struck their chosen rungs of the ladder. He swung violently back to the left, then clambered up the side and sat down at the end of the flat car.

The high sides kept him from seeing anything except the ridges of Monte Verde and the sun-faded blue of the sky with two or three buzzards adrift in the high light like a few ugly words on a blank page of white. Then the rattling of the flat car began to shake his wits into a thoughtless jumble for it was a rough bit of roadbed and the heavy flat car crashed and shook like a vast cargo of tin and iron junk. The vibration set the sky trembling.

It shivered the teeth of Liddell together and set a tingle in his lips and eyelids. No shadow of warning came over him, but he turned his head about suddenly and saw the big brakeman coming up behind him, still with the same smile. This fellow had a pair of small, watchful eyes that had no relation whatever to the smile on his lips. Liddell stood up and held out a dollar bill.

"OK, chief?" he asked. "I'm dropping off a few miles up the line."

The brakeman took the bill, looked at it a moment, tucked it into a trouser pocket, and struck Liddell violently across the head with a leather-covered blackjack. The blow knocked him back against the end of the car. He teetered far over, out of balance. Part of his brain remained alive to tell him that if he fell the wheels that rushed behind the flat car would finish him, but his hands had no sense of them. They would not grip the edge of the car and maintain a secure grip. The heavy jolting was helping to unbalance him. And then he saw the big brakeman coming at him again with the blackjack in the hollow of his hand, the knob of it just inside the tip of his fingers. Still only a small instinct in Liddell told him to fight. The rest of his mind was telling him that this was a dream and that the still-smiling face of the brakeman was that of a friend.

The brakeman took his time. He set his feet wide apart. His smile broadened. Even the little eyes twinkled with pleasure, now. Then he slapped the blackjack at Liddell's head. He was so sure of himself that it was easy to duck the blow. Liddell spilled forward and threw his arms around the fellow's body.

It was like embracing a barrel sheathed with India rubber, the bones were so big, the muscles so hard. He took Liddell by the throat, pushed him off to arm's length and struck at his face with the blackjack.

The car heeled at a curve. That was why he missed that stroke. Otherwise he should have smashed Liddell's face to a pulp. As it was, he not only missed but lost his grip and Liddell hit him twice about the head.

There was no force in the punches. His shoulders were soggy and his elbows were cork. The brakeman kept on smiling. Some of the deliberate surety had left him, however. He freshened his grip on the blackjack. He came in like a boxer, with short, shuffling steps, his long left hand out.

Liddell paid no heed to that. A man with a club strikes hard only with the club hand. Liddell watched the blackjack. The life was coming back to him. The pain in his head was burning away the fog. The top of his skull seemed to be off. But he was glad of the torment. It was whiskey to him.

It made him hot all over with strength. The wits came back into his feet. They made sense as they leaped to the side and let the brakeman's rush go by. Liddell buried his fist in the soft of the body. It went right in, deep. It creased the brakeman like a piece of paper and doubled him over.

Liddell crouched. Only the shudder and jouncing of the car unsteadied his target. So he got in two lifting punches that straightened his man. The brakeman was back on his heels making a futile swipe through the air with the blackjack. A thin line of blood, like a stroke of red paint, appeared on his mouth.

Liddell hit for that mark. Then he stepped back and let the brakeman fall on his face. The blackjack, as though there was intelligent malice in it, flew out of the nerveless hand and rapped against Liddell's shin. He picked it up and threw it away, then he sat down to wait.

He was scarcely aware of the weariness in his body because the pain from his head was reaching down through him and touching all his nerves. Each rattling bounce of the car brought him taut with pain.

The head of the brakeman kept jouncing up and down. He had red hair, long and thin. The dust on the floor of the car blew into it and clogged with the blood, for he was still bleeding. A good pool of it gathered around his head. When he tried to sit up, his hand slipped in the blood. He fell on his face again. He lay there for another long moment, his body jouncing loosely. After a while he managed to sit up and his face was bad to see. He covered it with his hands and sat there with his back bowed as though there were no spine in it.

Liddell squatted on the quivering car, leaning on one hand to steady himself, and stared at the man he had beaten. The brakeman was silent and slack, as if he were still unconscious.

He was very big. He must have weighed two hundred and twenty or thirty pounds and Liddell knew that he had never been beaten before. Now the manhood was gone out of him. This shack never would be able to bully a tramp again. Before long he would not be able to look any angry man in the face. It made Liddell sick to think of what was coming. Still the fellow sat there with his hands over his face and the blood leaking out between his fingers and running down over his wrists.

Now the ridges of Monte Verde were diminishing rapidly in height; the country began to smooth out. Off to the left lay a flat land with a reddish-brown mist gathered low down over it. It made the throat of Liddell dry to look at it for he had spent time enough on the desert.

The wheels of the train began to rattle in an increasing staccato. They had passed the long grade, at last, and were heading down. He went over the side of the car, hung on the lowest rung of the ladder, and looked back to see if the brakeman were in sight, but the big man was still hidden from view.

The rough of the tiles beside the track now gave way to a broad, cinder-spread shoulder. Liddell swung back, slanted his body, and let go. By the time he had come to a walk the caboose of the train was going by, with a dirty flag blowing and snapping off the rear of it.

Now that he was on the ground, there was no wind whatever. The sun burned down through his hat. Two hot thumbs pressed against the top of his head as though there were no bone to shelter the brain itself. His right hand was painful, also. He had used it for the last, finishing punch and one of the brakeman's teeth, cutting straight through his lip, had driven into Liddell's middle finger just below the knuckle, cutting to the bone. It still bled. His whole hand was red.

For a hundred yards or so he followed the rails until he came to a faintly traced path. He thought, as he turned into the rough along the side of Monte Verde, that brakemen are a queer lot. Usually they are as tough as shoe leather but this fellow had been too big. All big men are soft, somewhere. They have some small dimension somewhere. Usually it's the neck. Big heads set on small necks are no good. Even he himself was too big. He was three inches too tall. Five feet ten is plenty. Condense a hundred and eighty pounds in five feet ten and you have plenty of man, rubbery with strength, compact, hard all over. If you're closer to the ground, you don't have so far to fall. If you're closer to the ground, you're not apt to break your back when you lift.

He kept thinking of these things in a monotone of the mind, a dreary repetition, pacing out the words of his thinking with the steps he took, and the pain got worse and worse in his head.

He came near to a little song of running water. It was a rill that went among the rocks quick as the flash of a fleeing snake. The water was no good for drinking. It was brackish with alkali. But it did pretty well for washing his hand and his head. There was not much of a lump on top of his head but the scalp was cut, and he was perfectly certain that the skull was fractured. At last he made himself take the full strength of his hands and work on each side of the pain. He had a feeling that if there were a fracture, he would feel and even hear the bone edges rasp together. When he heard nothing, he felt much better. The seasickness left the pit of his belly when he stood up and marched ahead.

When you go west out of San Jacinto, there is only one easy way of climbing Monte Verde. If you take the easy way, it leads you off into a shallow depression that deepens and narrows to a valley and at last the valley cuts down to a gorge that is not twenty feet wide in places. It is cut by water that only runs down that draw during the spring rains. In seasons of light rainfall there is no run of water at all.

The gorge has straight sides. The bottom of it is set with boulders as big as a horse and rider, and there are some shrubs growing, too, because the rain water never runs down the draw long enough to drown a plant. But it's a desolate gorge.

Up the mountain sides there is some smoky green of paloverde, and cactus sticks out catclaws at you, and the rocks are hand-polished by the sun so that they hurt your eyes at midday. This was where Liddell sat down on the shady side of the boulder to wait.

VII

He worked himself up to such a point as he sat there in the airless swelter that it seemed to him the brakeman, who he'd fought on the freight, had not used the blackjack. It was as though Skeeter had beaten him over the head. Then he began to feel a horrible riot of nerves as he realized how the time was drifting past him because there *were* other ways, of course, by which the mare could have been taken out of San Jacinto and into the west. He had come to a grim certainty that he never would see the silk and shine and beauty of Cicely again, when he heard a horse dog-trotting down the gorge, and of course that was Cicely with blue-jeaned Skeeter on her back.

He got himself back behind the rock and coiled his strength into one big spring. He had made up his mind that he would make Skeeter take all that was possible. There would be no more horse stealing in that career after he had tied Skeeter's hands to that thorn bush and used the buckle end of a belt thoroughly.

That was the trouble with youngsters. They could not even be disciplined. There was nothing you could close your hands on or sink your teeth into, so to speak. But Cicely's hoofs rapping over the rocks were like beats on a drum, coming closer and closer until the noise was right upon Liddell.

Then he leaped out.

Cicely was a little quicker than a cat, but she was not quick enough to get away from that surprising charge, or perhaps she recognized her master even faster than she felt fear. At any rate, he got in a flying leap, fastened his hand on the nape of Skeeter's neck, and brought that young rider to the ground with a sound like a loud hand clap.

Breath and senses were knocked out of Skeeter at the same instant, and as the body turned inertly from the side to its back, the big cap spilled off the head and allowed the hair to go tumbling down around the ears.

Well, some of the boys, when they feel their

blood, can wear hair as long as that, but Liddell was using his eyes all the way, now, and as he looked at the hands and the turn of the throat and the delicate care with which the nose and the lips had been fashioned, he felt a strong, new horror come up in him.

His mark was distinctly on this act. It was the little red trickle of blood that formed at the corner of her mouth, exactly like the line of red that had been the target on the brakeman's face not so very long before. Liddell fell into a mighty sweat, for it seemed to him that heads were lifting from the shadows of the rocks and staring at him, and that a whisper ran up and down the gorge.

Once, in his earliest school days, he had seen a boy hit a girl. Her head bobbed right back as though her neck were only a loose spring. She hadn't run away. She hadn't even screamed. She just stood there, bewildered. And then the whole schoolyard descended on that lad and winnowed him small with fists and feet. Once in his life, also, he had seen a man who was known to beat his wife.

Liddell, before the girl was half conscious, had her up off the ground, not at all worried about her health but only concerned to get the dust brushed from the blue jeans and the blood from her face. When he handled her, the soft of her body sort of slid from his grasp and he kept swearing under his breath and sweating. He felt as though he were losing a frightful race against public opinion.

All at once, he saw that although she let her body remain as limp as ever, she was smiling a little. He sat her down rather hard and stood back. He took off his hat. She permitted herself to be conscious.

"I'm seven kinds of a fool," Liddell said in an uncertain voice, "but this morning I wasn't half awake when you were sitting up there in the window . . . the duststorm had knocked the tar out of my eyes."

He picked up her cap, dusted it conscientiously, and gave it into her hands. She kept on smiling a little, and looking him up and down. He said huskily: "I'm giving you my word of honor . . . I didn't see you well enough. I thought you were a boy. I beg your pardon," said Liddell.

She pulled out a handkerchief and dabbed at her lip, and then looked at the drop of blood on the white cloth. She said nothing.

"If I'd known . . . if I'd guessed . . . if I hadn't been such a stupid fool," said Liddell, his agony increasing with her silence.

He hoped that her smile meant kindness, but he could not be sure. She kept looking at the drop of blood on her handkerchief. Another speck of blood was forming at her lip. "Suppose I'd just been a boy . . . ?" she suggested.

"Why, that would have been different," said Liddell. He started to make himself a cigarette with nervous hands. He offered the makings to her.

"I don't smoke," she said.

"I beg your pardon," said Liddell.

"If I'd been a boy, you'd have torn the hide right off my back, wouldn't you?" she asked, still with that smile. It was like the smile of the brakeman. It could mean anything in the world.

"I didn't guess," stammered Liddell. The cigarette went to pieces in those sure fingers of his.

"Man or woman, I'd still be a horse thief, wouldn't I?" she asked.

"I wouldn't dream . . . ," said Liddell. "Of course everybody likes a joke."

"How'd you get here, anyway?" she asked.

"I hopped a freight," he answered. "When I found out that you'd ridden west, I hopped a westbound freight, because I remembered how this trail came to a narrow . . ."

"Tell me," asked Skeeter, "why I grabbed that Cicely mare of yours?"

"You had to get somewhere and you didn't have time . . . ," he began politely.

She put her chin on her fist and studied him curiously. The wind kept knocking her hair to one side. Sometimes a flicking of it came across her face. Even the stillness was gone from the air, since she arrived.

"I stole that horse because I knew you'd follow," she said. "And if you stayed in San

Jacinto, I knew that those apes would do you in sooner or later. So I thought that I'd lead you a paper chase. Because I knew that you wouldn't give up Cicely without a fight. Believe me?"

"Certainly," said Liddell. "Of course I believe you."

"What's the matter with you?" asked the girl. She stood up suddenly. She put her fists on her hips—what a fool he had been not to see at a glance the woman in her—and said: "I see what it is. You're afraid that I'll go back and tell people that you beat me up. Afraid I'll say that you manhandled a girl, eh? Listen, Slip, what sort of a hound would that make you?"

He was pale with the thought of it. His face was the color of grease.

"Go on and tell me," insisted the girl. "If I went back and said that, and showed 'em the place on my mouth, what would they think of you?"

"You wouldn't do it," said Liddell. "Of course it's a joke." He tried a laugh that was a poor, staggering excuse for mirth.

"I'll tell you what," she answered, "if you try to turn back into San Jacinto now, I'll spill the news all over the place."

He made a two-handed gesture of appeal clumsily, because he was not used to making gestures of appeal. "But I've got to go back," he said.

"You gotta go back, why?" she demanded. "You

gotta go back and be lynched, why? Mind you, those fellows Pudge and Soapy and that bright young Mark Heath, they won't stop till they've started a lynching mob after you."

"Were any of the three of them spending a lot of money last night?" he asked.

"No. But what's that got to do with it?" she asked. "I'm saying . . . how'll you have it? Do you keep away from San Jacinto or do you have me spill the beans about how the big guy slammed the girl around?"

He fought through a real agony. He sat down on his heels and took one of her hands in his. "There'll be nothing hard for me in San Jacinto," he said. "And I've got to get back there and stay until . . ."

"What's all this?" she asked. She took her hand away from him. "Some crazy matter of honor . . . or is it a bet?"

"It's more than honor."

"You're going back?"

"I have to go," he told her.

"Then I spill the beans about you all over town."

He held himself so hard that he trembled. After a while he said: "Get up on the mare, then, and I'll take you back to town."

"You've got to go back and take it, do you?" she asked. "Slip, what's come over you? What's the matter with you, anyway? Do you think I don't

78

know what those mugs can do and will do? What is it that pulls you back to San Jacinto?"

"Business," he said.

"Five thousand dollars in blood money?"

He made no answer.

"Listen," she said. "Tell me one thing. If you hadn't grabbed me with Cicely right here, would you have gone on trekking farther west to trail me?"

"No," he said.

"Then it doesn't matter," she sighed. "I would have lost anyway."

He said: "If I hadn't caught up with you here . . . you would have come back to San Jacinto?"

"Of course I would," she said. "Hi, quit it, Slip! Don't be polite and doubting. I'm for you. Can't you see that?"

"Are you?" he asked, bewildered more than ever, and still very nervous.

"What do you make of that?" she murmured to herself. And then aloud and with anger she demanded: "You don't think I'm a *horse* thief, do you, Slip?"

"No," he said, following a sudden light. "You're not a thief, Skeeter."

"No?" she echoed. She began to laugh. "When I hit the stem, you watch my smoke. And when I'm on the road with Pop, who finds the chickens in the dark and wishes them off the roost so soft they keep right on sleeping till they find themselves in the mulligan? Oh, Slip, I could swipe eyelashes and never make the eyes blink, but I'm a regular sort of guy, at that. Do you think I could be?"

"I think you could be," said Liddell. "I think you are." He swung into the saddle on Cicely. "Hop on behind," he said.

She stepped on his stirrup and was suddenly seated behind the cantle with an arm lightly around him.

"You're breathing deep and feeling better," she observed. "Did you think I'd really go to town and pull a phony on you?"

"I wasn't thinking straight," he answered as the mare picked her way among the boulders.

"They're talking in the streets about you," she said. "Those people will never rest easy till they've done something about you, and, when they start, they'll have ropes in their hands. You know that?"

"I know that," he said.

"And still you're not scared of death?"

"I suppose I'm scared," he answered.

"But you've got to go back?"

"I've got to go back."

"All right," she answered chiefly to herself. "Will you let me see a lot of you while you last?"

"All you can stand."

"D'you ever suppose things?"

"Yeah, once in a while."

"Well, suppose that I was dolled up in fluff

and zingo and perfume, would you like me a lot better?"

"I like you fine the way you are."

"Fine?" she repeated.

"Yeah, fine."

"Once I was at a masquerade and I swiped a dress and made up like a girl," said Skeeter. "I tell you what I did. I went and combed out my hair and brushed it up, and a million waves and curls came into it, and it shone like nobody's business."

"It shines plenty right now."

"Yeah, but you got no idea," said Skeeter. "And I got myself into a red dress with a yellow kind of a what-not around the neck. It had a lot of zingo, is what that old dress had, and believe you me."

"I believe you, all right," said Liddell.

"And there was red slippers that squeezed my toes," said Skeeter, "because from going barefoot my feet are kind of spread. But they're not very big feet, at that? Would you say?" She stuck out a foot.

"They're OK feet, I'd say," replied Liddell.

"But those slippers went with the dress, and when you start getting fashionable, the pain don't count," she observed. "I had on a lot of things underneath, too, so it was kind of hard to breathe. But the point I make is what I did to the men at that party. I knocked 'em right out of their chairs."

"I'll bet you did," agreed Liddell.

"If I was to take and lean forward and look at

you, I'd see a smile on your pan, right now," she declared.

"No, you wouldn't," he replied. "Except enjoying what you're saying. That's the only smile you'd see."

"Honest?" she asked.

"Honest."

"Well," she said, "they certainly were a dizzy lot . . . but the slippers wore me out and I pretty near died before the last dance was over. And I walked home barefoot, and I'll tell you what, Slip, I kind of felt sorry for men, the way a skirt and a dish of perfume knock 'em for a row of loops. What kind of perfume do you like, Slip?"

"Soap," he answered.

"What?" she demanded.

"Just a kind of a clean smell," he told her.

"Geez, you're a funny kind of a guy," she remarked after thinking this over. "But take you by and large, you're the most man that I ever bumped into."

"Thanks," said Liddell, "and you're the most . . ."

"Wait a minute," she interrupted. "You don't half know about me, yet. You haven't even read the headlines. You wait and see."

"All right. I'll wait," said Liddell.

VIII

It was dusk when they came to the edge of San Jacinto. "You get off here," he told her. "I've got to get to an appointment and I'm nearly late now."

"Is it a blonde?" she asked. She stood by the mare with her arms akimbo, looking up.

"It's not a blonde," he told her, smiling down.

"I know," said Skeeter. "It's old lipstick . . . old powder-her-nose . . . that Dolores, the poor dummy that couldn't get past the third grade."

"She's not a bad sort of a girl. You ought to know her," said Liddell. "Where do you stay, Skeeter?"

"You know the second bridge, and a string of little white shacks down south of it? I live in one of those."

"Thanks," said Liddell. "I'll be seeing you."

"Thanks for asking," said the girl. And then as he cantered the mare away, she was adding: "Thanks for nothing . . . thanks for being a sap-head . . . I never saw such a cock-eyed bozo in my life. Can't he see I'm eating my heart like bread, because of him?"

But suddenly she broke into a run, following behind him when she saw him turn the mare onto the river road.

It would have done you good to see her run. You know how most girls scamper, leaning forward as though they were about to fall on their faces, and their feet stuttering along behind them and their hands catching at the air? Well, Skeeter ran with a good knee lift and her legs blowing out behind her the way a champion runs when he means business. She slid along through the shadows as easy as you please, keeping close to the side of the lane so that the willows would cover her, because she wanted to know what Liddell had to do down the river road, that time of the day.

The road took a good dip from the town level down to the waterside and the big San Jacinto went drifting along and, through the gaps in the tulles, she could see the last golden, rusting, tarnishing stain of the sunset afloat on the water. Then there was nothing but tulles, and the dust raised by the galloping mare burned the lungs of Skeeter because the wind had fallen away to nothing as it generally does out there at sundown and the dust hung where the heels of the mare kicked it.

The light grew dull, also, but she was able to see her man turn off the road and go into the tulles. They were tall enough to cover him to the neck. Just his head moved along above the feathery tips of the tulles. And Skeeter dropped down on a bank and watched, and panted, and listened.

She could hear the plopping of the hoofs of the

mare as Cicely entered the muck out of which the tulles grew, and far back of her, out of the town, floated the voice of the fiesta, made up of the bawling of cattle—they had been doing some roping that day—and the pattering hoofs of horses, and the barking of dogs that made no sense at all, and the shrill of children calling out as they played, and the trembling of musical strings.

That sharp, accurate ear of hers dissolved the cloud of sound into these thin elements but still she could hear the mare working her way out into the marsh land. It took nerve to ride the mare out there into the dark, where a quicksand might grab her legs any moment.

Then she heard something else that stopped her heart, for some reason. It was a whistle composed of three notes—one long and two short. It was repeated, on a high pitch. In that musical brain of hers she recorded the pitch and the rhythm faultlessly.

Three or four times the whistle was repeated. Then a silence set in, and out of the silence grew the faint noise of oars groaning in their locks. This noise also ended, and the silence closed in, and the damp coolness of the night covered her body and rose to her lips. She was listening so hard that she almost forgot to breathe.

Minutes of this followed. At last the noise of hoofs plumping through the marsh came back again toward the riverbank. The black silhouette of a horseman lurched out of the tulles and turned up the road.

Skeeter, lying flat behind the trunk of a tree, peered out, and she knew against the stars the outline of the rider. She could tell him by the angle of his hat and the cant of his head. The mare wanted to gallop hard but he reined her in. She heard his voice saying gently: "Easy, Sis! Easy does it, honey. Easy, girl."

The words did something to her. She smiled all the way down the line to the shack where old Pop was waiting. They had two ground-floor rooms, to the back, where they could hear the swish-swash of the river currents all night long. When Pop heard her, he did not turn his head at once. He was sewing up a second-hand pair of trousers—because when you buy second-hand stuff, it's always better to go over the seams, first, and tighten up the bad places, and all the buttons can do with a stitch or two. That way, they last twice as long. So when he heard her come in, he stopped sewing but he did not turn his head. Neither of them spoke.

There was a little, round, rusted iron stove in a corner with an iron pot simmering on top of it and filling the room with a greasy smell. She took a granite cooking spoon off the table, went over to the pot, and stirred the contents. She lifted a spoonful and let it slop back. There were carrots, beans, some sort of greens, tomatoes, and strings and fragments of meat all mushed up from long cooking. She piled a good heap of the mulligan stew on a paper plate and sat on the table with the plate in her lap. She used the graniteware spoon to eat with and a big chunk of bread as a pusher. When the end of the bread was well-smeared with gravy, she bit off the wet part. Otherwise the bread was too stale and hard to bite into.

Pop said: "I been knowing all the time that you'd turn soft. And today's the time. I been trying for years and years to keep you clean and straight. But the dirt that's under the skin has gotta come out. So you went and run off with somebody, did you? He gives you a whistle and you go right off with him. I been seeing it come over you."

She looked calmly upon him, working hard over a mouthful. Time had put its hands on him, and twisted. Time had taken him by the nape of the neck and pushed his head forward and bent a crook in his back. A shag of greasy gray hair stuck down over the collar of his shirt.

He was old. He was like a man going downhill, a long step every day. So she merely said: "What's been happening in town?"

He answered: "You don't wanna talk about where you been?"

"What's been happening in town?" she repeated.

"Money. That's what's been happening. Everybody's had his hand in his pocket all day long, shelling out cash. If you'd been here to do the dance, we'd've taken in a hundred bucks. Even me alone doing jigs on the accordion with my hat on the sidewalk, even me, I took in more'n eight dollars."

"That's good." She nodded.

"Not that you get any share nor hide nor hair of it!" he shouted. "You didn't take a step to help in the making of it."

"OK," said the girl. "Nothing else important?"

"Nothing except what they're all talking about. This bozo that you went to warn this morning . . . this Slip Liddell . . . he's yella. He took a run-out powder. He blew out of town. He'll never be seen in San Jacinto again. He's got no more name than a Chinaman, right now. The people are laughing at him."

"Maybe I made a mistake," she said as she finished her meal. She got down from the table, filled a tin bucket with water from the tap, and went into the next room.

"Whatcha gonna do?" demanded Pop.

"I'm taking a bath," she said.

"Why you gonna take a bath?" he asked. "You ain't done any dancing today or sweated yourself up any."

For answer, the key turned into the lock. Drowsily he heard the swishing of water in the next room. Before his mind turned two more gloomy corners, she was back again, still toweling her hair.

"That perfume is over there in the second drawer . . . ," he said.

"I got a new kind of perfume."

"Whatcha mean?" asked Pop.

"Soap," she said.

"You gone and lost your mind?" cried Pop. "A good, sweet smell on you is what you need, particular after you been dancing hard. It'll turn dimes into quarters when the boys come to chuck money into the hat."

"A good clean smell is good enough for me," said Skeeter. "How come they all say that Liddell is yellow? Because they didn't find him around town?"

"I'll tell you what it's come to," answered Pop. "There's a young feller by the name of Heath . . . remember him?"

"I remember him," she answered.

"He's been telling the world that, if it can find Liddell, he'll be waiting for him up in the Royal Saloon."

"He's been telling what?" exclaimed Skeeter.

"Telling the whole world . . . that he's waiting there in the Royal for Liddell, if Slip has the nerve to come and have a showdown with him," said Pop. "He's daring Liddell to show his face inside the Royal Saloon, and he'll change his looks for him. Because he says that the longer he thinks, the surer he is that he can't leave in the world the sort of rat that took and murdered poor Frank Pollard. And if . . ."

He started up from his chair, shouting: "Hi, Skeeter! Where are you . . . ?"

But Skeeter was gone through the door and up the street. She ran the entire way and her knees were gone under her when she reached the Royal Saloon. She cut right in across the vacant lot beside it to save time, and in this way came to the open window. Something was very odd about the place. She realized, as she hurried up, that not a sound was coming from the Royal at what should have been one of its busiest moments of the day. When she looked through the window, she saw the reason at a glance and the heart went out of her.

For everything inside the Royal was as still as paint. It looked, in fact, as though an artist had snapshot the scene. Some of the men at the tables, half risen, rested their weight on the arms of their chairs as though still in the act of rising. Instead of the long line at the bar, a dozen or so had stepped back to leave it clear for two people, and these were Liddell and young Mark Heath.

The pause must have lasted for some time.

Heath was green-white but his eyes were fixed and dangerous. He said now in a strained, high-pitched voice: "I'm telling you again. You've got a gun. Fill your hand and we start."

It was like something out of a ghost of an old barroom in the West. He must have remembered it out of stories of the past, that phrase about filling the hand with a gun. His own hand was back behind his hip and he was leaning forward a little as though to balance the weight of the draw.

She saw Pudge McArthur and Soapy Jones, too. They were at a table near the bar. Pudge had his hand under his coat; Soapy's gun was out in plain view and it pointed steadily toward Liddell. It looked too big—a caricature of a weapon, a funny-paper revolver.

She wanted to yell out something as a warning to Liddell, but she had become a part of that frozen scene inside the Royal, and no voice would issue from her lips.

Then she heard Liddell saying: "I've got something better than a gun to fill my hand. I've got a drink here, Heath. Here's to you and here's to everybody." He lifted the whiskey, waved it left and right to the crowd, and poured it down his throat.

"Keep the change, Chuck," he said, and walked out of the place with a deliberate step. The swing-door was still oscillating when Pudge McArthur jumped out of his chair and shouted: "I told you he was yella, Mark! I told you he'd lost his guts! Foller him up! Give him hell!"

But whatever Mark Heath was prepared to do in the future, he was at this moment wiping the sweat from his face and reaching an uncertain hand for his own drink.

IX

Skeeter felt very sick. Twice as she went down the street she paused to rest her hand against a wall and regain breath and strength. There was a great bustling everywhere and the voices of girls giggling and laughing, for almost the gayest moment of the fiesta came this night with the open-air dance on the platform under the cypresses by the river. This stir of expectancy and happiness sickened her more than ever. For her, this was a funeral moment. She walked wretchedly in procession after the death of a man's reputation.

She was at the mouth of the narrow street on which the silversmith had his shop when two men went by, stepping large and fast, and she heard them saying: "Did you see the kind of a fool smile he wore when he picked up his drink?"

"Yeah, like a punch-drunk bum in the ring . . . grinning . . . pretending he's not hurt. This here Slip, he's had the whole world buffaloed with a big bluff. Say, maybe that's why they call him *Señor* Coyote. . . ."

"You'd think he'd rather have died."

That was it. That was what one would think.

She went down the alley into the little cramped courtyard of Pinelli, with the sense of winter dampness underfoot and in the air. When she leaned through the window, she could see the length of big Liddell stretched on the bed. He did not have a lamp lit. Enough illumination came from the hall to show her he was face down. She slid through the window and dropped to the floor.

"Who's that?" asked Liddell.

"Nobody," Skeeter responded as she closed the hall door.

She was glad of the darkness. It would be easier to talk in the black of the night. It would have been better if no stars looked in through the window, showing the narrow roof of the next building and letting the thought of the exterior world come to them. In the murk she found the bed and sat on her heels beside it.

"Listen, Slip," she said. "I know how you feel. Once I went to school and, having the girls look at me and my funny rig, it made me terrible sick. I used to be so happy when Friday night came, that I cried. Yeah. Me. I really cried. And I used to nearly cry again when Monday morning came. I know what I felt when I had to hop my first freight, too. That was five years back, when Pop still had some spring in his legs."

"Is he your father?" asked Liddell.

"That old . . . what do you think?"

"No, I don't think he is."

"Thanks, Slip. But he's been pretty good to me in a lot of ways . . . and I'm going to take care of him when he gets too old and mean to make his way. I didn't come to talk about him and me. Slip . . . I was at the window of the Royal and I saw. And the whole town is saying that you took water."

She heard his body turn but she said nothing. After a moment she reached through the darkness and by a sure instinct found his hand. It closed hard and suddenly over hers.

She said: "Sometimes it looks to me like we only have so much stuff in us. Just so much and no more. You've been all over. I know where you've been. All up and down the line I've met shacks and tramps and straight people that told me things you've done. Now·the nerve is gone out of you. Courage, that's like strength. It can't last forever. It's like some people live fast and die young, and some people live slow, and last a long time. But each of them do the same amount of living. Isn't that true?"

"Perhaps it is," said Liddell.

She could feel a tension in him, and knew he was listening as no one ever had listened to her before. "Look at you," said the girl. "The way you've lived is half a dozen lives. That's why it doesn't matter so much if you should have to stop living."

"D'you think I have to die, now?" asked Liddell.

A sob came up in her throat and almost strangled her. She choked it back. The effort knocked her voice to pieces when she spoke. "You've gotta go out and meet Heath, and McArthur, and Soapy Jones," she said.

He was silent.

"There's thousands and thousands of folks that know about you, Slip. They've heard about you and they wouldn't want to hear that you'd shown the white feather. Right now there's something alive that belongs to you. It's part of your name. Young fellas that get into a pinch ask themselves what Slip Liddell would do at a time like that. But if they were to hear what happened tonight . . ."

"It's already happened. I'm dead to the world."

"The dead could up and rise again," panted the girl. "You could go and laugh in Heath's face, even with Pudge and Soapy behind him. You *gotta* go and laugh in his face. What's three men to the real Slip Liddell? To *Señor* Coyote? What did he do to the three shacks down in the yards at Phoenix? But unless you stand up to 'em, everything good that's ever been said about you is gonna die in the throats that said it. It's better for *you* to die, Slip. Don't turn your name into cheapness, Slip. A coyote would run away, Slip. . . ."

"I wonder," said Liddell.

"Listen to me," remarked the girl, "if I could have my way, I'd follow you around the world like a squaw and I wouldn't care. I know what you've been, and that would be good enough for me. And I'd take you off somewhere up in the mountains where you'd never have to bump into tough mugs any more. I'd fix you up fine, Slip. If you wanted to marry me, that would be swell. If you didn't want to marry me, I wouldn't care. I'd cook for you, and make the house shine, and keep your clothes right . . . and you'd always have a slick horse to ride and money in your pocket and me and Pop would go out once in a while and just rake in the dough. We'd play the big joints and just rake it in."

"It sounds good to me," Liddell said softly. "But can't we do that anyway?"

"We can't, Slip," said the girl.

She got up and stood at the window, drinking in deeper breaths of the air. The silence drew out long between them.

"Come back to me a minute, Skeeter, will you?" he asked.

"If I touch you again, I'll be crying like a fool," she said.

"You want me to go back to the Royal now?" Liddell asked.

"You mean that you *would* go?" gasped Skeeter.

"I'd try to," said Liddell.

"Did me coming and talking, did that help?"

"It put a different kind of a heart in me," he told her.

"Then thank God that I came. Dying isn't hard, Slip. You'll find out that it isn't hard. . . ."

"Are you sure?" asked Liddell.

"I know it isn't. Once I nearly drowned. I got

under the ice and I couldn't break through. I was nine or ten or something. And it wasn't so bad. A funny thing was the way the world looked through the ice. The naked trees sort of blurred over, like there was leaves and things on them. And somehow it seemed to me that the whole world was full of summer, outside of the ice. But it wasn't bad. Just kind of choking a good deal."

"Come here," said Liddell. She came to the edge of the bed. "Sit down by me," said Liddell.

"One way or another, I've been telling you that I like you a lot," said Skeeter. "That wouldn't make you be foolish with me, would it?"

"I hope not," said Liddell.

"Because that wouldn't be a very good last thing for you to do in the world," said Skeeter.

"No, it wouldn't," he agreed.

She sat down beside him. He put a big arm around her, turning on his side.

"How did you get out from under the ice?" asked Liddell.

"Don't say anything," whispered Skeeter. "It's sort of wonderful, just being here close. I mean, it's wonderful for me."

He said nothing, obediently. One of her hands found his face and remained touching it, the fingertips moving softly as though it were a blind hand, reading.

After a long time she said: "Suppose that sky pilots and the preachers and the teachers were right? Suppose that praying did any good? Wouldn't that make a fool out of me? Suppose that praying would jam the gun of Soapy Jones and make Pudge McArthur miss and leave only Heath for you to face. Just supposing that prayer was worth a damn and that I could somehow save you . . . ?"

"You ever come close to praying, Skeeter?" asked Liddell.

"What's the good?" she answered. "In the jungle or on the main stem or on the rattlers, or wherever you are, a fast hand and a quick lam are what get away with the goods, so far as I can see . . . there wouldn't be time for praying except afterward. What do *you* think, Slip? Is there a God tucked away somewhere?"

After a bit of consideration he said: "Not the kind that will stop a roulette wheel at the right place."

"Or make your old shoes last," she suggested.

"Or give you another stake," said Liddell.

"Or take the frost out of a midnight ride on the rods," she added. "But I don't want to talk about Him. I want to talk about you. What chance would you have, if you went down there to the dance, this evening? If you went down and faced them?"

Instead of answering, he countered with rather a queer question. "Up there at the Royal you saw Heath and Pudge and Soapy, all three?"

"Yes," she answered, "and Soapy with his rod out ready to shoot."

"Were any of them spending a lot of money?" he asked.

"Not that I saw. I only saw you, at the last minute, taking the drink."

She buried her face in her hands, shuddering. The big hand of Liddell patted her back.

She broke out: "Am I wrong, Slip? Had you better get out of here and run for it? If you take it on the lam, I'd go with you."

"No, you wouldn't," answered Liddell. "You'd rather run away with a ghost than with me after my name's dead."

"Maybe that's right. I wonder," said the girl. "You get a name by just playing around and doing the things that are fun when you want to do them. And the name gets bigger and bigger. And after a while, it's so big that you've got to die for it. That's a funny thing, Slip, isn't it?"

He was silent till she exclaimed: "You wouldn't go and change your mind back to the other side again, would you?"

"No," said Liddell.

"That's having the old nerve again," said the girl. "I can hear what they're gonna say. They're gonna say . . . 'We thought there was only this kid. We thought there was McArthur and Soapy Jones on the side all the time, with their guns ready. And that was why Slip hesitated a little. But finally he crashed through. He went down with his guns smoking. He never did a finer thing than the day he died.' They'll talk about you like that. Everybody that ever speaks about you is gonna look up, is what they're gonna do." Her voice broke into bits again. "I'll be going along," she said.

She stood up. Liddell rose with her.

"If I had clothes or something, I could be down there at the finish," said Skeeter.

"Take this money and get clothes," Liddell suggested.

"All the stores are closed up tight."

"Take this money and see if you can't pry a store open, Skeeter."

"Yeah. Maybe I could." Her hand closed feebly over a wad of bills. "You want me there?" she asked.

"I sure want you there," said Liddell. "But so far as I'm concerned, these clothes of yours are plenty good."

"Everybody'd laugh at me," she answered. "Slip, it's kind of funny. This morning I was thinking that we had years and years and years laid out ahead when we'd be seeing each other now and then, and you'd be laid up in the back of my mind like a bit of summer weather, and all that. And now here it is the end, already. It makes me feel queer. It makes me feel kind of sick in the stomach. . . . And good bye."

She was out the window in a flash, but in the

open air she turned again. "Should I come back? Would you kiss me good bye?" she asked.

"You don't have to come back for that," he said. And he picked up her hand and leaned over and kissed it with a long, light pressure of his lips.

Afterward she lifted the hand to her cheek. She began to laugh, but the laughter staggered and went out suddenly.

"Slip," she whispered. "I'm not going to live long after you."

"Stop talking rot!" he commanded.

"I never could be another man's," said Skeeter.

"Wait, Skeeter . . . ," he called, leaning across the window sill.

But she already was gone into the night.

After that he paused for a moment, lit the lamp in his room, and then smoked half of a cigarette before his brain cleared. He went up to the second floor and tapped on a door.

"Hello?" called Dolores.

"Come to the dance with me," invited Liddell.

She pulled the door open. She was only partly dressed. Some of her makeup had not been put on so that she seemed to stand half in light and half in shadow.

"Did you ask me to go with you, *Señor* Jimmy?" she repeated. Her face had no expression.

"That's right. We haven't stepped out for a long time," said Liddell.

"Ah, but I'm not the right size, am I?" she asked.

"You'd do fine for me," said Liddell.

"Ah, but I wouldn't, I wouldn't!" cried Dolores. "I'm not nearly big enough for you to hide behind my skirts, am I, *Señor* Coyote?" There was shrill irony in her voice as she said it. She pinched and flashed her eyes with malice as she delivered the insult, and a hearty, husky roar of laughter came from the corner of the room. That was mama, waddling into view with her fat arms folded over her fat stomach, shaking herself with mirth and contempt.

Liddell closed the door softly and went back down the stairs.

X

Skeeter, under the first street lamp, counted the money in her hand and found $165. It stopped her brain. It took the reality out of the night and set the stars spinning. She had dreamed of a man like that, who handed out a whole fistful of money without counting, and here was the money in her grasp.

Then she went on. It was queer to feel that stab, that upthrusting of joy, and know that it came from a dead man.

Once she went to a funeral home in southern California to do a little honor to a famous hobo's death. They got a church funeral for him, some way. And the church was filled with flowers and organ music and she almost had fainted. Now the air of San Jacinto was sweetened with flowers at every window and music was never still in the air from one side of the town to the other. So that sense of death remained with her constantly. Nevertheless, her mind was grimly determined to see the end even if to give testimony later on against the numbers that were sure to combine against him.

Besides, there was some sort of a ghost of a hope remaining in her that help would come in the final moment. Yet as she remembered how quiet he had been in the dark of his room, listening to her, she knew that she was wrong. He had submitted his will to hers, his judgment to hers, almost like a child. At this thought, the tears went suddenly down her face. She did not know they were there and let them dry in the warm air of the night.

She had in mind a Mexican shop well out of the polite center of town. It could be opened by a little extra money if any store in the town could be unbarred at this time of the night. But she found it securely closed. Even this place obeyed the custom on the nights of the fiesta.

This brought her to a pause. She stood gloomily on a corner, her head hanging, as an open automobile swung past filled with laughter and color. It turned the next corner toward the river and the laughter was shut out instantly, as though a velvet-edged door had closed between them. But other automobiles followed, and now a long, low, luxurious limousine with two men in front in uniform and a hint of ladies and gentry pointed out by street lamps as the car went by. They came, no doubt, from one of the houses on San Jacinto Hill.

It was not much of a hill. Probably it did not rise a hundred feet above the river, but the swells and rich people who had their houses on it were fond of speaking of the superior stir of air, and the purity of the wind that blew through their precincts. For there were plenty of rich people in San Jacinto—Mexicans, most of them.

When she thought of that, Skeeter moved straight into that superior section of the town. This was a region of iron grilles and barred lattices across windows and over balconies so that modesty could take the air and see the world at the same time. The same devices offered very perfect ladders, and Skeeter, after walking a few swift blocks to pick the best prize, selected her mansion and was up a second-story balcony in no time at all. The balcony window was not even locked. In a moment she was in a boudoir that fairly loosened her knees and made her sit down to take stock. But she could not sit down.

The *señorita*, on this evening, had not been able to suit her fancy at once. Across the bed lay a cloud of green, a shimmer of white, a mist of rose, and then a dashing design of all colors that she could think of. Skeeter made up her own mind while she was locking the door, with her head turned over her shoulder. She would take the green and use the scarf of the rose.

The overalls came off with a few pulls and kicks. The rest of her clothes followed. Sometimes her face was a bit of a trial to her but the whole of herself was a great satisfaction, always. She stood for half of a priceless moment within the angle of a great triple mirror made of three expensive pier glasses, and with her arms folded behind her head she admired every slightness and every curve, for, as though gifted with new eyes, the mirror showed her more than she ever had seen before.

But time counted. It might be desperately important.

Her hands found their way to spider-webbing of lingerie, and to stockings that could be felt, but hardly seen, a mere overlaying of pink mist on the gold brown that she had picked up at a thousand swimming holes. Then the dress. Then the makeup. But who could choose with ease among ten colors of lipstick?

She made a choice, however, cursing the flight of time a little as she did so. And then she could darken those pale eyebrows with such effect that she hardly knew her own face. She worked on with frantic hands until the picture was such that she trembled a little at sight of it while she brushed out the tangle and left the curl of her hair. Over all, a black cloak. And she was ready.

For what? To climb again down that irregular ladder of lattice and bars? She thought the thing over while she bundled up the overalls that were her stock in trade. After all, that descent should not be a big problem to one who could climb a rope like a sailor. She tied the bundle of clothing to her shoulder, scanned the street, blessed its emptiness, and in a moment had swung down to the pavement.

What those clothes were worth she could not guess, but she had left a full hundred dollars on the dressing table of the room above. For she felt, somehow, that it would not do to go as a thief in a thief's apparel on this night, when she was to witness what seemed to Skeeter a sacred thing that only a church should house.

Her feet found their way across the town. Her mind was not on the streets and the turnings, but raced forward to deal with great images of struggle and death. So she found herself almost by surprise at the coolness of the river air.

She had come down onto the river road and now she was passing a familiar place. She stopped. For she remembered that this was exactly the spot at which earlier in the evening Liddell had ridden into the tulles.

She tried to walk on but some imp of the perverse made her step to the edge of the tulles. The infinitesimal waves that worked through the growth whispered against the shore. The faint night breeze went with shiverings through the tulles. And silently sounding the pitch in the back of her mind, she whistled a high, long note, followed by two short ones. When she waited, there was only the whispering sound of the little waves again and the hushing sound of the wind.

She had to get on to the dance under the cypresses and to the last scene of big Slip Liddell. Yet something held her there at the verge of the river, as fire is said to hold horses enchanted until they burn. Once more she whistled and listened.

And now she heard the dim noise of oars in their oarlocks. She heard something pushing through the tall reeds. Again she whistled, more softly, and almost at once the tulles were parted. A light skiff was barely distinguishable, and the loom of a man's figure against the paler rushes. He was standing in the boat.

"Hi . . . Slip?" he called softly.

That name, out of the dimness, did strange things to her. She said: "Are you a friend of Slip Liddell?"

The boatman thrust his skiff back into instant invisibility among the reeds. "Come back! There's no danger!" she called, careful of the pitch of her voice.

The boat returned, very slowly. "What you got? Money or just news?" asked the boatman.

"What's Slip to you?" asked Skeeter.

"He's OK to me," he answered.

"Would you lift a hand to help him?"

"Maybe I would, at that. Is he in a pinch?"

She found her voice altered, breathless, rapid with excitement as she said: "He's going to die. They've ganged up on him . . . because they say he killed Frank Pollard. He's going to the dance and they're going to gang up on him."

"That's easy," said the boatman. "Stop that fool from going to the dance. Why not?"

"Who can stop him when he's made up his mind?" she demanded. "But he's going to need his friends tonight."

"Did he send you to tell me that?" asked the man from the river.

She pretended not to hear and, waving her hand, turned and hurried down the bank.

"Why'd he send you?" called the boatman after her, but still she went on, hurrying, until she saw before her the cloudy heads of the cypress trees and heard the singing of the strings of the orchestra.

The big dance floor under the cypresses was swarming with people. They had hung the lights from the outstretching branches of the trees and placed some of them high in the foliage where they twinkled like stars, and each of those immense trees might have been called a separate heaven, a particular little firmament. Crowds of little tables surrounded the dance floor and off at one side had been erected an open-air bar draped with gaudy bunting where a long line of bar-tenders served a crowd that never diminished.

Everyone in San Jacinto seemed to be there, but in fact everyone was not, for there was a $2 admission and a good many were ruled out. They stood in compacted lines outside of the barrier that had been built shoulder-high around the place of festival. They were free to see and they were enjoying the sight to the full. This was no occasion for babies to be put to bed early. They were carried around on the shoulders of their mothers so that they could enjoy the color and the noise and their squealing and shouting made a background of sound that gave a certain unexpected privacy to the conversations at the tables inside the barrier.

Beyond all, certain lit, decorated floats stood out into the river, like stages in a green meadow, the waterlilies grew so thickly in the still shadows of the San Jacinto. She saw all this at once but her anxious eye had to wander a bit before it located Liddell. He sat at a table well back toward the barrier, looking very much like any of the other cowpunchers who were there except that, to her eye at least, something about the carriage of his head made him different from every other man in the world.

And now, as she passed the entrance toward the dance floor, she saw three figures take a place at a table not two away from Liddell. She knew them almost before her eyes could distinguish their faces clearly. They were Pudge McArthur, Soapy Jones, and Mark Heath, and they had not gone so near to Liddell except that they looked for trouble. She had come in time for the execution, then, and there were the three executioners.

A big cowhand, all silk and silver and jingle, plunged up to her and said: "Don't leave yourself without a man. Leave me try to fill in till your regular man comes around."

She did what the proud ones do in the movies. She walked ahead looking at nothing but her future, and she could feel the big fellow wilt behind her. She walked the way some of them do in the movies, too. That is to say, she put her feet down one exactly in front of the other. She could feel that make her body go forward on a level line. Somehow, she despised herself for doing this. A girl looked at her, looked down at her feet—smiled. She stopped walking with one foot placed exactly in front of the other.

Somewhere in the crowd was undoubtedly the girl from whom she had taken the green dress. Perhaps when she unveiled that dress it would be like exhibiting a face, well-known to all its friends. There might be an outcry of: "Thief! Thief!"

She slid off the black cloak and waited for the yell to begin. It did not begin.

She could see that Heath, McArthur, and Soapy Jones were seated on one side of their table so that they could face, not the dance floor, but Liddell. Other people, in nearby places, were moving hastily to distant tables. An open desert was forming around Liddell and his three enemies as she came up with the cloak fluttering over her arm and stood by Slip's table, saying: "I'm sorry, Slip, that I'm late."

His bewildered glance ran from her face to her feet and from her feet to her face again. Then he was up, taking her hand.

"How did you do it, Skeeter?" he asked. "Are you sitting or dancing?"

"Dancing," she said, throwing the cloak over a chair, and then they were out on the floor and swinging into the rhythm. He danced pretty well. He was not like one of those hobo specialists who have feathers on their heels and interpret the music better with their feet than a conductor can with his baton, but he danced well enough.

"Are you all right?" she asked.

"I'm all right."

"You look fine," she declared, with wonder. "You look steady and fine."

"Where did you find that much Paris in San Jacinto?" he asked.

"I bought it," she answered. "It doesn't matter where."

"You didn't get enough money from me to pay for it," he told her.

"A hundred bucks . . . everything from the skin out," said Skeeter.

"How many horses did you throw in to boot?" demanded Liddell.

"Slip, tell me what you've planned."

"I haven't planned, except I want to watch what the people spend. If you see anybody breaking loose with a lot of easy money, let me know, will you?"

"What has the spending of money to do with you, Slip? It's not money that *you* are going to spend tonight, is it?"

"I'm going to hand you something when we get into the thick of that bunch. Get that bag of yours open. And now take it." He pushed a sheaf of bills into the bag. "There's several hundred," Liddell said. "Use it to get back to civilization. And then stay civilized. Promise me that you'll stay off the road."

"I might have known that it would be this way," Skeeter said bitterly. "I might have known that you'd be clean, and right, and generous, and everything that I want in the world."

"Quit talking about me," said Liddell. "Watch the faces as they sail by you. See the men put on the brakes. Look at them lifting their heads.

They're seeing a new country, with gold in them hills, Skeeter. You grew two inches on your legs and let yourself out and pulled yourself in all over."

"I mugged myself up with makeup," said Skeeter. "And the rest is all clothes."

She saw Mark Heath dancing, but staring earnestly at her. On a sudden impulse, she gave Mark Heath her sweetest smile. A good Hollywood director would have known the star from whom that smile was copied, the slowness of it, and the melancholy.

When she looked again, someone had tagged Mark's girl and he was waiting on the edge of the dance floor.

"What did you say again about a cabin off in the mountains somewhere?" asked Liddell. "Say it again, will you?"

"I'll say it if you want," she answered. "I'll say it now and mean it all my life."

She looked up at his face and saw that he was smiling a little. He looked old. He looked the way a man in front of guns might have looked.

"I don't want you to say it," answered Liddell. He looked like a man at whom guns had pointed for a long time. If she could gain for him even an added hour of life, it seemed to Skeeter the most important objective in the world.

She had almost forgotten Mark Heath, but suddenly Liddell was stepping back and Heath was there, taking her in his arms to finish the dance.

"Get away and keep away," Heath said not too softly.

And he took her away, and she could see the insult strike the face of Liddell like a fist as he turned and went off.

"Was I wrong?" asked Mark Heath. "Did you give me the eye, or was I wrong?"

"You weren't wrong," she said.

"I thought you were glad to see him, but maybe that was my mistake," said Heath. "You know what kind of an *hombre* that one is? He shoots 'em in the back. He's murdered his partner for the blood money. He killed Frank Pollard. Why, that's"—he laughed—"*Señor* Coyote."

She saw big Liddell walking from the edge of the dance floor to his table. He was not waiting to cut in again. How much nerve was left to him, she wondered, if he accepted an insult in front of her? But that must not be the topic of her thought. Her one effort must be to stay close to Mark Heath. He could not pull guns, surely, when she was with him. And the other two, would they matter at all if Heath were not there to lead them?

XI

It wasn't a long dance because San Jacinto had an artist up from Mexico City, a girl who was all smile and eyes and a few ounces of fluff to protect her from the weather, and now they turned out the lights and flashed the spot for her and the orchestra started up some shudderingly fast rhythms. She had the footwork to go with it. Skeeter, taken from the floor as the regular dance ended, had been guided back not to Liddell's table, but to that of Heath and the other two. Soapy Jones was on one side of her, Mark on the other, and Pudge farther away watched the dance over his shoulder and made a sour face.

"It makes me kind of sick," confided Soapy Jones. "I mean the way they strip, nowadays. You'd think off here at the end of no place that they'd try to be a little decent."

"Legs like that . . . wouldn't it be a crime not to show 'em?" asked Skeeter.

"Legs like them? Scrawny things," said Soapy Jones confidentially. "When the knee sticks out like that, it don't mean anything to me."

"I know what you mean. You like 'em over-stuffed," said Skeeter. "Well, I've got a pair of shanks like those out there, and I'm proud of 'em."

"Why, you know what I mean . . . ," commenced Soapy.

"Shut up, Soapy. You don't know how to talk to her," declared Mark Heath. He explained to the girl: "Soapy's all right, but he don't understand."

She hated the complacency of Mark Heath with all her heart, and from the corner of her eye she watched Liddell seated alone at his table. He was trying to catch the eye of a waiter to order a drink, but they walked past him with a deliberate insolence. They did not want him there. Even his money seemed to be no good.

Then the dance ended. The flashlight went out. The regular lights came on.

"But *you* understand," she heard her voice saying to Heath as she kept herself smiling. "You know how to dance. You know how to talk. What else do you know?"

"You ask me questions," said Heath.

"Will you know the answers?" she asked.

"Ah, I get by most of the examinations," Heath answered with a grin, and his eyes began to take possession of her. "What are we drinking?"

"It ought to be a good drink," said Skeeter. "Because I'm meeting a fellow who knows all the answers, it ought to be the best. What about champagne?"

She waited for them to laugh, all three. She was ready to laugh herself. She never had tasted the stuff.

Pudge, in fact, said: "Aw, take it easy. That stuff puts a tingle up your nose and makes you sneeze, and it costs . . ."

"Who cares what it costs?" asked Heath. "We're going over to the bar where they got it good and cold. Come on over to the bar with me where we can get it cold. You come, Pudge . . . and you come along, Soapy. I'm going to show you what it's like."

They were all trailing across the dance floor. Then the orchestra was swinging into its beat again, and they were off the dance floor and at the long bar, with its gaudy drapings of bunting, and the crowd lined up three deep, and the cool damp of the river air kept drifting in and pinching at the bare shoulders of Skeeter with small, chilly fingers. But nobody else seemed to think that she was cold. It was very wonderful to see what clothes would do. It was she who made a place for them all at the bar, in fact. A dumpy fellow with enormous shoulders spread out his arms, when he saw her coming, and backed up, jostling many people behind him.

"Clear the track," he said. "Can't you bozos see the green light and give it the right of way?"

". . . and stick a couple more bottles into the ice," Mark Heath was saying. "We've gotta drink three times to get the taste. And fetch down those big glasses. Here's to you, sweetheart."

The bubbles came racing up and bursting at the

brim, but there were not as many bubbles as there are in ginger ale and the water didn't squirt up with the bursting of them in the same way. But the bubbles kept on rising from the bottom of the glass in the exact center, as though there were a magic source of life at that point.

The stuff had a funny taste. It tasted sour and it tasted sweet. It tasted sharp and brittle, and it tasted smooth and long-drawn out, like molasses. Then, while she was savoring it, Skeeter remembered that she was supposed to be having a good time with young Mark Heath and Pudge McArthur and Soapy Jones. So she finished off her glass and flourished the emptiness over her head. And she sang out: "Mark, Mark, here's to all the good fellows, all over the world . . . and down with the rats and the shacks wherever they are!" She turned her glass upside down and the last drops trickled away to the fate that should overtake all rats and shacks wherever they may be.

This gesture enchanted Mark Heath. He stood up on a chair so that he could make his eyes felt as well as his voice heard, and he shouted: "Open 'em up down the line, there! Everybody's gotta have a drink with me. Open 'em up right down the line of the bar, there. Crack out a dozen bottles!" shouted Mark Heath.

The bartenders looked at him for a moment, wildly. He laughed in their faces.

"A dozen of 'em!" he shouted.

The dozen bottles popped open with a lively cannonade. Then Mark Heath took a small billfold out of his hip pocket and carelessly tossed on the bar a $100 bill. It was the first bill of that denomination that Skeeter had ever seen. She snatched it up with a swift motion, like a bird picking up a seed. She looked at it on both sides, and then laid it down again with a sigh. It was rather strange, but there was no doubt about it that the possession of money made a man into a new thing. Mark Heath might be an enemy of Slip Liddell, but nevertheless a certain aura, a certain dignity attached to any man who could throw $100 bills around, in this fashion.

The head bartender came down the line, picked up that bill, glanced at both sides of it, and then stuck it into the cash register, calling out: "Sixty . . . out of a *hundred!*"

It was magnificent—$60 out, and still $40 left in that single little piece of paper, and a whole handful of crinkling change being brought to Mark Heath. Now the glasses were filled and lifted, and expectant, broad grins were turning to Heath. He held the drinkers from their wine for a moment.

"Nobody would wanna be any place but San Jacinto," he said, "but when there's a rat in the house, why don't you poison it? And there's a rat over there at that table. There's Slip Liddell.

There's the gent that pats his partner on the back with one hand and shoots him through the head with the other. D'you want *him* in San Jacinto? There ain't even any man in him. He's a yella, yella, yella hound."

Skeeter tasted those words far deeper than champagne, and a black agony rose like a mist across her eye. She stared at the table where Liddell was sitting, and now in fact she saw that he was rising and advancing straight toward the bar.

"He's coming right on over," someone said.

"He knows there's free drinks. And he feels a tickling in his ears, figuring we been talking about him so much. His ears is real hot so he's coming to join the good time."

Skeeter, who knew that this moment would be the most dreadful of her life, reached out desperately in her mind to find some way in which she could intervene, but a man who can be saved by a woman's strength is not a man at all.

She had a strange way of phrasing this moment to herself. She was hoping, bitterly, that there would be enough power in Liddell for him to reach his destiny like a man—just enough strength for him to die as one hero beaten down by many hands.

Near her, she heard a man say: "Jimmy, get that rope over there. We're gonna need a rope before we get through with Liddell."

Then Liddell came in on the crowd along the bar. Faces half cold and half smiling received him. Everyone turned to watch, and even the orchestra felt the nervous strain that was tensing the air and stammered and began to die out in the midst of a piece. It was strange, but every person inside the enclosure and perhaps most of those outside it seemed to know exactly what was happening and the dangers that lay ahead of Liddell as he walked down the length of the bar.

He walked straight on toward Skeeter herself. Her heart cringed in her with pity and with shame and with love.

Then she saw him step past her and take Mark Heath by the right wrist.

She recognized the cleverness of that move. You take a man by one wrist and he's helpless. If he tried to make a vital move, he draws you with him. All his physical efforts are muffled. Then she looked up at Liddell's face and realized that it was not a trick. Some mist of ennui or indifference was blown away from him. She thought she was seeing him for the first time.

He was saying: "Where did you get the money, Mark? Where did you get the big money? You were flat broke a couple of days ago."

Someone behind was saying quietly: "Give me the rope. I'll handle it."

But if Liddell heard that and knew what it meant, he gave no sign. He seemed unaware of the way the crowd was pooling around him, thick as lodgepole pines where one of the old forest giants has fallen and left an opening.

Mark Heath shouted out: "I got that money from roulette . . . and what made you a chum of mine all at once? Get your hand off me, you damned . . . !"

Liddell flicked his free hand across the face of Heath. The blow made a loud, popping sound. It struck the mind of Skeeter with a stunning force. It seemed to lift the hair on her head, and it knocked the closely thronging faces agape. It froze the lips of Mark Heath over the next few words he was about to utter. Everyone could hear Liddell, though he was not lifting his voice, when he said: "They don't pay you off with hundred dollar bills at roulette. But you can get 'em from a bank. You can rob a bank and get 'em! If you reach for a gun, I'll break your back, Mark."

Mark Heath cried out: "Soapy . . . Pudge . . . are you gonna just stand there . . . ?"

But Soapy and Pudge just stood there, and everybody else was just standing until an outcry from the side split that crowd apart as water splits under the forefoot of a boat, for the outcry said: "It's Pollard . . . that tall guy . . . that's Pollard or the ghost of him!"

He came slumping along with an awkward, shambling step and a foolish grin on his face, making gestures that might be construed as apologies. With him came Sheriff Chris Tolliver, tenderly licking his cracked lip with the tip of his tongue, with more of the sour wine in his face than ever before.

Mark Heath saw that tall figure coming and groaned half audibly.

Liddell said: "Frank, you're all kinds of a fool to show your face. It's too early."

This dead man who had returned to life put his hand on the shoulder of Liddell and said: "And leave them string you up to a cypress tree, Slip?"

"Gimme that hundred dollar bill," said the sheriff, and when it was brought to him from the register, he spread it out flat on the bar, and said: "There's the ink mark, all right. That's what the bank teller said that I'd find."

He put the bill in his pocket and, drawing out a bright little pair of handcuffs, fitted them over the wrists of Mark Heath with a click. Pudge McArthur and Soapy Jones were pawing at Frank Pollard, vainly trying to get attention from him.

Liddell said: "Did you know right along, Chris? Did you know I was faking right along?"

"It was a slick trick of yours," said the sheriff. "That bullet hole in the wallet, and the blood, and everything was pretty slick. But the fact was that the first word the bank gave out about the money it lost was wrong. They found a whole thousand bucks that the thief had overlooked. So when I counted twenty-seven hundred in the wallet, I knew that you put that money there. I knew Frank, here, never had a hand in the dirty deal. I knew you had his horse, but you hadn't put bullets into him. I knew you two were framing it to lie low till we got the real crook. But who would've thought that a bank robber would be fool enough to stay right in the town and start spending what he'd stole?"

Liddell said to Heath: "When I met you outside the sheriff's office and you looking at Pollard's horse and kind of white and sick, you were afraid that he'd come in and given himself up. Wasn't that it?"

But Heath could not answer. He kept moistening his lips and swallowing, for his brain was a cold blank, but the taste of the champagne was still in his mouth.

Skeeter, in the meantime, slid through that crowd, and got away from them. When she reached the river road, she ran through the darkness and the cool of the air. For she was burning with grief and with shame, and yet there was a triumphant joy in her, also. She ran down the road past the place where she had whistled the man out of the tulles. That man had been Frank Pollard, of course.

A horse at a swinging gallop came up behind her, so she drew over to the side of the road and reduced her run to a dog-trot. She was not far from the shack in which old Pop would be waiting. She was panting. It had been hard to run in the clinging fluff of that green dress.

The rider pulled up beside her.

"Hi, Skeeter," said the voice of Liddell.

"Yeah. All right. Go on and guy me," said Skeeter. "I thought you were scared, and you showed me up. You showed everybody up. I was a fool. Go on and yap at me, and then get out of my sight!"

Liddell dropped to the ground beside her. "Are you through talking?"

"Yeah, I'm through talking. Go on and say your piece."

"What's the good of talking?" asked Liddell. "You know me almost better than Sis does . . . so I suppose you know I love you, Skeeter?"

"Wait a minute," said Skeeter. "What are you trying to put over on me, Slip? Are you trying to make me cry or something? Because I won't."

"Are you old enough to marry me?" asked Liddell. "How old are you, Skeeter?"

"None of your business," said Skeeter.

"I told you it was no good talking," remarked Liddell.

"Yeah, but I'm terribly old, really," Skeeter said.

"Sure you are. Sure. You're as old as the hills," said Liddell.

They walked on down the road. He found her hand and drew it inside his arm. They passed the tulles. They did not speak. They could see the stars in the sky and in the flat of the river at the same time. Still they walked on, more and more slowly with Cicely following wearily behind.

The Power of Prayer

Only two years into his publishing relation-
ship with Street & Smith, which was almost
exclusive between 1921 and 1932, Faust was
asked to contribute two Christmas stories
to magazines the company published. The
first was to *Detective Story Magazine*—"A
Christmas Encounter" (12/23/22) under his
Nicholas Silver pseudonym—and the other
was the story that follows that he titled "The
Power of Prayer." It appeared under the John
Frederick byline in *Western Story Magazine*
(12/23/22). In it Gerald Kern embodies many
of those same qualities of a figure found in
several of Faust's Western stories, a gunman
who is also a gentleman.

I

One could not say that it was love of one's native country that brought Gerald home again. It would be more accurate to say that it was the only country where his presence did not create too much heat for comfort. In the past ten years, forty nations—no less—had been honored by the coming of Gerald and had felt themselves still more blessed, perhaps, by his departure unannounced. Into the history of forty nations he had written his name, and now he was come back to the land and the very region of his birth.

No matter if the police of Australia breathed deeply and ground their teeth at the thought of him; no matter if the sleuths of France spent spare hours poring over photographs of that lean and handsome face, swearing to themselves that under any disguise he would now be recognized; no matter if an Arab sheik animated his cavalry by recounting the deeds of Gerald; no matter if a South American republic held up its million hands in thanksgiving that the firebrand had fallen upon another land; no matter were all these things and more, now that the ragged tops of the Rocky Mountains had swept past the train that bore him westward.

When he dismounted at a nameless town and

drew a deep breath of the thin, pure, mountain air, he who had seen forty nations swore to himself that the land that bore him was the best of all.

He had been fourteen when he left the West. But sixteen years could by no means dim the memories of his childhood. For was not this the very land where he had learned to ride and to shoot? A picture of what he had been rushed upon his memory—a fire-eyed youngster with flaming red hair, riding anything on four feet on the range, fighting with hard-knuckled fists, man or boy, delving deep into the mysteries of guns, baffling his very brother with lies, the cunning depth of which were like the bottomless sea.

He smiled as he remembered. No one would know him now. The fire-red had altered to dark auburn. The gleam was banished from his eyes, saving on occasion. And the ragged urchin could never be seen in this dapper figure clad in whipcord riding breeches and mounted—oh, hardy gods of the Far West behold him!—in a flat English saddle.

But, for the nonce, an English saddle pleased him. Time was when he had made himself at home in a wild Tartar's saddle on a wild Tartar horse, emptying his carbine at the yelling pursuers—but that was another picture, and that was another day. For the present he was happier encased in a quiet and easy manner of soft-spoken gentility. It was the manner which this morning he had slipped into as another man slips into a coat. And for ten years, to do on the spur of the moment what the moment made him desire to do, had been religion with Gerald.

To be sure, when he came down to breakfast in that outfit and ate his bread and drank his coffee in the little dingy hotel dining room, people stared at him. But Gerald was not unaccustomed to being the cynosure of neighboring eyes.

Then he went forth to buy a horse, and the dealer, after a glance at those riding breeches, led forth a high-headed bay, with much profane commendation and a high price. But Gerald, in a voice as smooth as a hand running over silk, pointed out that the beast was bone-spavined and declined with thanks. And so he went on from horse to horse. But it seemed that his glance went through each beast like a sword of fire. One look, and he knew the worst that could be said of it. The horse dealer followed, sweating with discomfort, until Gerald pointed to a distant corral with a single dark-chestnut mare standing in it.

"That yonder," he said, "that one yonder, my friend, looks as though it might be for me."

The dealer glanced at the little English saddle that all this time Gerald carried over the crook of his arm.

"I'll saddle her for you in a minute," he said. "Yep. You picked the winner. I'd hate to see Sorrow go, but for a price I guess it could be fixed."

"Why is she called Sorrow?" Gerald asked.

"Because she's got sad eyes," said the horse dealer, and looked Gerald calmly in the face.

So the little English pad was placed on Sorrow, and she was led out, gentle-mannered as a lamb, until the rider dropped into his place. That jarring weight transformed Sorrow into a vivid semblance of dynamite exploding.

"She busted herself in sixteen directions all at once," said the horse dealer afterward. "And, when she went the sixteenth way, this fellow stopped follering. He sailed about a mile and landed on his head. I came over on the run. I sure thought his neck was broke. But he was on his feet before I got to him. And the light of fighting fire was in his eye. He up and jumped onto that mare in no time. Well, she sun-fished and she bucked and she reared, and did she shake him this time? Not a bit of it! He stuck like a cactus bur. And after she'd tried her last trick, she realized she had an unbeatable master, and she quieted down like a pet kitten. He rode her away as if she had been raised by him and ridden by him for years."

Which was the truth. Sorrow stepped high and pretty, albeit obediently, back to the hotel. Here Gerald left her at the hitch rack while he threaded his way through the group of loungers on the porch and went in to freshen his appearance. In a few minutes he came downstairs, whistling. On the front verandah he spoke to the first comer, and the first comer was Harkey, the big black-smith.

"What is there to see around here?" he asked of Harkey. "Can you tell me of any points of interest?"

Harkey stared at him, and all he could see was the whipcord riding trousers and the tailor-made cigarette that drawled from a corner of Gerald's mouth.

"I dunno," said Harkey. "There ain't nothing that I've seen around here that would match up with you as a point of interest."

And he laughed heartily at his good jest, and along the verandah the loungers took up the laughter in a long chorus.

"My friend," said Gerald gently, "you seem to me to be a trifle impertinent."

"The devil I do," said Harkey.

"But no doubt," said Gerald, "you can explain."

"Me?" Harkey said, and he balled his sooty fists.

"Yes," said Gerald, "you."

"I'll see you and ten of your kind in hell first," said Harkey.

"My dear fellow," said Gerald, "how terribly violent you are."

And with that he stepped six inches forward with his left foot and struck with his left hand, swift as an arrow off the string, deadly as a barbed spear driven home. Vain were those thick muscles that cushioned the base of Harkey's jaw. The knuckles bit through them to the bone, and the shock, hammer-like, jarred his brain. The great knees of Harkey bent under him, benumbed. He slipped inert to the ground, his back against a supporting pillar, and Gerald turned to the rest.

"I have been asking," he said, "for the points of interest around the town. Can any of you tell me?"

They looked upon the fallen body of Harkey. They stared into the dead eyes of the giant. They regarded his sagging jaw, and they were inspired to speak. Yonder among the mountains, due north and a scant fifty miles away, where the Culver River had gouged for itself a trench, gold had been found, they said, not many months before. And in the town of Culver City there would be points of interest, they said. Yes, there would be many points of interest for one who wished to see the West.

When his back was turned, they smiled to one another. No doubt this fellow was a man of some mark. There lay the body of Harkey, now showing the first quivering signs of life. And yonder was he of the whipcord riding breeches mounted upon famous Sorrow, famous Sorrow now dancing down the road with her first-found master. But in spite of these things, what would happen when Gerald reached Culver City, where the great men of the West were gathered? He might ride a horse as well as the next man. He might crush the slow-handed blacksmith with one cunning blow. But what would be his ventures among those men of might, those deadly warriors who fairly thought a gun out of the holsters and smote an enemy with an inescapable lightning flash?

Such were the thoughts of the wise men as they shifted their quids and rolled fresh cigarettes, but among them all there was not one guessed the truth, that the West was meeting the West as Greek meets Greek.

Even wiser men than they might have been baffled, seeing those daintily tailored trousers, those shop-made cigarettes each neatly mono-grammed, and the high-stirruped, slippery saddle in which he sat. For who could have told that the same West that had fathered them in overalls and chaps and bandannas had fathered this returned prodigal also?

II

But Gerald knew. Ah, yes, Gerald knew, and the knowledge was as sweet to him as is the sight of a marked card to an expert gambler. Why had he roamed so long away from them? This, after all, was his country, in which he was to carve his destiny. Let Paris keep her laughing boulevards and Monte Carlo the blueness of her sea—these raw-headed mountains, these hard-handed men, spelled home to Gerald. What mattered it if, in his wallet, there was a scant $50, his all of worldly wealth, so long as here was a gun at his hip, smoke in his nostrils, and beneath him a horse that went as sweetly as a song?

Up the valley he wound, and, topping the first range, he looked down on a pitching sea of peaks. Somewhere among them was gold. Yes, due north from him he would find gold, and wherever there was gold, there was electric excitement thrilling in the air. Wherever there was gold, there were sure to be lovely women with clever tongues and brave men with hands of iron and other men with wits as keen as the glimmering edge of a Damascus blade. That was no meaningless simile to one who had learned saber play—and used it!

It was the dull time of the evening when he came in view of Culver City. The double-jacks and the single-jacks were no longer ringing in the valley. But up the valley road the teamster was still cursing his twelve mules to a faster walk, and up the valley road other men were coming on horseback or in old caravan wagons, a steady stream typical of that which flowed into Culver City all day and every day and never flowed out again. What became of them, then, since the city never grew beyond a certain size? That was an easy riddle. Superfluous life was needed. It was needed to be ground away in the mines that pock-marked with pools of shadow the valley here and there. It was needed still more to feed into the mill that ground out pleasure in the gaming halls and the dance halls in Culver City.

Gerald was new to mining camps. What he knew of the West was the West of the cow country, the boundless cattle ranges. But, with knowing one bit of the West, all the rest lies beyond an open door at the most. He who has burned the back of his neck in the sun and roped his cow and ridden out his blizzard, can claim knowledge of the open sesame that unlocks a thousand mysteries. So Gerald looked down upon the new scene with the feeling that he almost knew the men who he would find strolling through the long, crooked street of Culver City.

And know them he did, though not out of his knowledge of the West. He had seen all their faces before. He had seen them gather around the standard of that delightful revolution that had budded south of Panama and almost made him a famous man. He had seen them in politer garb around the gaming tables of the full forty nations. He had seen them hither and yon gathering like bees around honey wherever danger and hope went hand in hand.

But of course he had never seen one of them before. He was as safe under his true name in this little town as though he wore the most compli-cated alias and barbered disguise in Paris. And, ah, what a joy it was to be able to ride with eyes straightforward and no fear of who might come beside him or who from behind. Here in his own country, his home country, he was safe at last. He watched the yellow lights begin to burn out from the hollow as the evening thickened. And not a face on which those lights were now shining knew any ill of him.

He began to breathe more freely. He began to raise his head. Why not start life all anew? Hither and yon and here and there he had felt that life had pursued him through the world, and he had had no chance to settle down to labor and honesty. Now, however, he was quite free from controlling circumstance. He could carve his own destiny.

What if his capital were only honest resolution plus just a trifle more of capital than $50? Should he not spend one night at the gaming tables before he entered the sphere of the law-abiding, the law-reverent?

Sorrow had been going smoothly down the slope all this while. None like Sorrow to pick a way among the boulders, none like Sorrow to come through the rough going with never a shock and never a jar for her rider. And that day the mare had traveled farther into the land of knowledge than her rider had traveled into the mountains. She had learned that a human voice may be pleasantly low and steady. She had learned that a bit may be a helpful guide and not a torture instrument to tear her mouth. She had learned, for the mind of a man comes down the firm rein and telegraphs its thought into the brain of a horse. It was all very wonderful and all very strange.

A door slammed nearby. In the morning Sorrow would have leaped to the side first and turned to look afterward. But now she merely pricked her short, sharp ears. It was a girl singing in the door of a cabin, with the soft, yellow light of a lantern curving over arms that were bare to the elbow and glowing in her hair. Sorrow stopped short. In the old days of colthood and pasture and carelessness before she began the long battle against man, there had been even such a girl who would come to the pasture bars with a whistle that meant apples were waiting.

As for Gerald, he came on the view of the girl at that very moment when his thought was turning back toward the gaming tables and the necessary capital with which one might launch forth on a career of honesty.

"Good evening!" he called.

"Hello," said the girl. "Tommy dear, is that you?"

Gerald frowned. Who was "Tommy dear"? At any rate, though at that moment she moved so that the light struck clearly along her profile, he decided that he did not wish to linger.

"No," he said dryly, "this is not Tommy."

A touch on the reins, and Sorrow fled swiftly down the valley toward the place where the lights thickened, and from which the noise was drifting up. So he came into Culver City at a gallop, with a singular anger filling him, a singular desire to find Tommy and discover what manner of man he might be.

In the meantime, he must have a room. He went to that strange and staggering building known as the hotel. In the barn behind it he put up Sorrow in a commodious stall and saw that she was well fed. Then he entered the hotel itself.

He had quite forgotten that his garb was not the ordinary costume for Culver City and its mines. The minute he stepped into the flare of the lanterns that lit the lobby of the hotel, he was greeted with a murmur and then a half-stifled guffaw that warned him that he was an outlander to these fellows. And Gerald paused and looked about him.

Ordinarily he would have passed on as though he were deaf. But now his mind was filled with the memory of those rounded arms of the girl at the cabin door, and how the lights had glimmered softly about her lips and chin, and how she had smiled as she called to him. Who was "Tommy dear"?

It made Gerald very angry. So he stopped just inside the door of the hotel and looked about him, letting his glance rest on every face, one by one. And every face was nothing to him but a blur, so great was his anger and so sharply was he still seeing the girl at the cabin door. He drew out a cigarette case. It was the solidest gold. A jeweler in Vienna had done the chasing that covered it. A millionaire had bought it for a huge sum. And the millionaire had given the case to Gerald for the sake of a little story that Gerald told on an evening—a little story hardly ten words long. From that gleaming case he extracted his monogrammed cigarette. He lit his smoke. And then he shut the case and bestowed it in his coat pocket once more, while the laughter that had been spreading from a murmur to a chuckle suddenly burst out in a roar from one man's throat.

It was Red Charlie. He stood in the center of the room. Above his head was the circular platform around which the four lanterns hung—a platform some three or four feet wide and suspended by a single wire from the ceiling above. But Red Charlie laughed almost alone. The others preferred to swallow the major portion of their mirth for there was that about the dapper stranger that discouraged insult. The slow and methodical way in which he had looked from face to face, for instance, had been a point worth noting.

But Charlie could afford laughter. He had made his strike a week before, had sold his mine three days later, and he was now in the fourth stage of growing mellow. The more he laughed, the more heavy was the silence that spread through the room. And suddenly the laughter of Charlie went out, for there is a physical force in silence. It presses in upon the mind. And Charlie pulled himself together. The fumes of liquor were swept from his brain. He became cold sober in a trice, facing the slender figure of Gerald.

"I love a good joke," said the quiet voice of Gerald. "Won't someone tell me the point?"

There was no reply.

"I love a good joke," repeated Gerald. "And you, my friend, were laughing very loudly."

It was too pointed for escape. Red Charlie swelled himself to anger. "There's only one point in sight," he said. "And you're it, stranger."

"Really?" Gerald said. "Then I'm sorry to say that, much as I enjoy a good jest, I detest being laughed at. But of course you are sorry for the slip?"

"Sorry?" said Red Charlie. He blinked at the stranger and then grasped the butt of a gun. Had a life of labor been spent in vain? Had he not built a sufficient reputation? Was he to be challenged by every chance tenderfoot? "Why, damn your eyes!" Charlie exploded, and whipped out his weapon.

Be it said for Charlie that he intended only to splinter the floor with his bullets so that he and his friends might enjoy the exquisite pleasure of seeing the stranger hop about for safety that existed only outside the door. In all his battles it could never be said that Charlie had turned a gun upon an unarmed man.

But now a weapon was conjured into the hand of

the stranger. It winked out into view. It exploded. At the same instant the taut wire that held the platform and the lanterns snapped with a twanging sound. Down rushed platform and all and crashed upon the head of Red Charlie. Down went Charlie in a terrible mass of wreckage.

And Gerald walked on to write his name in the register. His back was turned when the platform was raised and Charlie was lifted to his feet. But as for Charlie, all thought of battle had left him. Mild and chastened of spirit, he stole softly through the door.

III

Two things were pointed out afterward—first, that the oddly attired stranger who wrote the name of Gerald Kern on the register had not lingered to enjoy the comments of the bystanders, and, second, it was noted that the wire that he had cut with his bullet was no more than a glimmering ray of light, though he had severed it with a snap shot from the hip.

The second observation carried with it many corollaries. For instance, it was made plain that this dexterous gunfighter would maintain his personal dignity at all costs, but it was equally apparent that he did not wish to shed human blood. Otherwise, he would have made no scruple of shooting through the head a man who had already drawn a weapon. Furthermore, he had quelled a bully and done it in a fashion that would furnish Culver City with an undying jest, and Culver City appreciated a joke.

And when Gerald came downstairs that evening, he found that the town was ready to receive him with open arms. Which developed this difficulty, that Gerald was by no means ready to be embraced. He kept the honest citizens of Culver City at arm's length. And so he came eventually to the gaming hall of Canton Douglas. A long residence in the Orient and an ability to chatter with the Chinese coolies accounted for the nickname. It might also have been held to account for the gaming passion in Douglas.

But he was famous for the honesty of his policy even more than for his love of chance. Gerald, the moment he stepped inside the doors of the place, recognized that he was in the domain of a gamester of the first magnitude. And he looked about him with a hungry eye.

Here was all that he could wish for. One glance assured him that the place was square. A second glance told him that the stakes were running mountain high, for these gamblers had dug their gold raw out of the ground, and they were willing to throw it away as though it were so much dirt. Gerald saw $1,000 won on the turn of a card, and then turned his back resolutely on the place and faced the open door through which new patrons were streaming. The good resolve was still strong as iron in him. The clean life and the free life still beckoned him on. And, with a heart that rose high with the sense of his virtue, he had almost reached the door when he heard someone calling from the side.

"Hello, Tommy!" said the voice. "Here's your place. Better luck tonight!"

Gerald turned to see what this Tommy might be, and he found a fellow in his late twenties, tall, strong, handsome, a veritable ideal of all that a man should be in outward appearance. But there was a promise of something more than mere good looks in him. There was a steadiness in his blue eyes that Gerald liked, and he had the frank and ready smile of one who has nothing to conceal from the world.

He knew in a thrice that this was the "Tommy dear" of the girl. And Gerald paused—paused to take out his cigarette case and begin another smoke. In reality, he was lingering to watch the other man more closely. And how could he linger so near without being invited?

"We need five to make up a good game," the dealer for Canton Douglas was saying. "Where's a fifth? You, Alex? Sit in, Hamilton? Then what about you, stranger?"

Four faces turned suddenly upon Gerald.

After all, he said to himself, he would make a

point of not winning. He would make a point of rising from the table with exactly the same amount with which he sat down.

"I'll be very happy to sit in," said Gerald. He paused behind his chair. "My name is Kern, gentlemen," he said.

They blundered to their feet, gave their names, shook hands with him. As he touched each hand he knew by the awe in their eyes that they had heard the tale of the breaking of the wire in the hotel. Nay, they had heard even more, for the news of the riding of Sorrow and the encounter with Harkey had followed him as the wake follows the ship. After all, Harkey was a known man for the weight of his fists, and scientific boxing seems always miraculous to the uninitiated.

So Gerald sat down facing Tommy Vance, and the game began. As for the cards and the game itself, Gerald gave them only a tithe of his attention. They were younglings, these fellows. Not in years to be sure, but their experience compared with his was as that of the newborn babe to the seer of three score and ten. Even Canton Douglas's dealer was a child. In the course of three hands, Gerald knew them all. In the course of six hands, he could begin to tell within a shade of the truth what each man held, and automatically he regulated his betting in accordance. In spite of himself, he was winning, and twice he had to throw money away on worthless hands to keep his stack of chips down to modest proportions.

In the meantime, he was studying Tommy Vance. And what barbed every glance and every thought he gave to Tommy was the picture of the girl in the cabin door. It was odd how closely she lingered in his mind. The ring of her voice seemed always just around the corner in his memory. Through the shadow on her face, he still looked back to her smile. And why under heaven, he asked himself, did he dwell so much on her? There had been other women in the past ten years. There had been a score of them, and not one had really mattered. But when he had paused on that dark hillside, it seemed that the door of his soul had been open and the girl had stepped inside.

So he watched every move of Tommy Vance, for every move of a man at a poker game means something. What better test of a man's generosity or steady nerve or careless good nature or venomous malice or envy or wild courage? And the more he saw of Tommy the more good there was in him, and the more dread grew like the falling of a shadow in Gerald.

Men who have seen much evil, and stained their hands with it, are still more sensitive to all that is good. They scent it afar. And all that Gerald saw of big Tom Vance was truest steel. He gambled like a boy playing tag, wholeheartedly, carelessly. When the strong cards were in his hand, how could he keep the mischievous light out of his blue eyes? And yet when his hand was strongest and one of the five had been driven to the wall, Gerald saw him push up the betting and then lay down his cards.

It was a small thing, but it meant much in the eyes of Gerald. He prided himself on his manner and his courtesy, but here was a gentleman by the grace of heaven, and by contrast Gerald felt small and low indeed.

Then Tommy Vance pushed back his chair.

"I've dropped enough to make it square for me to draw out, fellows?" he asked.

"You're not leaving, Tommy?" asked the dealer earnestly. "If you go, the snap is out of the game."

"There's another game for Tommy," and a hard-handed miner chuckled on Gerald's right. "She's waiting for you now, I guess. Is that right, Tommy?"

And Tommy flushed to the eyes, then laughed with a frankness and a happiness that sent a pang of pain through the heart of Gerald.

"She's waiting, Lord bless her," he said.

"Then hurry," said the dealer, "before another fellow steps in and takes up her time."

"Her time?" said Tommy, throwing up his head. "Her time? Boys, there ain't another like her. She's truer than steel and better than gold. She's . . ." He checked himself as though realizing that this was no place for pouring forth encomiums on the lady of his heart.

"This breaks up the game, and I'm leaving," Gerald said, rising in turn.

"Are you going up the hill?" Tommy Vance asked eagerly.

"I'll walk a step or two with you," said Gerald.

They walked out together into the night, and as they passed down the hall, Gerald felt many eyes drawn after him. Yes, it was very plain that all Culver City had heard of his adventures. But now they were out under the stars. Not even the stars that burn low over the wide horizon of the Sahara seemed as bright to Gerald as this heaven above his home mountains.

"Now that we're out here alone," said Vance, "I don't mind telling you what everybody else in Culver City is thinking . . . that was pretty neat the way you handled Red Charlie. That hound has been barking up every tree that held a fight in it. The town will be a pile quieter now that he's gone. Only, how in the name of the devil did you have the nerve to take a chance with that wire?"

"How in the same name," answered Gerald quietly, "were you induced to lay down that hand of yours that must have been a full house at least . . . that hand you bet on up to fifty dollars and then laid down to the fellow on my right?"

"Ah?" laughed Tommy Vance. "You knew that? Well, you must be able to look through the backs of the cards. It was a full house, right enough. Three queens on a pair of nines. It looked like money in the bank. But I saw that I'd break poor old Hampton. And that would have spoiled his fun for the evening."

"You're rich in happiness, then," said Gerald. "A good time for everyone when you're so happy yourself, eh?"

"Yes," Tom Vance said, and nodded. "I feel as though my hands were full of gold . . . a treasure that can't be exhausted. And . . . well, I won't tire you out talking about a girl you've never seen. But Jack Parker brought her into the talk, you know," he apologized.

"I like to hear you," said Gerald. "It's an old story, perhaps. But what interests me is that every fellow always feels that he is writing chapter one of a new book. I remember hearing a man who was about to marry for the third time. By the Lord, he was as enthusiastic as you. It's the eternal illusion, I suppose. A man cannot help thinking, when he's in love, that a woman will be true and faithful . . . pure as the snow, true as steel. That's the way of it." And he chuckled softly.

It was entirely a forced laugh, and from the corner of his eye he was studying the effect of his talk upon Tommy Vance. He was studying him as the scientist studies the insect and its wriggling under the prick of the needle and the acid. And certainly Tommy Vance was hard hit. By his scowl and the outthrust of his lower jaw, Gerald gathered that his companion would have fought sooner than submit to such observations as these had they been made in other than the most casual and good-natured manner.

"You sort of figure," said Tommy Vance, "that women are pretty apt to . . . pretty apt to . . ." He was stuck for words.

"I hate to generalize on such a subject," said Gerald. "Every idiot talks wisely about women. But a man in love is a blind man. He wakens sometimes in a short period. Sometimes he stays blind until he dies. But I never see a pretty girl that I don't think of the spider, so full of wiles . . . and such instinctive wiles. She can't help smiling in a certain way which you and I both know. And that smile is like dynamite. It's a destructive force. Am I not right, Vance?"

So saying, he clapped his companion lightly on the shoulder, and Vance turned a wan smile upon him. It was delightful to be treated so familiarly by one who had so lately made himself a hero in the town. But still the brow of Tommy was clouded.

"Maybe there's something in what you say," he admitted. "But still, as far as Kate Maddern is concerned, I'd swear . . ." His voice stumbled away to nothing.

"Your lady?" said Gerald gaily, forcing his casual tone with the most perfect artistry. "Of course she's the exception. She would be true to you if there were an ocean and ten years between you."

But here Tommy Vance came to an abrupt halt and faced Gerald, and the latter knew, with a leaping heart, that he was succeeding better than he had ever dreamed he could.

IV

"Look here" said Vance, "of course I know you're talking about womenfolk in general, but every time you speak like that I keep seeing Kate's face, and it's uncomfortable."

Oh, jealous heart of a lover! Masked by the black of night, Gerald smiled with satisfaction. How fast the fish was rising to the bait!

"As I said before," said Gerald, "I haven't her in mind at all. She's all that you dream of her, of course."

"That's just talk . . . just words," said Tommy Vance. "Between you and me, you think she's most apt to be like the rest."

"If you wish to pin me down . . ."

"Kern," Vance said, "if I was to go away tonight and never come back for twenty years, she'd still be waiting for me."

"My dear fellow."

"Well?"

"If you actually failed to keep your appointment with her?"

"Actually that."

"Well," said Gerald carelessly, "putting all due respect to your lady to the side so that we may speak freely . . ."

"Go ahead," said Tommy Vance.

"Well, then, speaking on the basis of what I've seen and heard, I'd venture that if you go away tonight and don't come back for ten days . . ."

"Well?" exclaimed Tommy.

"When you came back, you'd find a cold reception, Tommy."

"I could explain everything in five seconds."

"Suppose she'd grown lonely in the meantime? If she's a pretty girl and the town's full of young fellows with nothing to do in the evening . . . you understand, Vance?"

There was a groan from Vance as the iron of doubt entered his spirit. "It makes me sort of sick," he murmured. "How do I know what she'd do? But no, she'd never look at another gent!"

"How long have you been engaged?" asked Gerald.

"Oh, about a month."

"Have you been away from her for more than twelve hours during that time?"

"No," Tommy admitted reluctantly.

"My dear fellow, then you know that you're talking simply from guesswork."

Tommy was quiet, breathing hard. At length he said: "If she was to draw away from me simply because I missed seeing her one night and was away for ten days, why, I'd never speak to her again. I'd never want to see her again!"

But Gerald laughed. "That's what they usually say," he declared. "But after the smoke has cleared away, they settle back to happiness again. They wear a scar, but they try to forget. They wish themselves back into a blind state. And so they marry. Ten years later they begin to remember. They hearken back to the old wounds, and then comes the crash. That's what wrecks a home . . ." He broke off and changed his tone before he went on: "But of course no man dares to test a woman before he makes her his wife. He tests a horse before he buys it . . . he tests gold before he mines for it . . . but he doesn't get a proof in the most important question of all. Pure blindness, Tom Vance!"

"Suppose . . . ," groaned Tommy Vance, his head lowered.

He did not finish his sentence. He did not need to, for Gerald could tell the wretched suspicion that was beginning to grow in his companion.

"But you see there's never a chance for it," said Gerald. "There's a small, prophetic voice in a man that tells him that he dare not make the try. He knows well enough that, if the girl is ready to marry, she'll marry someone else, if she doesn't marry him. It's the home-making instinct in her that's forcing her ahead. That's all as clear as daylight, I think."

"Good Lord!" groaned Tommy. "Suppose I should be wrong."

"Come, come," Gerald said. "I didn't mean that you should take me seriously. I was merely talking about girls in general."

"I wish I'd never heard you speak," said Tommy bitterly.

"You'll forget what I've said by tomorrow . . . by the time she's smiled at you twice," said Gerald.

"Not if I live a hundred years," Tommy said. "And why not do it? As you say we test gold before we dig for it . . . and only ten days." He rubbed his hand across his forehead.

"You won't do it," said Gerald. "When it comes to the pinch, you won't be able to get away."

"What makes you so sure?" Tommy asked in anger.

He was boy enough to be furious at the thought that anyone could see through him.

"Why, as I said before," went on Gerald, fighting hard to retain his calmness and keep his voice from showing unmistakable signs of his excitement, "there's something inside of you that keeps whispering that I'm right."

"By the Lord," groaned Tommy, "I won't admit it."

"No, like the rest you'll close your eyes to it."

"But if at the end of ten days . . ."

"That's the point. If at the end of ten days, you

came back and found her dancing with another man, smiling for him, laughing for him, working hard to make him happy, why . . ."

"I'd kill him," breathed Tommy Vance.

"Of course you would," said Gerald. "And that's another reason you must not go away. It might lead to manslaughter."

Tommy tore open his shirt at the throat as though he were strangling, and yet the wind was humming down the valley, and the night air was chill and piercing. It was late November, and winter was already on the upper mountains, covering them with white hoods.

"You're so cussed sure . . . ," said Tommy Vance.

"Of course."

"What gives you the right to talk so free and easy?"

"I'd wager a thousand dollars on it," said Gerald.

"The devil you would!"

"I'm not asking you to take up the bet," tempted Gerald.

"I could cover that amount."

"But a thousand dollars and a girl is a good deal to put up."

"Kern, I'll make the bet."

"Have you lost your wits, Tom Vance?"

It was too wonderfully good to be true, but now he must drive the young fellow so far that he could not draw back.

"I mean every word of it," Tom said.

"I don't believe it. Think of what will go on in the girl's head, Tom. She's waiting for you now. She'd worry a good deal if she didn't hear from you till the morning, and then got only a little bit of a note . . . 'Dear Kate, have to be away on business. No time to explain. Back in ten days.' A note like that, my boy, would make her wild with anger. A girl doesn't like to be treated lightly."

"But," Tommy Vance insisted, "I am going to send her just such a note."

"Tush! That's mere bravado even from you."

"Kern, is my word good for my money?"

"Good as gold."

"Then I'm gone tonight, and when I come back in ten days if she's . . . she's as much as cold to me, you win one thousand dollars!"

He turned away. Gerald caught him by the shoulder.

"Tom," he said, "I'm not going to let you do this. I'd feel the burden of the responsibility. And mind you, my friend, if the girl is not as strong as you think she is, and as constant, it is simply the working of Mother Nature in her. Will you try to see that?"

"I've come to my conclusion, Kern, let me go!"

"It's final?"

"Absolutely!"

"Ten whole days?"

"Ten whole days!"

"With never a word to her during all that time?"

"With never a word to her during all that time!"

The hand of Gerald dropped away. He stepped back with an almost solemn feeling of wonder passing over that crafty brain of his. How mysterious was the power of words that could enter the brain and so pervert the good sense of a man as the sense of Tommy Vance had been changed by his subtle suggestions.

"Well," he said when he could control his voice, "you're a brave fellow, Tom Vance."

"Good night!" snapped Tommy over his shoulder.

"And good luck!" sang out Gerald.

He watched his late companion melt into the shadows, and then Gerald turned to saunter on his way. It was all like the working of a miracle. Without the lifting of his hand, he had driven from Culver City the only man who stood between him and a pleasant visit with lovely Kate Maddern.

No matter if she were already engaged to another man. One curt note, and then ten days of silence could do much. Oh, it could do very much. Wounded pride was an excellent sedative for the most vital pangs of love. And silence and the leaden passing of time would help. Ten days to a lover were the ten eternities of another person.

Would it be very odd if she came to pay some attention to a stranger who was not altogether ungracious, whose manners were easy, whose voice was gentle, who could tell her many tales of many lands, and the story of whose manhood was even now ringing through Culver Valley—if such a man as this were near while Kate Maddern struggled with grief and pride and angry pique, would there not be a chance to win $1,000 from Tom Vance—and something more?

V

He went lazily on up the slope of the mountain. Behind him the town was wakening to a wilder life. And, staring back, he could see a thickening stream that poured in under the great light in front of Canton Douglas's place.

Yes, it would be very pleasant to sit at one of those tables and mine the gold out of the pockets of the men who were there with their wealth. But a game even more exciting was ahead of him. He turned up the hill again, walking lightly and swiftly now. Yonder was the cabin, with the door open and a spurt of yellow lamplight over the threshold and dripping down half a dozen stone steps.

He arrived at the path and turned up it, and in a moment she came whipping through the door and down the steps with a cloak flying behind her shoulders.

"Tommy, Tommy dear!" she was calling as she came dancing to him. Her arms flashed around his neck. She had kissed him twice before she realized her mistake. And then horror made her too numb to flee. She merely gasped and shrank away from him.

"I beg your pardon," said Gerald. "This is the second time I've been mistaken for 'Tommy dear'. Do I look so much like him in the darkness?"

"What have I done," breathed poor Kate.

She went up the steps backward, keeping her face to him as though she feared that he would spring in pursuit the moment she turned her back. But at the top step, near the door of the cabin, she paused.

"Who are you?" she queried from this post of vantage.

"My name is Gerald Kern," he said.

"Have you come to see Dad?"

"No."

"Are you one of the men from the next cabin?"

"No."

"Well?" inquired Kate tentatively.

"I came to see you," said Gerald.

"You came to see me? I don't remember . . ."

"Ever meeting me?"

"Have I?"

"Never! So here I am, if you don't mind."

She hesitated. It was plain that she was interested. It was also plain that she was a little alarmed.

"I came down the hill this afternoon," he went on. "Rather, it was in the dark of the twilight, and someone called from the door of the cabin to 'Tommy dear'."

"I'm so ashamed," said Kate Maddern.

"You needn't be. It was very pleasant. It brought me back up this mortal hill in the hope that you might let me talk to you for five minutes. To you and your father, you know."

"Oh, to me and to Dad."

There was a hint of laughter in her voice that told him that she understood well enough.

"I didn't know anyone who'd introduce me, you see."

"I think you manage very nicely all by yourself," said Kate Maddern.

"Thank you."

"You are just new to Culver City?"

"Yes. All new this evening."

"But you haven't come to dig gold . . . in such clothes as those."

"I'm only looking at the country, you know."

"And you don't know a single man here?"

"Only one I met at Canton Douglas's place."

"That terrible place! Who was it?"

"His name was Vance."

"Why, that's Tommy!"

"Your Tommy?"

"Of course!"

"Lord bless us," said Gerald. "If I had known that it was he, I should never have let him go."

"Go where?"

"He's off to find a mine . . . or prospect a new ledge, I think."

"He left tonight?" There was bewilderment and grief in her voice.

"Yes. I'm so sorry that I bring bad news. Shall I go back to find him?"

"Will you?"

"Of course. If I had guessed that he was your Tommy, I should have tried to dissuade him." He turned away.

"Come back!" she called.

He faced her again.

"Don't go another step. I . . . I mustn't pursue him, you know."

"Just as you wish," he answered.

"But what a strange thing for Tommy Vance to do."

"Wasn't it?"

"And to start prospecting in the middle of night . . ."

"Very odd, of course. But all prospectors are apt to do queer things, aren't they?"

"Without saying a word to me about it," she said, and stamped her foot.

"Hello?" called a voice beyond the cabin, and then a man turned the corner of the shack.

"Dad!"

"Well, honey?"

"What do you think of Tommy?"

"The same as ever. What do you think?"

"I think he's queer . . . very queer."

"Trouble with him?"

"Dad, he was to come to see me tonight. It was extra specially important."

"And he didn't come?"

"He left town!"

"Terrible," murmured her father, and laughed.

"Dad, he's gone prospecting. Without a word to me."

"Leave Tom alone. He's a good boy. Hello, there."

He had come gradually forward, and now he caught sight of Gerald, a dim form among the shadows.

"That's the man who has just told me about Tom."

"Hmm," growled Maddern. "Did Tommy ask you to bring us the news?" he asked of Gerald.

"No, Mister Maddern."

"You know me, do you?"

"I know your name."

"Well, sir, you might have let Tom talk for himself."

"It was quite by accident that I told your daughter," he said.

"I don't believe it," said Maddern. "A pretty girl hears more bad news about young men from other young men than an editor of a paper. Oh, I was young, and I know how it goes. It was by accident you told her, eh?"

"Dad, you mustn't talk like that."

"You don't need to steer me, honey. I'll talk my own way along. I've got along unhelped for fifty years. It was accident, eh?"

"It was," Gerald said.

"And that's a lie, young man."

"You are fifty, are you not?"

"And what of it?"

"You are old enough to know better than to talk to a stranger as you talk to me."

Maddern came swooping down the steps. There was no shadow of doubt that he was of a fighting stock and full of blood royal that hungered for battle.

"Dad!" cried the girl from above.

"Don't be alarmed," said Gerald. "Nothing will happen."

"What makes you so infernally sure of that?"

"A still small voice is speaking to me from inside," said Gerald.

And suddenly rage mastered him. It was the one defect in his nature that from time to time these overmastering impulses of fury would sweep across him. He lowered his voice to a whisper that could not reach the girl, but what he said to Maddern was: "You overbearing fool, step down the hill with me away from the girl, and I'll tell you some more about yourself."

To his amazement, Maddern chuckled.

"This lad has spirit," he said cheerfully. "Ain't you going to introduce me, Kate?"

"This is my father?" said Kate.

"I have gathered that," said Gerald.

"And, Dad, this is Gerald Kern, who was just . . ."

"Gerald Kern?" shouted Maddern, leaping back a full yard. "Are you the one that . . . come up here?"

He caught Gerald by the arm and literally dragged him up the stairs and into the shaft of light that streamed through the open door. "It's him!" he thundered to the girl as he stood back from Gerald, a rosy-cheeked, white-haired man with an eye as bright as a blue lake among mountains of snow. "It's the one that kicked Red Charlie out of town. Oh, lad, that was a good job. Another day, and I'd've got myself killed trying to fight the hound. When he talked to me, it was like a spur digging me in the ribs. But Charlie's gone, and you're the man that started him running. Gimme your hand!" And he wrung the fingers of Gerald Kern with all his force.

This was pleasant enough, but in the background what was the girl doing? She was regarding the stranger with wonder that went from his odd riding boots to his riding trousers, thence up to his face. But anon her glance wandered toward the trail outside the house again, and the heart of Gerald sank. Truly, she was even more deeply smitten than he had dreaded to find her.

But William Maddern was taking him into his house and heart like a veritable lost brother.

"Come inside and sit down, man," went on Maddern. "Sit down and let me hear you talk. By heaven, it did me good to hear the story. I'd have given a month of life to see Red Charlie when the lanterns and the other truck landed on him. Kate, you can stand watch for Tommy." Gerald was dragged inside the house.

"Why should I watch?" said Kate.

"Make yourself busy," said Maddern. "We're going to have a talk."

"Am I too young to hear man-talk?" Kate asked angrily, standing at the door.

"Now there's the woman of it," said her father with a grin. "Lock a door, and she's sure to break her heart unless she can open it, even if she has all the rest of the house to play in. But if you're inside, you'll be sure to wish you were out to wait for Tommy Vance."

She tossed her head. "Let him stay away," she said. "But not to have sent a single word, Dad!"

And Gerald bit his lip to keep from smiling. It was all working out as though charmed.

"When I was a youngster in Montana," began Maddern, "I remember a fellow in the logging camp as like Red Charlie as two peas in a pod. And when . . ."

With one tenth of his mind, Gerald listened. With all the rest he dwelt on Kate. And she was all that he had hoped. The glimpse had been a true promise. Now for a season of careful diplomacy and unending effort.

Were not ten days long enough for a great campaign?

VI

But ten days were not enough! Not a day that he left unimproved. Not a day that he did not manage to see Kate Maddern. But still all was not as it should be. He felt the shadowy thought of big, handsome Tom Vance ever in her mind. It fell between them in every silence during their conversation.

Not that he himself was unwelcome, for she liked him at once and showed her liking with the most unaffected directness. But sometimes he felt that friendship is farther from love than the bitterest hate, even.

Meanwhile, he had become a great man in Culver City. The sinews of war he provided by a short session every evening in Canton Douglas's place—a very short session, for it must never come to the ear of the girl that he was a professional gambler who drew his living from the cards. To her, and to the rest of Culver City, he was the ideal of the careless gentleman, rich, idle, with nothing to do except spend every day more happily than the days before it.

Neither was there any need for more battle to establish his prowess. It was taken for granted on all hands that he was invincible. Men made way for him. They turned to him with deference. He was considered as one apart from the ordinary follies of lesser men. He was an umpire in case of dispute; he was a final authority. And the sheriff freely admitted that this stranger had lessened his labors by half. For quarrels and gun play did not flourish under the regime of Gerald Kern.

There was the case of Cheyenne Curly, for instance. Cheyenne had built him a repute that had endured upon a solid foundation for ten years. He was not one of these showy braggarts. He was a man who loved battle for its own sake. He had fought here and there and everywhere. If he could not lure men into an engagement with guns, he was willing to fall back upon knife play, in which he was an expert after the Mexican school, and if knives were too strong for the stomach of his companion, he would agree to a set-to with bare fists. Such was Cheyenne Curly. Men avoided him as they avoided a plague.

And in due time, stories of the strange dandy who was *running* Culver City drifted across the hills and came to the ear of the formidable Curly. It made him prick his ears like a grizzly scenting a worthy rival. Before dawn he had made his pack and was on the trail of the new battle.

None who saw it could forget the evening on

which Cheyenne arrived in Culver City. He strode into Canton Douglas's place and held forth at the bar, bracing his back against a corner of the wall. There he waited until the enemy should arrive.

Canton Douglas himself left his establishment and went to give Gerald warning. He found that hero reading quietly in his room, reading the Bible and . . .

But that story should be told in the words of Canton himself.

"I come up the hall wheezing and panting, and I bang on Gerald's door," he narrated. "Gerald sings out for me to come in. I jerk open the door, and there he sits done up as usual like he was just out of a bandbox.

" 'Hello,' he says, standing up and putting down the big book he was reading. 'I'm very glad to see you, Mister Douglas. Sit down with me.'

" 'Mister Kern,' I say, 'there's hell popping.'

" 'Let it pop,' he says. 'I love noise of kinds.'

" 'Cheyenne Curly's here looking for you,' I say.

" 'Indeed?' he says. 'I don't remember the gentleman?'

"I leaned ag'in' the wall.

" 'He's a nacheral-born hell-cat,' I say. 'He don't live on nothing less'n fire. He's clawed up more gents than would fill this room. He'd walk ten miles and swim a river for the sake of a fight.'

" 'And he has come here hunting trouble with me?' says Gerald.

" 'He sure has,' I say.

" 'But I'm a peaceable man and an upholder of the law, am I not?' says Gerald.

" 'Which you sure are, Mister Kern,' I say. 'When you play in my house, I know that there ain't going to be no gunfights or no loud talk. And that's the straight of it, too.'

" 'Very well,' he says. 'Then, if you won't stay with me and try a few of these walnuts and some of this excellent home-made wine . . . if you insist on going back immediately . . . you may tell Mister Cheyenne Curly that I am most pacifically disposed, and that I am more interested in my book than in the thought of his company.'

"I let the words come through my head slow and sure. Didn't seem like I could really be hearing the man that had cleaned up Red Charlie. I backed up to the door, and then I got a sight of the book that he was reading. And . . . by the Lord, boys, it was the Bible! Wow! It near dropped me. I was slugged that hard by the sight of that book! Yep, it was an honest-to-goodness Bible all roughed up along the edges with the gilt half tore off, it had been carried around so much and used so much.

"Well, sir, it didn't fit in with Gerald the way we knew him, so quick with a gun and so handy with a pack of cards. But, after all, it did fit in with him, because he always looked as cool and as easy as a preacher even when he was in a fight. It give me another look into the insides of him, and

170

everything that I seen plumb puzzled me. Here he was reading a Bible, and the rest of us down yonder wondering whether he'd be alive five seconds after he'd met Cheyenne Curly. He seen me hanging there in the doorway, and he started to make talk with me. Always free and easy, Gerald is. He sure tries to make a gent comfortable all the time.

"He says to me . . . 'I get a good deal of enjoyment out of this old book. Do you read it much, Mister Douglas?'

"'Mister Kern,' I say, 'I ain't much of a hand with religion. I try to treat every man as square as I can and as square as he treats me. That's about as much religion as I got time for.'

"'Religion?' he says. 'Why, man, the Bible is simply a wonderful story book.'

"Yes, sir, them was his words. And think of a man that could read the Bible because of the stories in it. Speaking personal, there's too many 'ands' in it. They always stop me.

"'Well,' I say to Gerald, 'I'll go down and tell Cheyenne that you're too busy to see him tonight. He'll have to call later.'

"'Exactly,' he says. 'One can't be at the beck and call of every haphazard stranger, Mister Douglas.'

"'No, sir,' I say. 'But the trouble with Cheyenne is that he ain't got no politeness, and that when I tell him that, he's mighty liable to come a-tearing

171

up here and knock down your door to get at you.'

"At that, Gerald lays down his book and shuts it over his finger to keep the place. He looks at me with a funny twinkle in his eye.

"'Dear, dear,' he says, 'is this Cheyenne such a bad man as all that? Would he actually break down my door?'

"'He would,' I say, 'and think nothing of it.'

"'In that case,' he says, 'you might tell him that I am reading the story of Saul, and that when I have finished, I may feel inclined to take the air. I may even come into your place, Mister Douglas. Will you be good enough to tell him that?'

"'Mister Kern,' I say, 'I sure wish you luck. And if he gets you, there ain't a chance for him to get out of this town alive.'

"At that he jumps up, mad as can be.

"'Sir,' he says, 'I hope I have misunderstood you. If there should be an altercation between me and another man, I know that the victor would never be touched by the mob.'

"'All right,' I say, and backed out the door, feeling as though I'd stepped into a hornet's nest.

"I come downstairs and back to my place. There's Cheyenne Curly still standing at the bar with his back to the wall. He ain't drinking none. And all the half of the bar next to him is empty. The boys are doing their drinking in front of the other half. And Curly is waiting and waiting and not saying nothing to nobody, but his shiny little pig eyes are clamped on the door all the time.

"I go up to him and say . . . 'Curly, Gerald is plumb busy reading a book, but when he gets through with it, he says that he's coming down to have a little talk to you.'

"Curly don't say nothing back. He just runs the tip of his tongue over the edge of his beard and grins to himself like I'd just promised him a Christmas dinner. Made my blood turn cold to look at him.

"Then we started in waiting . . . me and every other man in my place, and there was a clear path from the door to the place where Curly was standing at the bar. But outside that path nobody was afraid of getting hurt. When two like Gerald and Curly started the bullets flying, every slug would go where it was aimed.

"It wasn't more'n half an hour, but it seemed like half a year to all of us, before the swinging doors come open and in walks Gerald. He was done up extra special that night. He had a white silk handkerchief wrapped around his throat like he was afraid of the cold. His boots shined like two lanterns. And the gun he was carrying wasn't no place to be seen. Matter of fact, just where he aims to pack his gun we ain't been able to make out . . . he gets it out so slick and easy out of nowhere.

"I looked over to Curly. And there he was crouched a little and with his right hand glued to the butt of his gun, and he was trembling all over, he was so tensed up for a lightning-quick draw. But his hand hung on the gun. He didn't draw, and I wondered why.

"I looked down to Gerald. And by heaven, sir, he wasn't facing Curly at all. He'd turned to one side and he was talking to young Hank Meyers. Yes, sir, with that wildcat all ready to jump at his throat, Gerald had turned his back on him, pretty near, and he was standing over by the table of Hank.

"Everything was as silent as the inside of a morgue. You could hear every word Gerald was saying. And his voice was like silk, it was so plumb easy.

"'I haven't seen you since the last mail, Mister Meyers,' he was saying. 'What is the word from your sick mother now?'

"Well, sir, hearing him talk like that sent a shiver through me. It wasn't nacheral or human, somehow, for a gent to be as calm and cool as that.

"Hank tried to talk back, but all he could do was work his lips. Finally he managed to say that the last mail brought him a letter saying that his mother was a lot better. And Gerald drops a hand on Hank's shoulder.

"'I'm very glad to hear the good news,' he says. 'I congratulate you on receiving it. I have a little engagement here, and when I'm through, I'll come back to you and hear some more, if I may.'

"You could hear every word clear as a bell. He turns back again.

"Curly was still crouched, and now he yanks his gun half clear of the holster, but Gerald leans over and takes out a handkerchief and flicks it across the toe of his boot.

"'Beastly lot of dust in the street,' he says.

"Well, sir, there was a sort of a groan in the room. We was all keyed up so high it was like a violin string breaking in the middle of a piece. I was shaking like a scared kid.

"But finally Gerald straightened and come right up toward Curly. I looked at Curly, expecting to see his gun jump. But there was nary a gun in his hand. Maybe he was waiting for Gerald to make the first move, I thought. And then I seen that Curly's eyes were glassy. His mouth was open, and his jaw was beginning to sag. And he was shaking from head to foot.

"I knew what had happened. That long waiting had busted his nerve wide open the same as it had busted the nerve of the rest of us.

"Up come Gerald straight to him.

"'I understand,' says Gerald, 'that your name is Cheyenne Curly, and that you've come to see me. What is it you wish to say to me, sir?'

"Curly moved his jaw, but didn't say nothing. I could hear the boys breathing hard. Speaking personal, I couldn't breathe at all.

"'I was given to understand further,' says

Gerald, 'that you intend to wipe up the ground with me.'

"Curly's hand moved at last. But it swung forward . . . empty! And I knew that there wasn't going to be no shooting that night. But it was like a nightmare, watching him sort of sag smaller and smaller. Straightened up, he must have been about three inches taller'n Gerald. But with Gerald standing there so straight and quiet, he looked like a giant, and Curly looked like a sick boy with a funny beard on his face.

"Hypnotism? I dunno. It was sure queer. Pretty soon Curly manages to speak.

"'I was just riding this way,' says Curly, his voice shaking. 'I ain't meaning any harm to you, Mister Kern. No harm in the world to you, sir.'

"He starts forward. I felt sick inside. It ain't very pretty to see a brave man turned into a yaller dog like that. Halfway to the door Curly throws a look over his shoulder, and then he starts running like he'd seen a gun pointed at him. He went out through the door like a shot. And that was the end of Curly.

"But, speaking personal, you and me, I'd rather hook up with a pair of tornadoes than have to face Gerald with a gun."

VII

There were other tales of that famous encounter between Gerald and Cheyenne Curly, that bloodless and horrible battle of nerve against nerve. And certainly the sequel was true, which related how terrible Curly sank low and lower until finally he became cook for a gang of laborers on the road, a despised cook who was kicked about by the feeblest Chinaman in the camp.

There was another aftermath. From that time on, men shunned an encounter with Gerald as though he carried a lightning flash in his eye. For who could tell, no matter how long his record of heroism, what would happen if he should encounter Gerald Kern in Culver City? Who could tell by what wizardry he accomplished his work of unnerving an antagonist? And was it not possible, as Canton Douglas had so often suggested, that there was a species of hypnotism about his way of looking a man squarely in the eye?

Even Kate Maddern was inclined to believe. And Kate was, of all people, the least likely to be drawn by blind enthusiasms. But she talked seriously to Gerald about it the next day.

It was a fortnight since Tommy Vance had disappeared, and Gerald himself was beginning to wonder at the absence of Tom. Was it possible that the young miner had determined to double the test to which he was subjecting himself? December was wearing away swiftly, and still he did not come. It troubled Gerald. It was incomprehensible to him, for he had not dreamed that there was so much metal in his rival. But perhaps it could be explained away as the result of some disaster of trail or camp that had overwhelmed Tommy Vance.

In fact, he became surer and surer as the days went by that Tom would never return—that somewhere among those hard-sided mountains lay his strong young body, perhaps buried deep beneath a snowslide or the thousand tons of an avalanche.

And yet there was no feeling of remorse in Gerald, even though it was he whose cunning suggestion had thrust Tom out of the camp. His creed was a simple one: *Get what you can from the world before the world gets what it can from you.*

In his own life he had never encountered mercy, and for mercy he did not look in his dealings with others. He gave no quarter, because he expected none. And if, from time to time, the honest and happy face of Tom Vance rose before him, Tom Vance with his eyes shining with the thought of Kate—if that thought rose for a moment, it was quickly forgotten again. Did not an old maxim say that all was fair in love or in war?

And he loved Kate profoundly, beyond belief.

He could no longer be alone. The thought of her followed him. It fell like a shadow across the page of the book he was reading. It whispered and stirred behind his chair. It laid a phantom hand upon his shoulder and breathed upon him in the wind.

Yet for all the vividness with which he kept the thought of her near him, she was always new. And on this bleak morning, as December grew old, it seemed to Gerald that it was a new girl who welcomed him at the door of her cabin.

He studied her curiously. All these days he had been waiting and waiting. There was something in her that kept certain words he was hungry to say locked behind his teeth. But this morning, with a bounding heart, he knew that there was a change. He told her so in so many words.

"Something has happened," he said. "There's been some good news since I saw you yesterday. What is it, Kate?"

"Didn't you see when you came up the steps?"

"Nothing," he said thoughtfully. "I saw nothing changed."

She brought him to the door again and threw it open. The strong wind, sharp with cold from the snows, struck them in the face and tugged her dress taut about her body.

"Don't you remember the boulder that used to be beside the door?" she inquired.

"I remember now," he said, looking down to the

ragged hollow near the threshold, where the great stone had once lain.

"Now look down the hillside. Do you see that big wet brown stone among all the black ones?"

A hundred yards away, across the road and down the farther slope, he saw the stone she pointed out.

"I pried the boulder up this morning," she said. "All last night I lay awake thinking about it, but finally I made up my mind. This morning I pried it out of its bed, and it rolled down the mountain. It sprang across the road in one bound, and then it fell with a crashing and smashing away off yonder."

She closed the door. They turned back into the room, and Gerald sat down with her near the fire.

"Well," she cried at last, "aren't you going to ask me what it all means?"

"I'd very much like to know," said Gerald.

"You're always the same," Kate Maddern said gloomily. "You keep behind a fence. You're like a garden behind a wall. One never knows what is going on inside. And it isn't fair, Gerald. It's like reading a book that has the last chapter torn out. One never has the ending of the yarn."

He smiled at her anger and said nothing.

"Well, the stone was in the way when we built the shack," she went on at last, still a little sulky. "Dad is very strong, and yet he couldn't budge it. He was about to blast it when Tom Vance came up from the mine. He laid hold of the stone . . . he's a perfect Hercules, you know . . . and he tugged until his shoulders creaked. He stirred it, but he couldn't lift it.

" 'It's no good,' Dad said. 'You can't budge the stone, Tommy. Don't make a fool of yourself and break your back for nothing.'

"Tommy simply looked at him and at me. Then he jumped back, caught up the stone, and staggered away with it. He dropped it yonder, and when we built the house the stone was by the door." She paused. Gerald had leaned forward, and she said the rest looking down to the floor. "I've never been able to see that boulder," she said, "without thinking of Tommy. It meant as much to me as the sound of his voice, and it was just as clear. Can you understand what I mean?"

"Of course," Gerald said sadly. "Of course I can understand."

"But finally," she went on, "I made up my mind last night. Tommy was not coming back. Perhaps he had found some other girl. Perhaps he was tired of me, and he hadn't the words or the courage to tell me about it. So he simply faded away. And this morning I got up and pried out the stone and watched it roll away."

He could raise his eyes no higher than her throat, and there he saw the neckband of her blouse quiver ever so faintly with the hard beating of her heart.

"And after the boulder rolled away," said Gerald at last, "what did you do then?"

"What do you think I did?"

He looked up to her face. She was flushed with a strange excitement.

"You came back and lay on your bed and cried," said Gerald.

"Yes," she whispered. "I did."

"And then . . . ," continued Gerald. He interrupted himself to draw out a cigarette, and he smoked a quarter of it in perfect silence before he completed his sentence. "And then," he concluded, "you jumped up and wiped the tears out of your eyes and vowed that you were an idiot for wasting so much time on any man. Is that right?"

"My father saw me, then . . . and he told you all about it."

"Not a word."

"But how do you know so well?"

"I make a game of guessing, you see."

She stared at him with a mixture of anger and wonder. "I wonder," she said, "if there is something about you . . . something queer . . . and do you really see into the minds of people?"

"Not a bit," he assured her.

"Do you think I believe that?"

Her head canted a bit to one side, and she smiled at him so wistfully that his heart ached.

"Now that the boulder is gone, Kate, won't you be lonely?"

"On account of a stone? Of course not. And then I have you, Gerald, to keep the blues away, except when you fall into one of your terrible, terrible, endless silences. I almost hate you then."

"Why?"

"Because, when a man is silent too long, it makes a girl begin to feel that he knows all about her."

"And that would be dreadful?"

"Dreadful," Kate Maddern said, and laughed joyously. As though she invited the catastrophe.

"But I'm only a stuffed figure, I'm afraid," said Gerald. "You're like a little girl playing a game. You call me Gerald to my face, but you call me Tommy to yourself, and when you are talking to me you are thinking of him."

She flushed to the eyes. "What a terrible thing to say!" cried Kate.

"Then it is true?"

"Not a word."

"Ah, Kate," he said, "I guessed it before, but that doesn't lessen the sting of knowing that my guess was right."

She sprang out of the chair. "Do you imagine that I'm still dreaming about him?" she challenged him.

"I know you are."

"You're wrong. I won't be treated so lightly by any man!" She added: "Besides, I think I always cared for him more as a brother than a sweetheart. We were raised together, you know."

"Ah, yes," Gerald said.

"You're not believing me again?"

"I haven't said that."

"It's gospel truth! And I'll never care for him again. I really never want to see him again. I'm only furious when I think of all the sleep I've lost about his going away."

How easy, now, to say the adroit and proper words. She had opened the way for him. That was plain. She had thrust the thought of Tom Vance away from her, and she wanted Gerald to fill the vacant room. And yet there was an imp of the perverse in him. He fought against its promptings, but he could not fight hard enough.

He found himself studying her shrewdly. Would it not be delightful to show her how truly weak she was—and make her in another moment weep at the very thought of Tom Vance? He spoke against his saner, inner promptings.

VIII

"I'm going to tell you a true story," he said. "It will change your mind about Tommy, and it will make you hate me, among other things."

"Do you want me to do that?"

"I can't help telling you," said Gerald. "The devil seems to be in me this morning, making me undo all my hard work. But let's go back to that first evening when I passed you on the hillside."

"Of course I remember."

"I never told you why I came back. But naturally you guessed."

"Naturally," she said. "There aren't many girls in Culver City."

He raised his thin-fingered hand and brushed that thought away. He waved it into nothingness.

"I heard you call," he said, "and then I had a shadowy glimpse of your face in the lamplight. That was enough to catch me. Mind you, it doesn't take much . . . just the right touch, the right stir of the voice, a glimmer of the eyes, and a man is gone forever. I was riding on a bus in London once. A girl crossed the street and looked up to me with a smile. Not that she was smiling for me, you understand . . . but there was an inner joyousness . . ."

He paused to recall it. And Kate Maddern was still as a mouse, listening, her fingers interlaced.

"She was very beautiful," said Gerald. "And if there had been something more, I think I should have climbed off that bus and followed her. But something was lacking."

"A second look, perhaps," suggested the pagan heart of Kate.

He smiled at her. "You miss my point," he said. "What I am trying to say is that men are sometimes carried away by shams. They think they have found the true thing, and they wake up to learn that their hands are full of fool's gold. But when the reality comes, it has an electric touch. And when I saw you and heard your voice, Kate, I knew that you were the end of the trail."

"Gerald," she said, "you are making love to me shamelessly."

"I am," he said, and lit another cigarette. "But to continue my story . . . unless it bores you?"

"I am fascinated. Of course I am."

"Very well. That night I went into Canton Douglas's place, and almost at once I heard someone speak to Tommy. Of course I looked, and the moment I laid eyes on him I knew that this was the man you had called to. He was handsome, clean-eyed, young, strong. He was everything that a man should be. And I managed it so that I should be asked to sit in at their game. I wanted to know more of Tommy Vance. I wanted to test the mettle of my enemy."

"Enemy?"

"Because I knew that one of us had to win, and the other one had to lose."

She sat, stiff and straight, and watched him out of hostile eyes. Whatever kindliness she might feel for him now, might she not lose it if she learned the rest of his story? And yet he kept on. That imp of the perverse was still driving him as it had driven him, on a day, to lead his army of brown-skinned revolutionists into the jaws of death, tempting chance for the very sake of the long odds themselves.

"I watched Tommy Vance like a hawk," he went on. "I was hunting for weaknesses. I was hunting for something that would prove him to be unworthy of you. And if I had found it"—here he raised his head and met her startled glance squarely—"I should have brushed him from my path with no more care than I feel when my heel crushes a beetle. But as the game went on I saw that he was a fine fellow to the core, brave, generous, kind, and true as steel."

He wrung those words of commendation from himself one by one.

"And I saw," he went on, "that as long as he was on the ground my case was hopeless." He paused again. "Well, in love and in war, Kate, men do bad things. I managed it so that I could leave the card game when he did. He was walking up the hill to meet you, and I set myself to prevent him from coming to your cabin. I told myself that if I succeeded, there was still a fighting chance for me. But if I failed, I would pack up and leave town and forget you if I could, or at least try to obscure the memory of you with other faces and other countries. But luck helped me. There is a jealous string in every lover. I plucked at that until I had Tommy in agony."

"How horrible," breathed Kate Maddern.

"Yes, wasn't it? But I was fighting for something better than life, and I took every weapon I could lay my hands on. He was a wide-eyed young optimist. But I planted the seed of eternal doubt in him. He began with an unquestioning faith in you. And before half an hour had passed, I had made a wager of a thousand dollars with him that if he left Culver City for a while and let you wonder why he had gone, when he returned, he would find that you had forgotten him. Well, he made the wager, and he left the town that same night. And that's where he is now."

"Oh, poor Tommy!" she cried. "And I've doubted him and hated him all these days, when all the time . . ."

"When all the time he was simply making the test. But he was right, after all, and I was hopelessly wrong. At least, Kate, I've made a good hard fight out of it. And the other day when I taught you how to manage Sorrow . . . just for an instant when you leaned and laughed down to me, I thought my dream was to come true after all."

He rose from his chair and confronted her courteously.

"But to send him away by trickery . . . and all these days to let me think . . . oh, it was detestable!"

"It was detestable," he admitted gravely.

And, encountered by that calm confession, her fire of anger was smothered before it had gained headway. She began to regard him with a sort of blank fear.

"What is it that you do to people?" she asked suddenly, throwing out her hands in a gesture of helplessness. "There is Red Charlie, who stood as though his hands were chained while you shamed him. And there is poor Tommy, of whom you made a fool and sent away. And then there is Cheyenne Curly, who you have turned from a brave man into a coward. Is it hypnotism?"

"Do you think it is?" he asked. "At least, they have seen the last of me around here." He tossed his cigarette into the fireplace. "Perhaps the devil inspires me to mischief, but the good angel who guards you, Kate, forced me to confess, and so all the evil I have done to Tommy is undone again. I'll leave tonight and trail him until I find him. I'll give him back to you as I found him. And, having been tried by fire, you'll go on loving each other to the end of time."

He picked up his hat. "You see that I retain one grace in a graceless life. I shall not ask you to forgive me, Kate."

"You are going . . . really?"

"Yes."

"To get Tommy?"

"Yes."

"For heaven's sake, Gerald, don't do that."

The hat dropped from his fingertips. "What on earth do you mean?"

"I mean . . . nothing. Only, don't you see . . . ?" She had fallen deeper and deeper into a confusion of words from which she could not extricate herself. Now she looked around her as though searching for a place of retreat. "Won't you understand?" she pleaded.

"Understand what?" Gerald asked huskily.

Then, as some wild glimmer of hope dawned in his brain, he sprang to her and drew her to the window so that the gray and pale light of the winter day beat remorselessly into her face.

"Kate!" he cried. "Speak to me."

She had buried her face in the crook of her arm.

"Let me go," whispered Kate.

Instantly his hands fell away from her. And there she stood, blindly swaying.

"Oh," she said, "it is hypnotism. And what have you done to me? What have you done to me?"

"I've loved you, my dear, with all the strength that is in me."

"Hush."

"It is solemn truth."

She broke into inexplicable tears and dropped into a chair, and Gerald, white-faced, trembling as Cheyenne Curly had trembled in Canton's place, stood beside her.

"Tell me what I can do, Kate. Anything . . . and I'll do it. But it tortures me with fire to see you weep."

"Only don't leave me," she whispered.

He was instantly on his knees beside her.

"I didn't know until you spoke of going," she sobbed. "And then it came over me in a wave. I had never really loved Tommy. He was simply a big brother. I was simply so used to him. You see that, Gerald?"

"I'm trying to see it, dear. But my mind is a blank. I can't make out what is happening, except that you are not hating me as I thought you would, Kate. Is that true?"

"Come closer."

He leaned nearer her covered face. And suddenly she caught at him and pressed her face into the hollow of his shoulder.

"How can you be so blind?" she breathed. "Oh, don't you see, and haven't you seen almost from the first, that I have loved you, Gerald? And, oh, even when you tell all that is worst in you, it only makes me care for you more and more. What have you done to me?"

"Kismet," Gerald murmured, and, raising his head high, he looked up to the raw-edged rafters and through them and beyond them to the hope of heaven.

IX

An hour later, Gerald was riding Sorrow straight into the heart of a snow-laden wind, for some action he must have to work out the delirious joy that filled him, and that packed and crammed his body to a frenzy of recklessness. The very edge of the wind was nothing to him, and, when the driven snow stung his lips, he laughed at it. For this was his home land, his native country, and all that it held was good to him, for was it not the land, also, that held Kate Maddern?

Lord bless her, and again, Lord bless her. He laughed to himself once more, and this time with tears in his eyes, to think how blind he had been to the truth. And he remembered how, with tears and with laughter, she had confessed that the rolling away of the boulder and the telling of that story to him had all been anxiously planned before in the hope that he would speak then, if ever.

And I shall be good to her, Gerald thought solemnly to himself. *I shall be worthy of her. Yes, I shall be very worthy of her, so far as a man may be. I shall make her a queen. I shall give her all the beauty of background that she needs. Her hand on velvet . . . a jewel at her throat and another in her hair. . . .*

His thoughts darted away, every one winged. The energy that he had wasted here and there and everywhere he would now concentrate upon the grand effect. No matter for the wild failures that had marked his past. Was not even the young manhood of Napoleon filled with vain effort and foolish adventures? There was still time and to spare for the founding of an empire.

It was a glorious ride, and the flush of glory was still in his cheeks and bright in his eyes when he came back to the hotel. And there, in the window, he saw a great, rough wreath of evergreen. He studied it in amazement. It was not like Culver City to waste time and energy on such adornments when there was gold to be dug.

Of the proprietor, behind the stove inside, he asked his question.

"And you don't know?" asked the latter with a twinkle in his eye.

"Of what?" asked Gerald.

"It's Christmas, man! Tomorrow will be Christmas. And tonight will be Christmas Eve."

Gerald stared at him, then laughed aloud with the joy of it. This surely was the hand of fate, which brought him for a present, on the eve of the day of giving, Kate Maddern and all her beauty and all her heart and soul, like a great empire.

He went up the stairs still laughing, with the voice of the proprietor coming dimly behind him: "There's a gentleman waiting in your room for you, Mister Kern. He looked like I might tell him to go up and make himself to home . . ."

The rest was lost and Gerald, kicking open the door of his room, looked across to no other than Louis Jerome Banti sitting in Gerald's chair and pouring over Gerald's own Bible. The act in which he was engaged shocked Gerald hardly less than the sight of Banti's face in this place. It was like seeing the devil busy over the word of God.

"In the name of heaven, Banti," he said, "how do you come here?"

"In the name of despair, *Monsieur* Lupri, what keeps you here?"

"Hush," cautioned Gerald, raising his finger. "There are ears in the wall to hear that name."

"Are there not?" Banti chuckled, rubbing his hands together. "Yes, ears in the stones to hear, and a tongue in the wind to give warning of it."

They shook hands, and, as their fingers touched, a score of wild pictures slid through the memory of Gerald, fleeter than the motion picture flashes its impressions on the screen—a cold winter morning on a road in Provence, with the crackle of the exhaust thrown back to them from the hills as their machine fled among the naked vineyards—and a night on the Bosporus when they were stealing, with their launch full of desperadoes, toward the great hulk of the Turkish man-of-war—and a day in hot Smyrna when the . . .

"Banti here . . . Banti of all men, and in this of all places."

"And you, my dear Gerald?"

"How did you find me? How on earth did you trail me?"

"How does one follow the path of fire? By the burned things it has touched."

"But I left you with the death sentence . . ."

"Over my head, and three days of life before me."

"Yes, yes. I had done my best. . . ."

"And it was better than you knew. The poor girl loved you, Gerald. On my soul, I sorrowed for her when I heard her talk. But she it was who came to me at last. With her own hand she opened the doors for me. She guided me to the last threshold. She put a purse fat with gold in my pocket. She pointed out the way to escape, and she gave me the blessing of Allah and this little letter in French for you . . . for her beloved . . . her hero of fire and steel."

"Be still, Banti, in the name of heaven. . . ."

He took the little wrinkled envelope. He tore open the end of it. Then, pausing, he lit a match and touched it to the paper. The flame flared. The letter burned to red-hot ash, fluttered from his fingertips, and reached the floor as a crumbling and wrinkled sheet of gray. A draft caught it and whirled it into nothingness.

"And that is the end?" said Banti, who had

watched all this from a little distance. "And yet there was an aroma in the words of that letter, I dare swear, that would have drawn the winged angels lower out of heaven to hear them."

"It is better this way," said Gerald. "I burn the letter, and I send the fair thoughts back to the fair lady."

"And her fat papa," said Banti.

"And to her fat papa. And now . . . Banti, you have not changed. You are the same."

"The very same," said Banti, and drew himself up proudly to the full of his height. He was a glorious figure of a man. And the cunning of his hand was second only to the cunning of his brain. Well did Gerald know it. Had he not, for three long months in wintry Moscow, dueled with this man a duel in the dark, a thousand shrewd strokes delivered and parried under cover of the darkness of polite intrigue? They had learned to read each other then, and they had learned to dread and respect each other, also. Victory in that battle had fallen to Gerald, but it was a Pyrrhic conquest.

"It is gold, then," Banti said. "It is gold that keeps you here?"

"No."

"A mystery, then?"

Gerald shrugged his shoulders.

"No matter. You will come with me?"

Gerald shook his head.

"No?" Banti smiled. "But listen . . . there is a kingdom in the sea."

"Damn the sea and its kingdoms," said Gerald. "This is my country. And here I stay."

"There is a kingdom waiting in the sea," Banti said. "Ah, I laugh with the joy of it, *monsieur*, when I think. Gerald, dear fellow, we are rich men, great men. The task awaits us."

"Banti, I shall not listen. And it is useless for you to talk."

"In two words, Gerald, what has happened to you?"

"I have a charm against your temptations. I have a flower to defy Circe, Louis."

"A woman?"

"My wife-to-be."

"She shall go with us, then. Where there is a king, may there not be a queen?"

"You are talking to the wind."

"You have not heard me yet."

"I don't wish to."

"You are afraid, then, in spite of your charm?"

"Talk if you must, and the devil take you."

"There is a kingdom in the sea . . . there is an island in the sea, *Monsieur* Caprice. Four great powers of Europe and Asia have reached for it . . . their hands met . . . and not a finger touched it. So, in mortal fear of one another, they withdrew. They made a compact. They erected the savage chief into a king. They erected the island into a kingdom in the sea, and they swore neutrality. But kings need wars for diversion, and, since he could do no better, this amiable idiot of a fat man-eater began to fight with his own subjects. In a trice, a musical comedy set.

"Yonder stands the commerce of the world licking its chops at the sight of the spices of that island and the river dripping with unmined gold and the mountains charged with iron ores and coal, the swamps foul with oil . . . but yonder is the king fighting his subjects. The island is split into halves. The king holds all the lowlands and the rich towns. The young cousin, with more brains in his little finger than in the whole sconce of the king, holds the uplands with a few hundred stout brigands and makes a living by inroad. Commerce is at a standstill. They kill a white man for the sake of his shoes. And the great, neutral nations and the great, neutral merchants stand about like a circle of lions and find one consolation . . . that no one is getting a piece of the dainty.

"But now, Gerald, enters a man of brains and money. He sees inspiration. He comes to me. He says . . . 'I give you money and a shipload of arms and a score of good men. Not too many, or my hand will be too apparent. I send you away. Your ship is wrecked . . . by unlucky chance . . . on the shore of the island. You go inland. You open communication with the young prince in the highlands. You offer him money and guns if he will give you the direction of his war. You, with your tact and your diplomacy, make a conquest of that young prince, who is man enough to appreciate a man. He takes you to his heart and into his councils. He turns over his army to you. The guns and the money are brought up. Your few white men are your bodyguard. You train the army of natives for a month. When they can strike the side of a mountain at fifty paces, you invade the domains of the king. In another month, you have routed him. You establish a new régime. You admit my money into your interior. And of the profits that come out of my ventures, one half goes to the kingdom . . . that is, to you . . . and the other half goes to me.'

"This, Gerald, is what the man of money and brains says to me. And I reply . . . 'This is all very well. If I were a Napoleon, I should undertake the task. I should agree to do all these things, ingratiate myself with the colored potentate, become ruler of him and his army, and conquer the kingdom. But I am not Napoleon. I am, however, one of his marshals. In a word, I know the man. Give me only six months to bring him to you.'

"That, Gerald, was my reply, and here I am. Pack up your luggage. Pay your bills . . . I have ten thousand, and half of it is yours . . . and come with me at once. We can reach a train by tomorrow morning."

He stopped, panting with the effort, and he found that Gerald was twining his hands together and then tearing them apart and staring down at the floor. But at last he raised his head.

"No," he said, "I cannot."

"In the name of heaven, Gerald. It is all as I have said. All that is needed to turn the dream into real gold is your matchless hand, your brain!"

"No again. A month ago, I should have gone with you. Today, not if you offered me England and its empire. Banti, you waste words."

Banti was pale with despair, but he had learned long years before that words are sometimes worse than wasted. He maintained a long silence.

"Gerald," he said at last, "if I may see the lady, my long trip will not have been wasted."

X

Footfalls stormed up the stairs, clumped down the hall, and a heavy hand beat on the door.

"Come," Gerald said as Banti discreetly turned his face to the window.

The door was thrown open by Canton himself.

"Kern," he said, "there's some devilish bad luck. Young Vance . . ." He stopped as he caught sight of Banti.

"This is my friend, Mister George Ormonde," said Gerald. "And this is my friend, Canton Douglas."

Gravely, having received a glance, Banti advanced, bowed, and shook hands.

"You may say anything you wish," Gerald said, "before Mister Ormonde."

"It's Tommy Vance come back raving and crazy," said Canton. "He's been out, and he struck it rich . . . rich as the very devil. He came back, went to see Kate Maddern, and then came down to town like a lion. I dunno what happened between them two. Maybe you know that better than me. But Vance calls you all kinds of names and says that he'll prove 'em on you when he meets you. He's been in my place, saying that he'll come there again at eight tonight, and that he expects to find you there."

"Very well," said Gerald. "I'll meet him."

Was it not better, once and for all, to have the matter ended and poor Tommy Vance out of the way?

"It's got to be that?" Canton asked sadly. "But Tommy's white, Kern. Ain't there any other way?"

"There would have been," said Gerald, "if the fool had come in private to me. But now that he's challenged me before the town, can I do anything but meet him?"

"It don't look like there's no way." Canton sighed. "But it's a mighty big shame."

"It is," said Gerald. "He's a fine fellow. I've no desire to meet him with a gun."

"Suppose he were to be arrested and locked up till he got over this . . . ?"

"Do you think he ever will get over it?" asked Gerald.

Canton hung his head. "It's a mess," he muttered. "I dunno what to think . . . except that it's the devil."

"Go back and tell the boys that I'll be there," said Gerald, and Canton left the room sadly.

Banti sat down again, whistling softly to himself. "I suppose this man Vance is the former lover?" he surmised.

"He is," said Gerald.

"He will depart from this sorrowful world tonight, then?"

"He will," said Gerald.

"And then," said Banti, "I shall take you and the lady of your heart away with me."

Gerald paused in his walking, then frowned upon Banti. "Louis," he said, "let me make this clear to you. I would give up a kingdom rather than take a chance that might harm her. Carry her into an adventure like that? I had rather be burned alive."

"Really?" Banti said, arching his brows. "But, my dear Gerald, if you marry the lady, do you think that you will be able to trust yourself thereafter?"

"Louis, you have never seen her."

"To be sure. But marriage is a great blunder of good resolutions. They vanish like the rainbow under the sun. One never comes to the pot of gold. Consider yourself. Here in the full flush of a new love, Gerald, when I paint the picture of that kingdom that is waiting for you in the sea, I notice that your eyes roll and your lip twitches and your hand jumps as though you were already in the fight. And in your heart of hearts you are already down yonder in the fight, scheming, plotting, learning a Negro tongue, working your way into Negro hearts, drilling a savage army. Tush! I can see the pull on you. It almost shakes you even now. You are on the verge of saying that you will take the wife with you. But after marriage, Gerald, when time dulls the gold . . . what then, *monsieur*?"

"Then there will be no devil named Banti bringing temptations."

"I? I am only one weak ship bringing a single cargo to port. But you, Gerald . . . What of you? Your own mind is the fruitful hatchery of strange schemes. The love of adventure is born in the blood. It is in yours. The time will come, lad, the time will come. The good Lord watches. He will whisper into your ear of some strange land . . . by the pole . . . an oasis in the desert . . . a shrine in Persia . . . and you must be gone. The tiger cannot be tamed. It may be wounded. It may be subdued by pain and kept quiet for the moment. But when it is healed, when you are past the first pangs of love, what then, Gerald?"

"Curse you and your tongue, Louis. I'll hear no more of this."

"You love her, do you not?"

"Like a part of heaven . . . like all of heaven . . . and she is all of it that I shall ever see."

"If there is such a thing as punishment for sin, why, yes, Gerald, she is all of it that you will see. But, if you love her, you care for her happiness more than for yours."

"A thousand times."

"Then give her up!"

"Ah?"

"I say give her up. Come. You are capable of noble action. This will be one of them. Step out of her life while you may. Step out before you break her heart."

"Banti . . ."

"I shall not come back."

"No, no! I have to thrash this out with you!"

"Talk it over with yourself. You are a better judge than I."

"Banti, stay for five minutes!"

"I shall be waiting . . . at eight o'clock . . . on the edge of the town. I shall have a horse. Bring your own. And we will ride all night into the lowlands. Remember."

"Banti, for the sake of our friendship . . ."

"*Adieu*!"

The door closed in the face of Gerald. He leaned against it until a tumult of new thoughts rushed into his brain—things that he should have said. He tore the door open, but Banti was already out of sight, and Gerald turned slowly back into the room.

XI

Night came early on that Christmas Eve. The steep shadow dropped from the western peaks over the little town, and by 4:00 p.m. it was dusk, with a wild wind screaming about the hotel. It shook the crazy building. It blew a vagary of drafts through the cracks in the floor, through the cracks in the walls. But through it all Gerald lay forward on his bed with his hands over his face.

There had never been a torment like this before. Not that march across the desert when the mirage floated before them with its blue, cool promise of water—not that moment earlier in this same day when he had told the truth to Kate—nothing compared with that long time of loneliness.

If Banti had been there, if one human being had been near to argue with and convince and thereby convince himself—but there was no one, and the solitude was a terrible judge hearing his thoughts one by one and spurning them away.

He looked at his watch suddenly and saw that it was 7:00. In a single hour he must face poor Tom Vance in Canton Douglas's place and kill him. There would be no chance to shoot for the hip or the shoulder, for Tom Vance would himself shoot to kill his treacherous enemy, and it was life or death for Gerald.

Not that he doubted the outcome. He had met sterner men than Tom Vance and killed them. And he would drop Tom with the suddenness of mercy.

And yet his soul rebelled against it. Rather any other man he had ever met than this fellow who he had so wronged. But suppose he could meet him and talk with him, man to man, for ten minutes, might not something be done?

He hurried out into the night, filled with the blind hope. Through the slowly falling sleet—for the wind had fallen to a whisper—he went up the street to the cabin of Tom Vance far at the end. He could look past it up the hillside to the glimmer of light in the cabin of old Maddern. In that house were the only people in the town who did not know, for the story would be kept from their ears surely.

With his hand raised to knock at the door, he hesitated. To walk in suddenly on Tom might be merely to bring to a quick head the passion that was in the young miner. There might well be a reaching for guns—and then the tragedy even earlier than he had dreaded to meet it.

Full of that thought, he went around the shack to the window on the farther side. It was sheltered by a projection of the roof and was clear of snow or frost; he could look through to the interior. There was Tom Vance not the distance of an arm's reach away.

Gerald shrank back. Then, recalling that the

light inside would blind the man within to all that stood beyond the window, he came closer again. And he saw the pen scrawl slowly across the paper, hesitate, and then go on again, a painful effort.

It wasn't hard to make it out. The lantern light fell strongly upon the page, and the stub pen blotted the paper with heavy, black lines. So he read the letter with ease.

Dearest Kate:

If this comes to you, I shall be dead as you read it, and Kern shall have killed me. I have challenged him. We are to meet tonight at Douglas's place, and there will be only one ending. I know what he can do. He can almost think with a six-shooter. And, though I am a good shot, I cannot stand up to such a marksman. But I shall do my best.

I don't want you to think of me as a man who has thrown himself away as a sacrifice. I know that the chances are against me, ten to one, but the tenth chance is worth playing for. With the help of heaven, I shall kill him!

You may think that I am a hound for fighting with a man you have said you love. But once you told me that you loved me, and I believed you. And I still believe that you cared for me as much as you care for him now. But there is some sort of fascination about him. The boys have told me when they begged me to take back my challenge or else fail to appear at Canton's tonight. They have told me how he broke down the nerve of Curly. They had sworn that no one can stand up against him.

And wouldn't it be odd if a man who can break the nerve of trained fighters couldn't win over a girl just as he pleased?

That is why I'm taking the tenth chance. Not that you'll ever care for me afterward, but because at least I'll have cleared the road for some other good man more worthy of you than either Kern or me.

I know that he is not your kind of man. He's a stranger. He talks in a new way. He thinks in a new way. He acts as no one in the mountains acts. He has a manner of fixing his eye on a person and paralyzing the mind and making one think the thoughts he wishes to put into one's head. And that's what he has done with you.

You half admitted it when you told me that you no longer cared for me because of him. When I asked you if you really loved him, you looked past me—a queer, far-away look. You seemed half afraid to answer. You would love him someday, you told me, more than you could ever love any other man.

But I think that you will never come to that day. Kate, take this letter as my warning. I am dying for the privilege of telling you what I think in honesty. And I swear to you that you can never be happy with him.

Where has he been? What has he done? Who knows his past?

Have you ever thought of asking him those questions? Has he ever spoken to you about friends of his? No, and I think he never will. One thing at least I know. I know that he is a man who has been hunted. He has a quick, sharp way of looking at new faces that come near him. Sometimes, when people pass behind him, he shivers a little. And, when he is not speaking, his mouth is set, and his teeth are locked together. He looks in repose as though he were making up his mind to do some desperate act.

I saw all these things that one evening I was with him. And I knew then that danger—hours and days and months of deadly danger—had given him those characteristics.

So, in the name of heaven, Kate, learn more about his past before you marry him.

And remember this—that a man who is capable of cheating and betraying another man as he cheated and betrayed me is capable of no really good thing.

I know that you will hate me when you have read this letter. Warnings are never welcome. But because I love you, Kate, I cannot help writing. Good bye, my dear.

Tom

So the letter came slowly to its end, and Gerald stepped back into the blanketing night and the soft whisper of the wind.

Who was it that said that truth sits upon the lips of dying men? He could not remember, but he knew the truth of all the words that Tom had written. And it was new to Gerald. Yes, the power with which he had been able to break down the wills of strong men might surely be strong enough to break down the will of a young girl. And had she, indeed, come to care for him chiefly because he was strange? He was recalled to a dozen times when he had found her looking at him half in terror, looking at him and past him as though she were seeing the future and trembling at what she saw.

Sick at heart, he came slowly back to the window. In the farther corner Tom was strapping on cartridge belt and the heavy Colt hanging in the holster. He took up a broad-brimmed, felt hat and placed it carefully on his head. Over his shoulders he threw a slicker. Next he drew out the revolver and went carefully over its action. When he was assured that all was in working order, he dropped the gun back into its leather sheath and marched to the door.

"The fool," muttered Gerald. "To go twenty minutes ahead of time and then stand the strain of waiting."

But Tom was not yet ready to leave. He turned again. He hesitated with a strange, half-sad, half-bewildered look. Presently he dropped to his knees beside his bunk. He clasped his thick, brown hands together. He raised his head, and Gerald watched the moving of his lips in prayer—words that came slowly, a long-forgotten lesson, learned at his mother's knee, was brought back to him and delivered him from the evil he would have done.

XII

Assembled Culver City was packed into Canton Douglas's place, and yet not a dollar's worth of business had been done, except at the bar. And when the door finally opened, at three minutes before the great clock at the end of the hall showed 8:00 p.m., all heads jerked around and watched Tommy Vance step in.

It was noted that he was quite pale, and that his lips were compressed hard—a bad sign of the condition of his nerves. But he bore himself stiffly erect. He looked quietly over the crowd, made sure that the man he wanted was not yet come, and walked with deliberation to a seat near the clock, pulling up a chair well apart from the others. There he sat and crossed his legs and waited.

"Just like the time that Cheyenne Curly . . . ," muttered someone.

"Except that it's different," said another. "Curly was a skunk. And Tom Vance is as white as they make 'em."

"He is," agreed another. "It's a shame that they got to have this trouble. Women sure get at the bottom of all the mischief."

"And Christmas Eve, too."

"Is it? God damn me if I hadn't forgot that it was the Twenty-Fourth! Tomorrow's Christmas?"

"It sure is."

"There'll be no Christmas for poor Tom Vance this year."

"Why not? Maybe he'll have the luck against Kern."

"Luck? There ain't any luck against Kern. He's like fate. You can't get away from him. When his eye takes hold of you, you just feel that you're gone, that's all."

"There's a considerable talk about this Kern," said a grizzle-haired old-timer who was proud of being able to remember the early frontier and the men of those hardy days. "But what's he done? He scared out two low-lived bullies. And any white man that don't get scared can beat an ignorant hound that don't know nothing but picking trouble. This here will be different. This boy Vance is clean. He'll make a different kind of fight."

"If his nerve holds. Look here. He can't hardly roll a cigarette!"

Tom had ventured on this task and was dribbling tobacco wastefully over the floor. Finally the paper tore across. He crumpled it, dropped it, and drew out the makings again.

"There you are," said the gray-haired observer. "There's the right nerve for you. He's going to try again. He'll do better this time, too. Look!"

The second cigarette was deftly and smoothly manufactured, lit, and a cloud of smoke puffed from Tom's lips.

"That ain't nerve," said Canton himself, who was near. "That's the way a gent will act when he's facing a death sentence. He ain't got any hope. All he wants to do is to die game without showing no white feather. But why don't Kern show up? It's past time."

Here 8:00 began striking, the brazen chimes booming loudly through the hushed room, and when the last sound echoed away to a murmur, every man leaned forward, expecting to see the door fly open. The cigarette fell from the numbed fingers of Tom Vance. But the door did not stir. And slowly the crowd settled back.

"He's waiting so's he can break Tom's nerve just the way he busted Cheyenne Curly's."

"It's a mighty poor thing to do," Canton said with heat. "I don't mind saying that it's downright low to play that sort of game with poor Tom that ain't got a chance in a hundred, anyway."

They waited five minutes, ten minutes, and the scowls of the miners grew blacker and blacker. The trick of Gerald was patent to all, and it enraged them.

"Hey, Jerry!" Canton called suddenly to one of the men who was making a pretense at continuing a card game. "Run over to the hotel, will you? Tell Gerald that his friend is waiting for him plumb anxious, will you? And tell him that he's a mile overdue."

There was a growl of assent from a hundred throats, and Jerry went off reluctantly on an errand that might prove dangerous unless the message were phrased tenderly enough. In three minutes he came back, and he came with a rush that knocked the swinging door wide.

"Boys," he shouted as he came to a halt, "I looked up in his room! He ain't there, and his things are gone. I run down and looked into the stable. And Sorrow wasn't there. And nobody ain't seen nothing of Kern nowhere!"

"By heaven!" roared the old-timer of the gray hair, rising from his place. "I sort of suspicioned it! He didn't like this game. He knew he had different kind of meat to chew this time. He's been bluffed out. He's quit cold, the yaller dog!"

Tumult instantly reigned in Canton's place. Out poured the hundred searchers. They swarmed through the town, but they found no trace of Gerald Kern.

"Up yonder!" called an inspired voice at last, pointing to the light in the window of the Maddern cabin. "I'll bet a thousand that he's up there sitting pretty and talking to his girl. Let's take a look."

And up the slope they went with a willing rush. They reached the door. It was opened by Maddern, with Kate behind him.

"Where's Kern?" they demanded.

"Not here," they were told. "And what's up, boys?"

"The hound has run out on Tom Vance. He's showed yaller. He's quit without daring to show his face."

"No, no!" cried Kate.

"Here's a hundred of us to swear to it," Canton Douglas insisted furiously.

And Kate raised her hands to her face.

It was hard going over the mountains. Though the wagons had beaten out a trail, it was deep with snow, and the two horsemen let their mounts labor

215

on, giving them what aid they could to guide them until the clouds were brushed from the sky and the stars looked down to show them the way. A little later, they reached the last of the ridges. Below them spread the lowlands and a safer and an easier trail to follow.

Here they drew rein, and Gerald looked back.

"*Cher ami*," said Banti, "no halting by the way. The small waiting makes the great heart ache. Forward, comrade!"

"Hush, Louis. It is my last look."

"Ah, my friend, it will be far better when you have your first look at your kingdom yonder over the sea."

"But this is my country," he said. "And this is the last time that I shall see it."

So the silence grew, while Banti gnawed his lip with anxiety.

"It is my torment if you linger here," he said gently, at last.

"Louis," murmured his friend, "what is it that a woman detests most in a man?"

"A close string drawn on the pocketbook."

"We are not in France," Gerald said with a touch of scorn. "Tell me again."

"Long silences at the table," said Banti. "They drive the poor dears mad. Yes, a silent husband is even worse than a pinched wallet."

"Still wrong," said Gerald. "What a woman hates most of all in a man is cowardice. A woman ceases to love a man who runs away from danger."

"Eh?"

"Because that is rot at the heart of the tree."

"Perhaps you are right. But what of that?"

"Nothing," said Gerald. "Let us ride on again."

They passed on down the slope. And the steady trot of the horses covered the weary miles one by one. As for Banti, he whistled; he sang; he told wild tales of a dozen lands, and all without drawing a word from his companion until, as they drew near to a town, he said:

"What is in your head now, Gerald? Tell me the thought that has stopped that restless tongue of yours so long?"

"I shall tell you," said Gerald, "though it will mean nothing to you. I have been thinking of Christmas Day, Louis, and the power of prayer."

Louis considered a moment. "Ah, yes," he said at last. "I had forgotten. But this is Christmas, and on this day one goes back to the silly thoughts of one's childhood. Is it not so?"

The Cure of Silver Cañon

"The Cure of Silver Cañon" by John Frederick was the second short novel by Faust to appear in *Western Story Magazine* (1/15/21). In Faust's Western fiction the mountain desert is a country of the imagination where no man is ever a hero and no man is ever a villain, but rather a mixture of both. This certainly proves the case in this story in which both Lew Carney and Jack Doyle love Mary Hamilton and where we, as readers, can never know with certitude for whose soul it is that Mary Hamilton weeps. The story's opening is perhaps the most imagistic and at the same time eerie as Faust ever wrote.

I

This is a story of how Lew Carney made friends with the law. It must not be assumed that Lew was an outcast; neither that he was an underhanded violator of constituted authority. As a matter of fact there was one law that Lew always held in the highest esteem. He never varied from the prescriptions of that law. He never, as far as possible, allowed anyone near him to violate that law. Unfortunately that law was the will of Lew Carney.

He was born with sandy hair that reared up at off angles all over his head. His eyes were a bright blue as pale as fire. Since the beginning of time there has never been a man, with sandy hair and those pale, bright eyes, who has not trodden on the toes of the powers that be. Carney was that type and more than that type. Not that he had a taint of malice in his five-feet-ten of wire-strung muscle, not that he loved trouble, but he was so constituted that what he liked, he coveted with a passion for possession, and what he disliked, he hated with consummate loathing. There was no intermediate state. Consider a man of these parts, equipped in addition with an eye that never was clouded by the most furious of his passions and a hand that never shook in a crisis, and it is easy to understand why

Lew Carney was regarded by the pillars of society with suspicion.

In a community where men shoulder one another in crowds, his fiery soul would have started a conflagration before he got well into his teens. But by the grace of the Lord, Lew Carney was placed in the mountain desert, in a region where even the buzzard strains its eyes looking from one town to the next, and where the wary stranger travels like a ship at sea, by compass. Here Lew Carney had plenty of room to circulate without growing heated by friction to the danger point. Even with these advantages, the spark of excitement had snapped into his eyes a good many times. He might have become a refugee long before, had it not chanced that the men who he crossed were not themselves wholly desirable citizens. Yet the time was sure to come when, hating work and loving action, he would find his hands full. Someday a death would be laid to his door, and then—the end.

He was the happiest rider between the Sierras and the Rockies and one of the most reckless. There was no desert that he would not dare; there was no privation that he had not endured to reach the ends of his own pleasure. Not the most intimate of Lew's best friends could name a single pang that he had undergone for the sake of honest labor. But for that matter, he did not have to work. With a face for poker and hands for the same game, he never lacked the sources of supply.

Lew was about to extinguish his campfire on this strange night in Silver Cañon. He had finished his cooking and eaten his meal hurriedly and without pleasure, for this was a dry camp. The fire had dwindled to a few black embers and one central heart of red that tossed up a tongue of yellow flame intermittently. At each flash there was illumined only one feature. First, a narrow, fleshless chin. Who is it that speaks of the fighting jaw of the bull terrier? Then a thin-lipped mouth, with the lean cheeks and the deep-set, glowing eyes. And lastly the wild hair, thrusting up askew. It made him look, even on this hushed night, as though a wind were blowing in his face. On the whole it was a rather handsome face, but men would be apt to appreciate its qualities more than women. Lew scooped up a handful of sand and swept it across the fire. The night settled around him.

But the night had its own illumination. The moon, which had been struggling as a sickly circle through the ground haze, now moved higher and took on its own proper color, an indescribable crystal white. It was easy to understand why this valley had the singular name of Silver Cañon. In the day it was a burning gulch not more than five miles wide, a hundred miles long, banked in with low, steep-sided mountains in unbroken walls. Under the sun it was pale, sand-yellow, both mountains and valley floor, but the moon changed it, gilded it, and made it a miracle of silver.

The night was coming on crisp and cold, for the elevation was great. But in spite of his long ride Carney postponed his sleep. He wrapped himself in his blankets and sat up to see. Not much for anyone to see except a poet, for both earth and sky were a pale, bright silver, and the moon was the only living thing in heaven or on earth. His horse, a wise old gelding with an ugly head and muscles of leather, seemed to feel the silence, for he came from his wretched hunt after dead grass and stood behind the master. But the master paid no attention. He was squinting into nothingness and seeing. He was harkening to silence and hearing. A sound that the ear of a wolf could hardly catch came to him. He knew that there were rabbits. He listened again, a wavering pulse of noise, and far off was a coyote. And yet both those sounds combined did not make up the volume of a hushed whisper. They were unheard rhythms that are felt.

But what Lew Carney saw no man can say, no man who has not been stung with the fever of the desert. Perhaps he guessed at the stars behind the moon haze. Perhaps he thought of the buzzards far off, all-seeing, all-knowing, the dreadful prophets of the mountain desert. But whatever it was that the mind of Lew Carney perceived, his face under the moon was the face of a man who sees God. He had come from the gaming tables of Bogle Camp;

tomorrow night he would be at the gaming tables in Cayuse; but here was an interval of silence between, and he gave himself to it as devoutly as he would give himself again to chuck-a-luck or poker.

Some moments went by. The horse stirred and went away, switching his tail. Yet Carney did not move. He was like an Indian in a trance. He was opening himself to that deadly hush with a pleasure more thrilling than cards and red-eye combined. Time at length entirely ceased for him. It might have been five minutes later. It might have been midnight. He seemed to have drifted on a river into the heart of a new emotion.

And now he heard it for the first time.

Into the unutterable silence of the mountains a pulse of new sound had grown. He was suddenly aware that he had been hearing it ever since he first made camp, but not until it grew into an unmistakable thing did he fully awaken to it. He had not heard it because he did not expect it. He knew the mountain desert as a student knows a book, as a monk knows his cell, as a child knows its mother. It was the one thing on earth that he truly feared, and it was probably the only thing on earth that he really loved. The moment he made out the new thing, he stiffened under his blankets and canted his head down. The next instant he lay prone to catch the ground noise. And after lying there a moment, he started up and walked back and forth across a diameter of a hundred yards.

When he had finished his walk, he was plainly and deeply excited. He stood with his teeth clenched and his eyes working uneasily through the moon haze and piercing down the valley in the direction of Bogle Camp, far away. He even touched the handles of his gun and he found a friendly reassurance in their familiar grip. He went restlessly to the gelding and cursed him in a murmur. The horse pricked his ears at the well-known words.

But here was a strange thing in itself: Lew Carney lowering his voice because of some strange emotion.

The sound of his own voice seeming to trouble him, he started away from the horse and walked again in the hope of catching a different angle of the sound. He heard nothing new. It was always the same.

Now the sound was unmistakable, and unquestionably it approached him. And to understand how the sound could approach for so long a time without the cause coming into view, it must be remembered that the air of the mountains at that altitude is very rare, and sound travels a long distance without appreciable diminution.

In itself the noise was far from dreadful. Yet the lone rider eventually retired to his blankets, wrapped himself in them securely, for fear that the chill of the night should numb his fighting muscles, and rested his revolver on his knee for action. He brushed his hand across his forehead, and the tips of his fingers came away wet. Lew Carney was in a cold perspiration of fear! And that was a fact that few men in the mountain desert would have believed.

He sat with his eyes glued through the moon haze down the valley, and his head canted to listen more intently. Once more it stopped. Once more it began, a low, chuckling sound with a metallic rattling mixed in. And for a time it rumbled softly on toward him, and then again the sound was snuffed out as though it had turned a corner.

That was the gruesome part of it, the pauses in that noise. The continued sounds that one hears in a lonely house by night are unheeded, but the sounds that are varied by stealthy pauses chill the blood. That is the footstep approaching, pausing, listening, stealing on again.

The strange sound stole toward the waiting man, paused, and stole on again. But there are motives for stealth in a house. What motive was there in the open desert?

It was the very strangeness of it that sent the shudder through Lew. Presently he could feel the terror of that presence that was coming slowly down the valley. It went before, like the eye of a snake, and fascinated life into motionlessness. Before he saw the thing that made the sound, while the murmur itself was but an undistinguished whisper, before all the revelations of the future, Lew Carney knew that the thing was evil. Just as he had heard the voices of certain men and hated them before he even saw their faces.

He was not a superstitious fellow. Far from it. His life had made him a canny, practical sort in the affairs of men, but it had also given him a searching alertness. He could smile while he faced a known danger, but an unknown thing unnerved him. Given an equal start, a third-rate gunfighter could have beaten Lew Carney to the draw at this moment and shot him full of holes.

Afterward, he was to remember his nervous state and attribute much of what he saw and heard to the condition of his mind. In reality he was not in a state when delusions possess a man, but in a period of super-penetration.

In the meantime the sound approached. It grew from a murmur to a clear rumbling. It continued. It loomed on the ear of Carney as a large object looms on the eye. It possessed and overwhelmed him like a mountain thrust toward him from its base.

But for all his awareness the thing came upon him suddenly. Looking down the valley, he saw, above a faint rise of ground, the black outline of a topped wagon between him and the moonlight horizon. He drew a great sobbing breath and then began to laugh with hysterical relief.

A wagon! He stood up to watch its coming. It

was rather strange that a freighter should travel by night, however, but in those gold rush days far stranger things had come within his ken.

The big wagon rocked fully into view. The chuckling was the play of the tall wheels on the hubs; the rattling was the stir of chains. Carney cursed and was suddenly aware of the blood running in old courses and a kindly warmth. But his relief was cut short. The wagon stopped in the very moment of coming over the rise.

Then he remembered the pauses in that sound before. What did it mean, these many stops? To breathe the horses? No horses that ever lived, no matter how exhausted, needed as many rests as this. In fact it would make their labor all the greater to have to start the load after they had drawn it a few steps. Not only that, but by the way the wagon rocked, even over the comparatively smooth sand of the desert, Carney felt assured that the wagon carried only a skeleton load. If it were heavily burdened, it would crunch its wheels deeply into the sand and come smoothly.

But the wagon started on again, not with a lurch, such as that of horses striking the collar and thrusting the load into sudden motion, but slowly, gradually, with pain, as though the motive power of this vehicle were exerting the pressure gradually and slowly increasing the momentum. It was close enough for him to note the pace, and he observed that the wagon crept forward by inches.

Give a slow draft horse two tons of burden and he would go faster than that. What on earth was drawing the wagon through this moon haze in Silver Cañon?

If the distant mystery had troubled Lew Carney, the strange thing under his eyes was far more imposing. He sat down again as though he wished to shrink out of view, and once more he had his heavy gun resting its muzzle on his knee. The wagon had stopped again.

And now he saw something that thrust the blood back into his heart and made his head swim. He refused to admit it. He refused to see it. He denied his own senses and sat with his eyes closed tightly. It was a childish thing to do, and perhaps the long expectancy of that waiting had unnerved the man a little. But there he sat with his eyes stubbornly shut, while the chuckling of the wagon began again, continued, drew near, and finally stopped close to him.

Then at last he looked, and the thing that he guessed before was now an indubitable fact. Plainly silhouetted by the brilliant moon, he saw the tall wagon drawn by eight men, working in teams of two, like horses. And behind the wagon was a pair of heavy horses pulling nothing at all. No, they were idly tethered to the rear of the vehicle. Weak horses, exhausted by work? No, the moon glinted on the well-rounded sides, and when they stepped, the sand quivered under their weight. Moreover they threw their hoofs as they walked—a sure sign by which the draft horse can always be distinguished. He plants his hoofs with abandon. He cares not what he strikes as long as he can drive his iron-shod toes down to firm ground and, secure of his purchase, send his vast weight into the collar. Such was the step of these horses, and when the wagon stopped, they surged forward until their breasts struck the rear of the schooner. Not the manner of tired horses, which halt the instant the tension on the halter is released. Not the manner of balky horses, either, this eagerness on the rope.

But there before the eyes of Lew Carney stood the impossible. Eight forms. Eight black silhouettes drooping with weariness before the wagon, and eight deformed shadows on the white sand at their feet, and two ponderous draft horses tethered behind.

It is not the very strange that shocks us. We are readily acclimated to the marvelous. But the small variations from the commonplace are what make us incredulous. How the world laughed when it was said that ships would one day travel without sails, or that the human voice would carry three thousand miles! Yet those things could be understood. And later on there was little interest when men actually flew. The world was acclimated to the strange. But an unusual handwriting, a queer mark on the wall, a voice-like sound in the wind will startle and shock the most hard-headed. If that wagon had been seen by Lew Carney flying through the air, he probably would have yawned and gone to sleep. But he saw it on the firm ground drawn by eight men, and his heart quaked.

Not a sound had been spoken when they halted. And now they stood without a sound.

Yet Lew's gelding stood plainly in view, and he himself was not fifty feet away. To be sure they stood in their ranks without any head turning, yet beyond a shadow of a doubt they had seen him. They must see him. Still they did not speak.

In the mountain desert when men pass in the road, they pause and exchange greetings. It is not necessary that they be friends or even acquaintances. It is not necessary that they be reputable or respectable. It is not necessary that they have white skins. It suffices that a human being sees a human being in the wilderness and he rejoices in the sight. The sound of another man's voice can be a treasure beyond the price of gold.

But here stood eight men, weary, plainly in need of help, plainly scourged forward by some dreadful necessity, yet they did not send a single hail toward Lew.

No man among them spoke. The silence became terrible. If only one of them would roll a cigarette.

At that moment the smell of burning tobacco would have taken a vast load off the shoulders of Lew Carney.

But the eight stirred neither hand nor foot. And each man stood as he had halted, his hands behind him, grasping the long chain.

II

How long they stood there Lew Carney could not guess. He only knew that a pulse began to thunder in his temple and his ears were filling with a roaring sound. This thing could not be, and yet there it was before his eyes.

It flashed into his mind that this might be some sort of foolish practical jest. Some wild prank of the cattlemen. But a single glance at the figures of the eight robbed him of this last remaining clue. Every line and angle of their bent heads and sagging bodies told of men taxed to the limit of endurance. The pride that keeps chins up was gone. The nerve force that allows a last few springy efforts of muscles was destroyed. Without a spoken signal, like dumb brute beasts, the eight leaned softly forward, let the weight of their bodies come gently on the chain and remained slanting forward until the wagon stirred, the wheels turned, and the big vehicle started on. The sand was whispering as it curled around the broad rims of the wheels, and that was the only sound in Silver Cañon.

Stupefied, Carney watched it go without relief. Another man might have been glad to have the mystery pass on, but, after the first chill of fear, Lew began to hunger to get under the surface of this freak. Yet he did not move until there was a sudden darkening of the moonlight. Then he looked up.

As he did so he saw that the moon was obscured by a gray tinge, and he felt a sharp gust of wind in his face. Up the cañon toward Cayuse the air was thick with a dirty mist, and he knew that it was the coming of a sandstorm.

That dismal reality brushed the thought of the wagon from his mind for a moment. He found a bit of shrubbery a hundred yards away and entrenched himself behind it to wait until the storm should pass over, and he might snatch some sleep. The horse, warned by these preparations, came close.

They were hardly finished before the blast of the wind had a million edges of flying sand grains. And a moment later the sandstorm was raging well over them. Lew Carney, comfortable in his shelter except for the grit that forced itself down his neck, thought of the eight men and the wagon. Even in the storm he knew that they had not stopped, but were trudging wearily on. And if the wagon were halted and dragged back by the weight of the wind, still they would lean against the chain and struggle blindly. The imagined picture of them became more vivid than the picture as they had stood in the moonlight.

It was not a really heavy blow. In two hours it was over, but it left the air dim, and when Lew peered up the valley, the wagon was out of sight. For a time he banished the thought of it, wrapped himself again in the blankets, and was instantly asleep.

The first brightness of morning wakened him, and, tumbling automatically out of his blankets, he set about the preparation of breakfast with a mind numbed by sleep. Not until the first swallow of scalding coffee had passed his lips did he remember the wagon, and then he started up and looked again at the valley. He rubbed his eyes, but it was nowhere in sight.

Ordinarily it would not seem strange that a night's travel, even at the slowest pace, should take a wagon out of sight, but Silver Cañon was by no means ordinary. Through the thin, clear air the eye could look from the place where Lew stood clear up the valley to the cleft between the two mountains thirty miles away, where Cayuse stood. There were no depressions to conceal any object of size, but the floor of the valley tilted gradually and smoothly up. To understand the clearness of that mountain air and the level nature of the valley, it may be remarked that men working mines high up of the sides of the mountains toward the base of Silver Cañon could see the campfires of freighters on four successive nights, dwindling into stars on the fourth night, but plainly discernible through the four days of the journey. And a band of wild horses could be watched every moment of a fifty-mile run to the water holes, easily traced by the cloud of dust.

Bearing these things in mind, it can be understood why Lew Carney gasped as he stared up the valley and saw—nothing!

The big schooner had vanished into thin air or else it had reached Cayuse. This thought comforted him, but after a moment of thought he shook his head again. They could not have covered the thirty miles. Two hours' travel had been impossible against the storm. Deducting that time, there remained well under three hours. Certainly the eight men pulling the wagon could not have covered a quarter of that distance in three hours or double three hours. And even if they had harnessed in the two big horses, the thing was still impossible. An hour of sharp trotting would have broken down those lumbering hulks of animals. And as for keeping up a rate of ten miles an hour for three hours with a lumbering wagon behind them and through soft sand, why it was something that a team of blooded horses, drawing a light buckboard, could hardly have accomplished.

The rest of Lew's breakfast was tossed away

untasted. He packed his tins with a rattle and tumbled into the saddle, and presently the gelding was cantering softly toward Cayuse.

As he expected, the storm had blotted out all traces. There was not a sign of wheels. The sand, perfectly smooth except for long wind riffles, scrawled awkwardly here and there. Little hummocks had been tossed up around shrubs, but otherwise all was plainly in view, and the phantom wagon was nowhere on the horizon.

Of course, one possibility remained. They might have turned out of the main course of the valley and gone to one side, ignorant of the fact that those mountains were inaccessible to wagons. It required a horse with tricky hoofs, unhampered with any load, to climb those sliding, steep, sand surfaces. For the draft animals to attempt it with a wagon behind them was ludicrous. Yet he kept sweeping the hills on either side for some trace of the schooner, and always there was nothing.

As has been said, Lew was by no means superstitious, and now he had broad daylight to help steady his nerves and sharpen his faculties. Yet, in spite of broad daylight, he began to feel once more the eerie thrill of the unearthly, and he felt that even if he had stepped out to examine the tracks of the wagon as soon as it passed him, he would have found nothing.

At this he smiled to himself and shook his head. A ghost wagon did not make eight men sweat and strain to pull it, and a ghost wagon did not rumble as it traveled and make a whispering of the sand. No, a solid wagon and eight solid human beings, and two heavy horses, somewhere between his last dry camp and Cayuse, had vanished utterly and were gone!

Searching the walls of the valley on either side, he almost neglected the floor of the cañon, and it was only the bright flash of metal that made him halt the gelding and look to his right and behind. He swung the mustang about and reached the spot in half a dozen jumps. A man lay with his arms thrown out crosswise, and a revolver was in his hand.

At first glance Carney thought that the fellow lived, but it was only the coloring effect of the morning sun and the lifting of his long hair in the wind. He was quite dead. He had been dead for hours and hours it seemed. And here was another mystery added to the disappearance of the wagon. How did this body come here? What vehicle had carried the man here after he was wounded?

For, tearing away the bandages around his breast, Carney saw that he had been literally shot to pieces. The tightly drawn bandages, shutting off the flow of blood, perhaps, had bruised the flesh until it was a dark purple around the black shot holes.

One thing was certain—after those wounds the man had been incapable of travel on horseback.

He must have been carried in a wagon. But certainly only one wagon had gone that way before the sandstorm, and after the sandstorm any vehicle would have left traces.

After all then, there had been some freight in the ghost wagon, and this man, perhaps dead at the time, had been part or all of the burden that had passed under Lew's eyes.

But why had the wagon carried a dead body? And if it carried a dead body at all, why was it not taken on to the destination of the wagon itself? Certainly the burden of one man's weight was not enough to make any difference.

Two startling facts confronted him: first, here was a dead man, and second, the dead man had been brought this far by the ghost wagon.

Here, also, was the chance of learning not only the identity of the dead man, but of the man who had killed him. Carney searched the pockets and brought out a wallet that contained half a dozen tiny nuggets of pure gold, nearly $100 in paper money, and a pencil stub. Evidence enough that robbery had not been the motive in this killing. Besides the wallet, the pockets produced a strong knife, two boxes of matches, a blue handkerchief, a straight pipe, and a sack of tobacco.

There was no scrap of paper bearing a name. There was nothing distinctive about the clothes whereby the man could be identified. He was dressed in a pair of overalls badly frayed at the knees, with a smear of grease and an old stain of red paint, both on the right leg. Also, he had on a battered felt hat and a blue shirt several sizes too large for him. In appearance he was simply a middle-aged man of average height and weight, with iron-gray hair, and hands broadened and callused by years of heavy labor. His face was singularly open and pleasant even in death, but it had no striking feature, no scar, no mole.

Carney stripped him to the waist and turned the body to examine the wounds, and then he straightened with a black look. It was not a man-to-man killing. It was murder, for the vital bullet that eventually robbed the man of life had struck him in the center of the back. By the small size of the wound he knew that the bullet had entered here, just as he could tell by the gaping orifice on the breast where the bullet had come out. Yet the man had not given up without a struggle. He had turned and fought his murderer, for there were other scars on the front. In five distinct places he had been struck, and it was only wonderful that he had not been instantly killed.

Had they carried him as far as this and, then discovering that he was indeed dead, flung his body brutally from the wagon for the buzzards to find? No, at the very latest he must have died within two hours of the reception of these wounds. He must have been dead long before he passed the dry camp of Lew Carney. But if they had carried him as far as this, what freak of folly made them throw the dead body, the brutal evidence of crime, in a place where the freighters were sure to find him inside of twelve hours?

It was reasoning in a circle. One thing at least was sure. The murderer and the men of the ghost wagon were confident that their traces could not be followed.

As for the body itself, there was nothing he could do. The freighters would pick the man up and carry him to Cayuse where he would receive a decent burial. In the meantime, unless that wagon were indeed a ghost, it must have gone by means however mysterious to Cayuse, also. And toward that town Carney hurried on.

III

The mountains went up on either side of Cayuse, but from each side it was easy of access. It gave out upon Silver Cañon in one direction, and on the other side there was a rambling cattle country. As for the mountains, they were better than either a natural highway or a range, for there was gold in them. Five weeks before it had been found. The rumor had gone roaring abroad on the mountain desert, and now, in lieu of echoes, a wild life was rushing back upon Cayuse.

Its population had been more than doubled, but

by far the greater number of the newcomers paused only to outfit and lay in supplies before they pushed on to the gold front. The majority found nothing, but the few who succeeded were sufficient to send a steady stream of the yellow metal trickling back toward civilization. Of that stream a liberal portion never went farther than Cayuse before it changed hands. For one thing supplies were furnished here at doubled and redoubled prices. For another, a crew of legal and illegal robbers came to this crossing of the ways, to hold up the miners.

In perfect justice it must be admitted that Lew Carney belonged to the robbers, though he was of the first class rather than the second. His sphere was the game table, and there he worked honestly enough, matching his wits against the wits of all comers, and trying his luck against the best and the worst. It meant a precarious source of livelihood, but in gambling a cold face and a keen eye will be served, and Lew Carney was able to win without cheating.

His first step after he arrived was to look over old places and new. He found that the main street of Cayuse was little changed. There were more people in the street, but the buildings had not been altered. Away from this established center, however, there was a growing crowd of tents that poured up a clamor of voices. Everywhere were the signs of the new prosperity. There stood half a dozen men pitching broad golden coins at a mark and accepting winnings and losses without a murmur. Here was a peddler with his pack between his feet, nearly empty—everything from shoestrings to pocket mirrors, and hardly a man that passed but stopped to buy, for Cayuse had the buying fever.

Carney left the peddler to enter Bud Lockhart's place. It had been the main gaming hall and bar in the old days and, by attaching a lean-to at the rear of his house, Bud had expanded with the expanding times, and he was still the chief amusement center of Cayuse. In token of his new prosperity he no longer worked behind the counter. Two employees served the thirsty line, and in the room behind, stretching out into the lean-to, were the gaming tables.

As Carney entered, he saw a roulette wheel flash and wink at him, and then the subdued exclamations of the crowd as they won or lost. For the wheel fascinates a group of chance takers at the same time that it excites them. The eye of Carney shone. He knew well enough that where the wheel is patronized by a group, there is money to spend on every game. One more glance around the room was sufficient to assure him. There was not a vacant table, and there was not a table where the chips were not stacked high. Bud Lockhart came through the crowd straight toward Carney. He was a large man with a tanned face, which in its generous proportions matched his big body. What it lacked in height above the eyes it made up in the shape of a great, fleshy chin.

"Hey, Lew!" called the big man, plowing his way among the others and leaving a disarranged but good-natured wake behind him. Carney turned and waited. "I need you, boy," said Bud Lockhart as he shook hands. "You've got to break your rule and work for me. How much?"

The gambler hesitated. "Oh, fifty a day," he murmured.

"Take you at that price," the proprietor said, and Lew gasped.

"Is it coming in as fast as that?" he queried.

"Faster. Fast enough to make your head swim. The suckers are runnin' in all day with each hand full of gold and they won't let me alone till they've dumped it into my pockets. I've got a lot of boys workin' for me but most of the lot are shady. They're double-crossin' me and pocketin' two-thirds of what they make. I need you here to take a table and watch the boys next to you."

"Fifty is pretty fat," admitted Carney, "but I think I'll do a little gold digging myself."

Bud gasped. "Say, son," he murmured, "have they stuck you up with one of their yarns? Are you goin' in with some greenhorn and collect some callouses on your hands?"

"No, I'm going to do my digging right in your place, Bud. You dig the coin out of the pockets of the other boys . . . I'll sit in a few of your games and see if I can't dig some of the same coin out again."

"Nothin' in that," Bud Lockhart protested anxiously. "Besides, you couldn't play a hand with these boys I have. I've imported 'em and they have the goods. Slick crowd, Lew. You've got a good face for the cards but these fellows read their minds."

"I see." Carney nodded. "But there's ways of discouraging the shifty ones. Oh, they're raw about it, Bud. I saw that fat fellow who's dealing over there palm a card so slow I thought he was trying to amuse the crowd until I saw him take the pot. I think I could clean out that guy, Bud."

"Not when he's goin' good. You could never see him work when he tries."

"He wouldn't try the crooked stuff with me," remarked Carney. "Not twice, unless he packs along two lives."

"Easy," cautioned Lockhart. "None of that, Lew. I paid too much for my furniture to have you spoil it for me. Look here, you're grouchy today. Come behind the counter and have a drink of my private stock."

"This is my dry day. But what's the news? Who's been sliding into town? You keep track of 'em?"

"I'll tell a man I do! Got two boys out, workin' 'em as fast as they blow, and steerin' 'em down to my joy shop. Not a bad idea, eh?"

"What's come in today?"

The proprietor pulled out a little notebook and turned the pages with a fat forefinger. "Up from Eastlake there was a gent called Benedict and another called Wayne . . . cowmen loaded with coin. They're unloadin' it right now. See that table in the corner? Then there was Hoe . . ."

"I don't know the lay of the land east of Cayuse," protested Lew Carney. "No friends of mine in that direction."

"Out of the mountains," began Bud, consulting his notebook again. "There was . . ."

"Cut out the mountains, too. What came out of Silver Cañon?"

"What always comes out of it? Sand." Bud's fat eyes became little slits of light as he grinned at his own jest. He added: "Lookin' for somebody?"

"Not particular. Heard somebody down the street talk about a wagon that came off the desert with eight or nine men. What was that?" To conceal his agitation he began to roll a cigarette.

"One wagon?" asked Bud Lockhart.

"Yep."

"What'n thunder would eight men be doin' in one wagon?"

"I dunno."

Carney took out a match, scratched it, and then lit his cigarette hastily. Every nerve in his body was on edge, and he feared lest the trembling of his hand should be noticed.

"Eight men in one wagon," chuckled Bud. "Somebody's been kiddin' you, Lew. If this crowd has started kiddin' Lew Carney for amusement, it's got more nerve than I laid to it. But why's the wagon stuff eatin' on you, Lew?"

"Not a bit," said Carney. "Doesn't mean a thing, but, when I heard that the wagon came off Silver Cañon, I thought it might be from my own country, might find a pal in the crowd."

"I'm learnin' something every day," Bud replied with a grin. "Makes me feel young again. Since when have you started in havin' pals?"

"Why shouldn't I have 'em?" Carney retorted sharply, for he felt that the conversation was not only unproductive but that he had aroused the suspicion of the big man.

"Because they don't last long enough," replied the other, with perfect good nature. "You wear 'em out too fast. There was young Kemple. You hooked up with him for a partner, and he comes back with a lump on his jaw and a twisted nose. Seems he disagreed with you about the road you two was to take. Then there was Billy Turner that was goin' to be your partner at poker. Two days later you shot Billy through the hip."

"He tried a bum deal on me, on his pal," Carney stated grimly.

"I know. I told you before that Billy was no good. But there was Jud Hampton. Nobody had nothin' ag'in' Jud. Fine fellow. Straight, square dealin'. You fell out with Jud and busted his . . ."

"Lockhart," snapped the smaller man, "you've got a fool way of talking sometimes."

"And right now is one of 'em, eh?"

"I've given you the figures," said Carney. "You can add 'em up any way you want to."

It was impossible to disturb the calm of big Bud. "So you're the gent who is lookin' for some pals?" he chuckled. "Say, Lew, are you pickin' trouble with me? Hunt it up some place else. And the next time you start pumpin' me, take lessons first. You do a pretty rough job of comin' to the wind of me."

A lean hand caught the arm of Bud as he turned away. Lean fingers cut into his fat, soft flesh. He found himself looking down into a face at once fierce and wistful. "Bud, you know something?"

"Not a thing, son, but it's a ten to one bet that you want to know something that's got a wagon and eight men in it. What's the good word?"

The knowledge that he had bungled his first bit of detective work so hopelessly made Lew Carney flush. "I've talked like a fool," he said. "And I'm sorry I've stepped on your toes, Bud."

"That's a pile for you to say," replied Bud. "And half of it was enough. Now what can I do for you?"

"The wagon . . ."

"Forget the wagon! I tell you, the only thing that's come in out of Silver Cañon is you. Hasn't my spotter been on the job? Why he give me a report on you yourself, the minute you blew in sight. What d'you think he said? 'Gent with windy lookin' hair. Rides slantin'. Kind of careless. Good horse. Looks like he had a pile of coin and didn't care how he got rid of it.' It sure warmed me up to hear that kind of a description, and then in you come. 'There he is now,' says the spotter. 'Like his looks?' 'Sure,' I said to him. 'I like his looks so much you're fired.' That's what I said to him. You should've seen his face!" The fat man burst into generous laughter at his own joke.

The voice of Lew Carney cut his mirth short. "I tell you, Bud, you're wrong. Either you're wrong or I'm crazy."

"Don't be sayin' hard things about yourself," Lockhart retorted.

"It's gospel, is it?"

"It sure is."

"Then keep what I've said to yourself."

"Not a word out of me, Lew. Now let's get back to business. What you need to get this funny idea out of your head is a game. . . ."

But the head of Lew Carney was whirling. Had he been mad? Had it been an illusion, that vision of the wagon and eight men? He remembered how tightly his nerves had been strung. A terrible fear for his own sanity began to haunt him.

"Blow the game," said Carney. "I'm goin' to get drunk!"

"I thought you said this was your dry . . ."

But the younger man had already whirled and was gone among the crowd. He went blindly into the thickest portion, and, where men stood before him, he shouldered them brutally out of the way. He left behind him a wake of black looks and clenched hands.

Bud Lockhart waited to see no more. He hurried to call one of his bartenders to one side. "You see that gent with the sandy hair?" asked Bud.

"Yep."

"Know him?"

"Nope."

"He's Lew Carney and he's startin' to get drunk. I've known him a long time, and it's the first time I've ever heard of him goin' after the booze hard. Take him aside and give him some of my private stock. Keep a close eye on him, you hear? Pass the word around to all the boys. There's a few that knows him and they'll hunt cover if he starts goin'. But some of the greenhorns may get sore and try a hand with him. You're kind of new to these parts yourself, son. But take it from me straight that Lew Carney has a nervous hand and a straight eye. He starts quick and he shoots straight. Let him down as easy as you can. Put some tea in his whiskey if he's goin' too fast. And see that nobody touches him for his roll. And if he flops, have somebody put him to bed."

IV

All of these things having been accomplished in the order named, with the single exception that the *roll* of Carney was untouched, the gambler awakened the next day with a confused memory and a vague sense that he had been the center of much action. But he had neither a hot throat nor a heavy head. In fact after the long nerve strain that preceded the drunk, the whiskey had served as a sort of counter poison. The brain of Lew Carney, when he wakened, was perfectly clear for the present. It was only a section of the past that was under the veil.

Through the haze, facts and faces began to come out, some dim, some vivid. He remembered, for instance, that there had been a slight commotion when news came that a freighter had brought in the body of a man found dead in Silver Cañon. He remembered that someone had jogged his arm and spilled his whiskey, whereupon he had smote the fellow upon the root of the nose, and then waited calmly for the gun play. And how the other had reached for his gun but had been instantly seized by two bystanders who poured whispered words into his ears. The words had turned the face of the stranger pale and made his eyes grow big. He stared at Lew, then had apologized for the accident, and had been forgiven by Lew, and they had had many drinks together.

That was one of the incidents that was most vivid.

Then, somebody had insisted upon singing a solo, in a very deep, rough bass voice. Carney had complimented him and told him he had a voice like Niagara Falls.

A little, wizened man with buried eyes and hatchet face had confided to Carney that he was a Comanche chief and that he was on the warpath hunting white scalps; that he had a war cry that beat thunder a mile, and that when he whooped, people scattered. Whereupon he whooped and kept on whooping and swinging a bottle in lieu of a tomahawk until the bartender reached across the bar and tapped the Comanche chief with a mallet.

A tall, sad-faced man with long mustaches had poured forth the story of a gloomy life between drinks.

Once he had complained that the whiskey was too weak for him. What he wanted was liquid dynamite so he could get warmed up inside.

Later he was telling a story to which everyone listened with much amusement. Roars of laughter had greeted his telling of it. Men had clapped him on the back when he was finished. Only one man in the crowd had seemed serious.

Lew Carney began to smile to himself as he remembered the effect of his tale. The tale itself came back to him. It was about eight men pulling a wagon across the desert, while two horses were tethered behind it.

At this point in the restoration of the day before, Carney sat erect in his bed. He had told the story of the phantom wagon in a saloon full of men. The story would go abroad. The murderer or murderers of that man he had found dead in the desert would be warned in time. He ground his teeth at the thought, but then settled himself back in the bed and, with a prodigious effort, summoned up other bits of the scene.

He remembered, for instance, that after he told the story, somebody had pressed through the crowd and assured him in a voice tearful that it was the tallest lie that had ever been voiced between the Sierras and the old Rockies. Whereat another man had said that there was one greater lie, and that was old man Tomkins's story about the team of horses that was so fast that when a snowstorm overtook him in his buckboard, he put the whip on his team and arrived home without a bit of snow on him, though the back of his wagon was full to the top of the boards.

After that half a dozen men had insisted on having Carney drink with them. So he had poured six drinks into one tall glass and had drunk with them all, while the crowd cheered. After this incident he could remember almost nothing except that a strong arm had been beneath his shoulders part of the time, and that a voice at his ear had kept assuring him that it was "all right . . . don't worry . . . lemme take care of you."

Finding that past this point it was hopeless to try to reconstruct the past, he returned to the beginning, to the first telling of the tale of the wagon, and strove to make what had happened clearer. Bit by bit new things came to him. And then he came again in his memories to the man who had looked seriously, for one instant. It had been just a shadow of gloom that had crossed the face of this man. Then he had turned and gone through the crowd.

"By heaven," Lew said to the silent walls of his room. "That gent knew something about the wagon."

If he could recall the face of the man, he felt that two-thirds of the distance would have been covered toward finding the murderer, the cur who had shot the other man from behind. But the face was gone. It was a vague blur of which he remembered only a brown mustache, rather close-cropped. But there were a hundred such mustaches in Cayuse.

He got up and dressed slowly. He had come to the halting point. Dim and uncertain as this clue would be, even if the stranger actually had some connection with the murder, even if he had not been simply disgusted by the drunken tale, so that he turned and left in contempt. Yet in time his memory might clear, Carney felt, and the veil be lifted from the significant face of the man. It seemed as though the curtain of obscurity dropped just to the top of the mustache, like a mask. There was the strong chin, the contemptuous, stern mouth, and the brown mustache, cropped close. But of eyes and nose and forehead, he could remember nothing.

Downstairs, he found that he had been the involuntary guest of Bud Lockhart overnight in the little lodging house. He went to the big parlor to repay his host. Smiles greeted his entrance. He reduced his pace to the slowest sauntering and deliberately met each eye as he passed. The result was that the smiles died out, and he left a train of sober faces behind him.

With his self-confidence somewhat restored by this running of the gantlet, he found Bud Lockhart and was received with a grin that no amount of staring sufficed to wipe out. He discovered that Bud seemed actually to admire him for the drunken party of the day before.

"I'll tell you why," Bud said, "you get in solid with me. Some's got one test for a gent and some's got another. But for me, let me once get a gent drunk and I'll tell you all about how the insides of his head are put together. If a gent is noisy but keepin' his tongue down to make a bluff, he'll begin to shoutin' as soon as the red-eye is under his belt. And if he's yaller, he'll try to bully a fellow smaller than himself. And if he's a blow-hard, he'll start his blowin'. But if he's a gentleman, sir, it's sure to crop out when the whiskey is spinnin' in his head."

At this Carney looked Bud in the eye with even more particular care.

"And after I knocked a man down and insulted another and told a lot of foolish stories, just where do you place me, Lockhart?"

"Do you remember that far back?" Bud asked with a chuckle. "Son, you put away enough whiskey to float a ship. You just simply got a nacheral ability to blot up the booze."

"How much tea did you mix with my stuff?"

At this Bud flushed a little, but he replied: "Don't let 'em tell you anything about me. No matter what it was you drank, you put away just twice as much as was enough. Son, you done noble, and I tell it to you. You done noble. Only one fight, and seein' it was you, I'd say that you spent a plumb peaceable day."

"Bud," broke in the other, "I think I chattered some more about that ghost wagon. Did I?"

"Ghost wagon? What? Oh, sure, I remember it now. That funny idea of yours about seein' a wagon with eight men pullin' it? Sure, you told that yarn, but everybody put it down for just a yarn and had a good laugh out of it. I suppose you've got that fool idea out of your head by this time, Lew? Good thing if you have."

Lew Carney began to feel that there was far more generous manliness in Bud Lockhart than he had ever guessed.

"I'll tell you how it is," he said. "I'd put the thing out of my head if I could, but I can't. Know why? Because it's a fact."

The smile of the big man became somewhat stereotyped.

"Sure," he said. "Sure it's a fact."

"Are you trying to humor me?" Carney asked with a growl.

The older man suddenly took his friend by the arm and tapped his breast with a vast, confidential forefinger.

"Listen, son. The first time you pulled that story it was a swell joke, understand? The second time it won't get such a good hand. The third time people are apt to pass the wink when you start talkin'."

"But I tell you, man, I saw that thing as clearly . . ."

"Sure, sure you did. I don't doubt you, Lew. Not me. But some of the boys don't know you as well as I do. You'll start explainin' to 'em real serious, and then they'll pass the wink along. Savvy? They'll begin to tap their heads. You know what happened to Harry the Nut? Between you and me, I think he had just as good sense as you and me have. But he done that one queer thing over to Townsend's, and when he tried to explain, it didn't do any good. Then pretty soon he was doin' nothin' but explainin' and tryin' to make people take him serious. You remember? And after a while he got to thinkin' about that one thing so much that I guess he did go sort of batty. It's an easy thing to do. I'll tell you what, Lew. If you can't figure out a thing, just start thinkin' about somethin' else. That's the way I do."

There was something at once so hearty and so sane about this advice that the young gambler nodded his head. He had a wild impulse to declare outright that he knew there was a close connection between the ghost wagon and the dead man who the freighters had brought in the day before. But he checked himself on the verge of speech. For this tale would be even more difficult of explanation than the first.

Instead he took the big man's hand and made his own lean fingers sink into the soft fat ones of Bud Lockhart. "You got a good head, Bud," he said, "and you got a good heart. I'm all for you and I'm glad you're for me. If you ever hear me talk about the ghost wagon again, you can make me eat the words."

The big man sighed and an expression of relief spread visibly across his face. Oil had been cast upon troubled waters.

"Now the thing for you is a little excitement, son," he advised. "Go over to that table. I'll bring you the stakes . . . and you start dealin' for the house."

"Whatever you say goes for me today," Carney murmured obediently.

"And as for the coin," said the fat man, "you just split it with the house any way you think is the right way."

V

Only half of the mind of Lew Carney was on the cards, and west of the Rockies it needs very close attention indeed to win at poker. Once he collared a fellow clumsily trying to hold out a card. At the urgent entreaty of Bud Lockhart to do him no serious damage, he merely threw him out of the place. Luck now inclined a little more to his side, when the men who took their chances at his table saw that they could not crook the cards, but still he lost for the house, steadily. He had an assignment of experienced and steady players, and the chances seemed to favor them.

By noon he was far behind. By midafternoon Bud Lockhart was seen to be lingering in the offing and biting his lip. Before evening Carney threw down the cards in disgust and went to his employer.

"I'm through," he said. "I can't play for another man. I can't keep my head on the game. I'll square up for what I've lost for you."

"You'll not," said Lockhart. "But if you think

the luck ain't with you, well, luck takes her own time comin' around . . . and if the draw ain't with you, well, knock off for a while."

"I'm doing it. S'long, Bud."

"Not leavin' the house, old man?" The proprietor moved back before the door with his enormous arms outspread in protest. "Not goin' to beat it away right now, are you, Lew?"

"Why not? I want a change of air. Getting nervous."

"Sit down over there. Wait a minute. I'll get you a drink."

"Not now."

"Bah! You don't know what you need. Besides, I've got something to say to you." He hurried away, turned. "Don't move out of that chair," he directed, and Carney sank into it, as though impelled by the wind of the big man's gesture.

Once in it, however, he stirred uneasily. The events of the day before had served to make him a well-known character in the place. Wherever people moved, they often turned and directed a smile at the young gambler, and such glances irritated him. Not that the smiles were exactly offensive. Usually they were accompanied by some reference to the celebrated tale of the evening before, the amazing lie about the ghost wagon. Yet Carney felt his temper rise. He wanted to be away from this place. He did not know how many of these strangers he had drunk with the night before. Perhaps he had drunk with his hand on the shoulder of some. He had seen drunken men do that, and the thought made his flesh crawl. For Lew Carney was not in any respect a good democrat and there was very little society that he preferred to his own. Not that he was a snob, but his was a heart that went out very seldom, and then with a tide of selfless passion. And the faces in this room made him feel unclean himself. He dreaded touching his own cheek with the tips of his fingers for fear that he would feel the stubble left by the hasty shave of that morning.

Above all, at this moment, the thought of the vast flesh and the all-embracing kindliness of his host was irksome to him. He felt under an obligation for the night before, and the manner in which Lockhart had handled the delicate situation of the gambling losses deepened the obligation, made it a thing that a mere payment of cash could not balance. He had to stay there and wait for the return of Bud, and yet he could not stay. With a sudden, overmastering impulse, he started up from his chair and strode swiftly to the door.

His hand was upon the knob when a finger touched his shoulder. He turned. There stood Glory Patrick, the man who kept order in the parlor and gaming hall of Bud Lockhart. Glory was a known man whether with his bare hands or with a knife or gun. And Lew Carney had seen him working all three, at one time or another. He smiled kindly upon the rough man; his eyeteeth showed with his smile.

Glory smiled in turn.

Who has not seen two wolves grin at each other?

"The boss wants you, chief," said Glory. "Ain't you goin' to wait for him?"

"Can't do it. Tell Bud that I'll be back." He looked around rather guiltily. The big man was nowhere in sight. And then he turned abruptly upon Glory. "Did he send you to stop me just now?"

"Nope. But I seen that he was comin' back and would want you ag'in."

It was all said smoothly enough, but when Carney asked his direct question the eyes of the bouncer had flicked away for the briefest of spaces, a glance as swift as the flash of a cat's paw when it makes play with the lightning movements of a mouse.

Yet it told something to Lew Carney. It told him a thing so incredible that for an instant he was stunned by it. He, Lew Carney, battler extraordinaire, fighter by preference, trouble-seeker by nature, gunman by instinct, boxer by training, bull terrier by grace of the thing that went boiling through his veins, was stopped at the door of this place by a bouncer acting under the order of fat Bud Lockhart.

It shocked Carney; it robbed him of strength

and made him an infant. "Doesn't Bud want me to go?" he asked.

"Nope. Between you and me, I don't think he does."

"Oh," Carney said softly. "Wouldn't you let me go?"

"You got me right," said Glory.

Carney dropped his head back so that he could only look at Glory by glancing far down, with only the rim of his eyes. He began to laugh gently and without a sound. At length he straightened his head. All he said was: "Oh, is that what it means?"

Glory went white about the mouth, and his eyes seemed to sink in under his brows. He was a brave man, as all the world knew. He was a strong man, as Lew Carney perfectly understood. But he had not the exquisite nicety of touch; he lacked the lightning precision of the windy-haired youth who now stood with a devil in either eye. All of these things both of them knew, and both knew that the other understood. Glory was quite willing to take up an insult and die in the fight, but he would infinitely prefer that Lew Carney should withdraw without another syllable. And as for Carney, he balanced the chances. He rolled the temptation under his tongue with the delight of a connoisseur, and then turned on his heel and walked out.

It had all passed within a breathing space, yet the space of five seconds had seen a little drama begin, reach a climax of life and death, and end, all without sound, all without gesture of violence, so that a man rolling a cigarette nearby never knew that he had stood within a yard of a gun play.

The door swung behind Lew Carney and he stepped into the street and confronted the man with the close-cropped brown mustache. All at once he felt some power beyond him had taken him by the shoulder and made him start up from the chair where he had sat to await the coming of Bud Lockhart, had forced him through the door past Glory Patrick, and had thrust him out into the daylight of the street and into the presence of this man. It was no guesswork. The moment he saw the fellow the film of indecision was whipped away, and he distinctly remembered how this man had heard the tale of the ghost wagon begun and had turned with a shadow on his face and gone through the crowd. It might mean nothing, but a small whisper in the heart of Lew Carney told him that it meant everything.

He had not met the eye of the other. The man stood at the heads of two horses, before a store across the street, and his glance was toward the door of the shop. The source of the expectancy soon appeared. She was a dark girl of the mountain desert, but with a fine high color that showed through the tan. That much Lew Carney could see, and though the broad brim of her sombrero obscured the upper part of her face, there was something about her that fitted into the mind of Carney. Who has not thought of music and heard the same tune sung in the distance? So it was with Carney. It was as though he had met her before.

She went straight to one of the horses, and he of the brown mustache went to hold her stirrup and give her a hand. The moment they stood side-by-side, Lew felt that they belonged together. There was about them both the same cool air of self-possession, the same atmosphere of good breeding. The old clothes and the ragged felt hat of the man could not cover his distinction of manner. He did not belong in such an outfit. His personality broke through it with a suggestion of far other attire. He should have been in cool whites, Carney felt, and the cigarette between his fingers should have been tailor-made instead of brown paper. In fact, just as the girl had fitted into Carney's own mind, so now the man stepping up to her drew her into a second and more perfect setting. And it cost the gambler a pang, an exquisite small pain that kept close to his heart.

Another moment and the pain was gone. Another moment and the blood went tingling through the veins of Lew Carney. For the girl had refused the proffered assistance of her companion and she had done it in an unmistakable manner. Another woman in another time might have done twice as much without telling a thing to the eyes of Lew Carney, but now he was watching with a sort of second sight, and he saw her wave away the hand of the other and swing lightly, unaided, into the saddle.

It was a small thing but it had been done with a little shiver of distaste, and now she sat in her saddle looking straight before her, smiling. Once more Carney read her mind, and he knew that it was a forced smile, and that she feared the man who was now climbing into his own place.

VI

A moment later they were trotting down the street side-by-side, and the pain darted home to Lew Carney again. A hundred yards more and she would jog around the corner and out of his life forever. She would pass on, and beside her the man who was connected with the ghost wagon and the dead body in Silver Cañon. Yet how small were his clues. The man with the brown mustache had frowned at a story that made other men laugh, and a girl had shrugged her shoulders very faintly, refusing the assistance to her saddle.

Small things to be sure, but Carney, with his heart on fire, made them everything. To his excited imagination it seemed certain that this brown-faced girl with the big, bright eyes, was riding out of his life side-by-side with a murderer.

She must be stopped. Fifty yards, ten seconds more, and she would be gone beyond recall.

He glanced wildly around him. His own horse was stabled. It would take priceless minutes to put him on the road. And now the inertness of the bystanders struck him in the face. Could they not see? Did not the patent facts shout at them? A man sat on the edge of the plank sidewalk and walled up his eyes, while he played a wailing mouth organ. A youth in his fourteenth year passed the man, sitting sidewise in his saddle, rolling his cigarette, and sublimely conscious that all eyes were upon him.

A thought came to Lew. He started to the horse of the boy and grabbed his arm. "See 'em?" he demanded.

"See what?" said the boy with undue leisure.

"See that gent and the girl turning the corner?"

"What about 'em?"

"Do me a favor, partner." The word thawed the childish pride of the boy. "Ride after him and tell him that Bud Lockhart wants him in a deuce of a hurry."

For what man was there near Cayuse who would not answer a summons from Lockhart? The boy was nodding. He swung his leg over the pommel of the saddle, and, before it struck into place in the stirrup, he had shot his horse into a full gallop, the brim of his hat standing straight up.

Carney glanced after him with a faint smile,

then he started in pursuit, walking slowly, close to the buildings, mixing in with the crowd to keep from view. What he would say to the girl when he met her, he had not the slightest idea, but see her alone, he must and would, if this simple ruse worked.

And it worked. Presently he saw the man of the brown mustache riding slowly back down the street, talking earnestly to the boy. In the midst of that earnest talk, he checked his horse and straightened in the saddle. Then he sent his mount into a headlong gallop. Carney waited to see no more, but, increasing his pace, he presently turned the corner and saw the girl with her horse reined to one side of the street.

She had forgotten her smile and was looking wistfully straight before her. Behind her eyes there was some sad picture and Carney would have given the remnants of his small hopes of salvation to see that picture and talk with her about it. He went straight up to her, pushed by the fear that the man of the brown mustache might ride upon them at any moment, and when he had come straight under her horse, she suddenly became aware of him.

It was to Lew Carney like the flash of a gun. Her glance dropped upon him. A moment passed during which speech was frozen on his tongue and thought stopped in his brain. Then he saw a faint smile twitch at the corners of her lips as the color deepened in her cheeks. He became aware that he was standing with his hat gripped and crushed in both hands and his eyes staring fixedly up to her, like any worshipping boy. He gritted his teeth in the knowledge that he was playing the fool, and then he heard her voice, speaking gently. Apparently his look had embarrassed her, but she was not altogether displeased or offended by it.

"You wish to speak to me?" she said.

"I don't know your name," Carney said slowly, and as he spoke he realized more fully how insane this whole meeting was, how little he had to say. "But I've something to say to you."

He was used to girls who were full of tricky ways, and now her steady glance, her even voice, shook him more than any play of smiles and coyness.

"My name is Mary Hamilton. What is it you have to say?"

"I can't say it in this street . . . if you'll go . . ."

But her eyes had widened. She was looking at him with more than interest; it was fear. "Why?" she asked.

"Because I want to talk to you for two minutes, and your friend will be back in less time than that."

"Do you know?"

The excitement had grown on her with a rush, and one gauntleted hand was at her breast.

"I sent for him," confessed Carney. "It was a bluff so I could see you alone."

Momentarily her glance dwelt on him, reading his lean face in an agony of anxiety, and then it flashed up and down the street, and he knew that she would go with him.

"Down here and just around the corner," he said. "Will you? Yes?"

"Follow me," commanded the girl, and sent her horse at a trot out of the street and down the byway. He hurried after her, and as he stepped away, he saw the man with the brown mustache thundering down the street. There were nine chances out of ten that he would ride straight on to find the girl and never think of turning down this alley. But there was something guilty about that speed, and when Lew stood before the girl again, he felt more confidence in the vague things he had to say. All the color was gone from her face now; she was twisting at the heavy gauntlets.

"What do you know?" she asked, and always her eyes went everywhere about them in fear of some detecting glance.

"I think," said Lew, "that I know a few things that would interest you."

"Yes?"

"In the first place you're afraid of the gent with the brown mustache."

All at once he found her expression grown hard.

"He sent you here to try me," she said. "Jack Doyle sent you to me."

What a wealth of scorn was in her voice. It made the cheeks of Carney burn.

"He's the one that's with you?"

"Don't you know it?"

"I'm some glad to have his name," admitted Lew. Suddenly he decided to make his cast at once. "My story you may want to know has to do with a wagon pulled by eight men, with two horses and . . ."

But a faint cry stopped him. She had swung from the saddle with the speed of a man and now she caught at his hands. "If you know, why don't you save us? Why . . . ?" She stopped as quickly as she had begun and pressed a gloved hand over her lips. Above the glove her eyes stared wildly at him. "What have I said?" she whispered. "Oh, what have I said?"

"You've said enough to start me and something you've got to finish."

She dropped her glove. "I've said nothing. Absolutely nothing. I . . ." And unable to finish the sentence, she turned and whipped the reins over the head of her horse, preparatory to mounting.

The gambler pressed in between her and the stirrup. "Lady," he said quietly, "look me over. Then go back and ask the town about Lew Carney. They'll tell you that I'm a square-shooter. Now say what's wrong. Make it short, because this Jack Doyle is drifting around looking for you."

She winced and drew closer to the horse.

"Say two words," Lew Carney said, the uneasy spark bursting into flame in his eyes and shaking his voice. "Say two words and I'll see that Jack Doyle doesn't bother you. Lift one finger and I'll fix it so that you ride alone or stay right here."

She shook her head. Fear seemed to have her by the throat, stifling all speech, but the fear was not of Lew Carney.

"Gimme a sign," he pleaded desperately, "and I'll go with you. I'll see you through, so help me God."

And still she shook her head. It was maddening to the man to feel himself at the very gate of the mystery, and then to find that gate locked by the foolish fears of a girl.

"I got a right to know," he said, playing his last card. "Everybody's got a right to know . . . because there's one dead man mixed up with the ghost wagon, and there may be more."

She went sick and pale at that, and with the thought that it might be guilt, Lew Carney grew weak at heart. How could he tell? Someone near and dear to her might have fired that coward's shot from behind. Why else this haunted look? More than anything, that mute, white face daunted him. He fell back and gave her freedom to mount by his step. And she at once lifted herself into the saddle.

With her feet in the stirrups fear seemed in a measure to leave her. And she looked with a peculiar wistfulness at Carney.

"Will you take my advice?" she said softly.

"I'll hear it," said Lew.

"Then leave this trail you've started on. It's a blind trail to follow, and a horror at the end of it. But if you should keep on, if you should find it, God bless you."

And she spurred her horse to a gallop from that standing start.

VII

It was as though she had smiled on him before she slammed the door in his face. He must not follow the blind trail to the horror, but if he did persist, if he did go to the end of the trail, then let God bless him.

What head or tail was he to make of such a speech? She wanted him to come and yet she trembled at the thought. And at the very time she denied him her secret, she pleaded bitterly with her eyes that he should learn the truth for himself. When he mentioned the ghost wagon, she had flamed into hope. When he spoke of the dead man, she had gone sick with dread. But above all that her words had meant, fragmentary as they were, the tremor of her voice when she last spoke was more eloquent in the ear of Lew Carney than aught else.

Yet, stepping in the dark, he had come a long way out of the first oblivion. He was still fumbling toward the truth blindly, but he knew at least that the ghost wagon had not been an illusion of the senses. How it had vanished into thin air and what strange reason had placed eight men on the chain drawing it—all this remained as wonderful as ever. But now it had become a fact, not a dream. His first impulse, naturally enough, was to go straight to Lockhart and triumphantly confirm his story.

But two good reasons kept him from such a step. In the first place there was now a new interest equaled with his first desire to learn the truth of the ghost wagon, and the new interest was Mary Hamilton. Until he knew or even guessed how far she was implicated, he could not take the world into his confidence. And beyond this important fact there was really nothing to tell the world except the exclamation of the girl, and the frown of Jack Doyle.

These things he thought over as he hurried toward the stables behind Bud Lockhart's saloon. For on one point he was clear: no matter how blind might be the trail of the ghost wagon, the trail of the girl and her escort should be legible enough to his trained eyes, and he intended to follow that trail to its end, no matter where the lead might take him.

Coming to the stables he had a touch of guilty conscience in the thought that Bud Lockhart must be still waiting for him in the gaming rooms, for no doubt Glory had told the boss that Lew Carney had stepped out for only a moment and would soon return. But there was no sign of Bud in the rear of the saloon, and Lew saddled the gelding in haste and swung into place. He touched the mustang in the flank with his spur and leaned forward in the saddle to meet the lunge of the cow pony's start, but instead of the usual cat-footed spring, he was answered by a hobbling trot.

For a moment he sat the saddle, stunned. Lameness was not in the vocabulary of the gelding, but Lew drew him to a halt and, dismounting, examined the left front hoof. There was no stone lodged in it. Deciding that the lameness must be a passing stiffness of some muscle, Lew leaped into the saddle again and spurred the mustang cruelly forward. The answering and familiar spring was still lacking. The horse struck out with a lunge, but on striking his left foreleg crumpled a little, and he staggered slightly. Lew Carney shot to the ground again. If the trouble was not in the hoof, it must be in the leg. He thumped and kneaded the strong muscles of the upper leg and dug his thumb into the shoulder of the gelding, but there was never a flinch.

He stood back, despairing, and looked over his mount. Never before had the dusty roan failed him, and to leave him to take another horse was like leaving his tried gun for a new revolver. Besides, it would mean a loss of time, and moments counted heavily, now that the afternoon was waning to the time of yellow light, with evening scarcely an hour away. Unless the two took the way of Silver Cañon—and that was hardly likely—they would be out of sight among the hills if he did not follow immediately.

Looking mournfully over that offending foreleg, he noticed a line of hair fanning out just above the knee, as if the horse had rubbed against the stall and pressed on the sharp edge of a plank. He smoothed this ridge away thoughtlessly and then looked wistfully down the street. The lazy life of the town had not changed. Men were going carelessly about their ways, yet there were good men and true passing him continually. Charlie Rogers went by him, Gus Ruel, Sam Tern, a dozen other known men who would have followed him to the moon and back at a word. But what word could he give them? A hundred men would scour the hills at his bidding, yet what reason could he suggest? All that wealth of man power was his if he only had the open sesame that would unlock the least fragment of the secret of the ghost wagon. No, he must play this hand alone.

He looked back with a groan to the lame leg of the horse and again he saw the little ridge of stubborn hair. It was a small thing but he was in a mood when the smallest things are irritating. With an oath he leaned over and smoothed down the hair with a strong pressure of his fingertips, and at once, through the hair, he felt a tiny ridge as hard as bone, but above the bone. Lew Carney set his teeth and dropped to his knees. It was as he thought. A tiny thread of silk had been twisted around the leg of his horse, and drawn taut, and that small pressure, exerted at the right place over the tendons, was laming the gelding. One touch of his jackknife, and the thread flew apart while there was a snort of relief from the roan. And Lew Carney, lingering only long enough to cast one black look behind him, sprang into the saddle for the third time, and now the gelding went out into his long, rocking lope.

The gambler felt the pace settle to the usual stride but he was not satisfied. What if Doyle had given his horses the rein as soon as he found the girl? What if he had made it a point to get out of Cayuse at full speed? In that case he would be even now deep in the bosom of the hills. And many things assured him that the stranger was forewarned. He must have been given at least a hint by the same agency that had lamed the roan.

More than this, if someone knew that Lew Carney was about to take up this trail, and had already taken such a shameful step as this to prevent it, he would go still further. He might send a warning ahead. He might plant an ambush to trap the pursuer.

There is no position so dangerous as the place of the hunter who is being hunted, and, at the thought of what might lie ahead of him, Lew Carney drew the horse back to a dog-trot. Even if the odds were on his side, it might be risky work, but he had reason to believe that there were eight men against him, eight men burdened with one crime already, and therefore ready and willing to commit another to cover their traces.

The thought had come to Lew Carney as he broke out of Cayuse and headed west and south, but while the thoughts drifted through his mind, and all those nameless pictures that come to a man in danger, his eye picked up the trail of two horses that had moved side-by-side. And the trail indicated that both horses were running at close to top speed. For the hoof prints were about equally spaced, with long gaps to mark the leaps. The trail led, as he had feared, into the broken hills south of Silver Cañon where danger might lie in wait to leap out at him from any of twenty places in every mile he rode.

But Lew Carney at any time was not a man to reckon chances too closely, and Lew Carney, with a trail to lead him on, was close to the primitive hunting animal. He sent the roan gelding back into the lope, and in a moment more the ragged hills were shoving past him, and he was fairly committed to the trail.

It was a different man who rode now. With his hat drawn low to keep the slant sunlight from dazzling him, his glance swept the trail before him and the hills on every side. Men have been known to play a dozen games of chess blindfolded. Lew Carney's problems were even more manifold. For every half mile passed him through a dozen places where men might lie concealed to watch him or to harm him, and each place had to be studied, and all its possibilities reckoned with. He loosened his rifle and saw that it drew easily from the long holster. He tried his revolver and found it in readiness. Now and again he swung sharply in the saddle, and his glance took in half the horizon behind him, for in such a sudden turn a man can often take a pursuer by surprise. But the great danger indubitably lay ahead of him, and here he fixed his attention.

The western light was more and more yellow now, and before long the trail would be dim with sunset, and then obscured by the evening. When that time came, he must fix a landmark ahead of him, and then strike straight on through the night, trusting that Doyle had cast his course in a straight line. Unless by dint of hard riding he should come upon the two before dark. But this he doubted. Riding at full speed, Doyle and the girl had opened up a gap of miles before Lew was even started. Moreover, for all his leathery qualities of endurance, the roan was not fast on his feet over a comparatively short distance. It needed a two days' journey to bring out his fine points.

Lew preferred to keep to a steady gait well within the powers of the roan, and trust to bulldog persistence to bring him up with the quarry. He kept on with the hills moving by him like waves chopped by a storm wind. When the sunset reds were dying out, and the gloom of early evening beginning to pool in blues and purples along the gulches, he caught the first sign of life near him. It was a glint of silver far to his left, and it moved.

The ravine down which Carney rode was merely a flat plateau out of which mountain tops went up irregularly, and the glint of moving silver that he had caught to his left was not in the same ravine, or even in the same bottom, but far beyond in a similar rough and shallow valley. Between two hills he had caught this glimpse into the next gulch, and he rode thoughtfully for a moment.

Once more he passed a gap through which he could look into the next valley but this time he saw nothing. It occurred to him then that the flash of silver had been moving at a rate close to that of a horse galloping swiftly, and, setting his teeth, Lew Carney spurred the gelding to top speed.

Weaving through the boulders furiously, he reached the next gap after a half mile sprint, and here he pulled the gelding, panting heavily, to a halt.

Fast as he had traveled over the past furlongs, he had not long to wait before the silver flashed once more out of the thickening gloom of the early night, and this time he saw clearly that it was a gray horse that was being ridden at full gallop through the hills.

But the color of the animal meant a great deal to Lew. He had seen a tall gray, muscled to bear weight, in the stables behind Bud Lockhart's saloon, and he had been told that this was Bud's horse. Moreover, a long train of thought flashed back upon the mind of Lew, with this as the conclusion: he remembered the manner in which Bud had laughed at the story of the phantom wagon, the eagerness with which he had persuaded Lew to drop the tale, his strangely friendly endeavors to keep Lew inside the saloon when the man of the brown mustache was about to leave the room. Bud Lockhart was in some manner implicated. It was he who had posted Glory to keep the gambler in the saloon. It was he who had lamed the roan. And now, finding that his quarry had escaped in spite of all precautions, it was he who mounted his fine gray horse and rode furiously through the hills to carry warning.

VIII

Lust of murder filled the brain of Lew Carney when he thought of the fat face and its pseudo-amiability, the big, fat hand, and the fat cordiality. And yet he saw a way in which he could use the saloonkeeper. He could cut across to the next valley and, at a distance, follow the gray horse through the night, and so reach his destination. The warning of his coming would go before him but he felt that his gain would be equal to his loss.

He swung the gelding across through the gap and a little later sped into the second cañon. The turning to one side brought him out far behind Bud Lockhart and the speeding gray, but for this he cared little. The fat man had apparently assured himself of reaching his destination in time, and he had brought his horse back to a hard gallop that the slow roan could easily match, and, keeping carefully within eye range and out of hearing, Lew wove down the valley, putting an occasional rise of ground between him and his leader, and doing all that was in his power to trail unsuspected. One great advantage remained with him in this game. The roan's color blended easily with the ground tones and the gloom of evening, whereas the gray literally shone through the half-light.

But in spite of this handicap in his favor Lew presently discovered that his presence to the rear was known. For the gap between him and the gray suddenly increased. Coming up a rise of ground only a short distance to the rear, when he reached the top, he discovered the gray gleaming far off, and he knew with a great falling of the heart that his trailing had been at fault.

One hope remained. One bitter chance to take. He could never catch the gray with the roan in a journey that would probably end before the morning. Only one power could overtake the fugitive and that was lead sped by powder. He counted the chances back and forth through the tenth part of a second. His bullet might strike down Bud Lockhart instead of Bud Lockhart's horse, but Bud had played the part of a sneak, and his life to Lew Carney meant no more than the life of a dog. He jerked his rifle to his shoulder, caught the bull's-eye, and fired. As he watched for the effect of the shot he saw the gray horse pause, stop, and lean slowly to one side.

Before the animal fell, the rider had leaped to the ground, looking huge even at that distance. A gun gleamed in his hand but that was only the rash first impulse. A moment later Bud Lockhart's fat arms were heaved above his head and, with his rifle held ready, Lew cantered down to meet his prisoner.

As he came close so that his face could be more

clearly seen, there was a roar of mingled relief and fury from the saloonkeeper.

"Lew Carney! What d'you mean by this?" And he lowered his arms.

"Put 'em up and keep 'em starched. Quick!"

For the saloonkeeper, attempting to smile at the first of this remark, had slipped his hands upon his hips, but the last word sent his arms snapping into the air.

"It ain't possible," stammered Bud Lockhart. Even in the half light it was easy to see that his face was gray. "After what I've done for you, it ain't possible that you've double-crossed me, Lew." He allowed a nasal complaint to creep into his voice. "Look here, son, when a man's broke, he'll do queer things. If you're busted, say the word, and I'll stake you to all that you want. But you come within an inch of killin' me with that shot! And that's the best horse that I ever sat on!"

For answer, Lew replaced his rifle in its case and drew a revolver as a handier weapon for quick use. Then he spoke. "Yep," he said, "I figured on trimming you pretty close. But I'm sorry about the horse. The only way I could help you, though."

"There's an unwritten law about gents that kill horses," said Bud Lockhart, his voice hardening as he noted this apparent weakening on the part of Lew Carney.

"Sure there is," said the younger man. "That's

why I'm going to remove the witness. Your time's short, Bud, because I'm considerable hurried."

The vast arms of the saloonkeeper wavered.

"You can put your arms down now," Lew said kindly. "I'd rather that you tried a gun play. I'll give you a clean break." And he restored his own weapon to its holster.

The arms of the other lowered by inches, and all the time his eyes fought against those of Lew. But when finally the hands hung by his sides, he was limp and helpless. He had admitted defeat, and he was clay ready for the molding.

"I won't raise a hand," Bud protested with perverse stubbornness. "It's murder, that's all. You spend your life with guns, and then you go out and murder. And murder'll out, Lew, as sure as there's a God in heaven."

"Truest thing you ever said. That's why I'm here."

"Eh?"

"I'm here because a murder is coming out."

"What in thunder d'you mean, Lew? D'you suspect me of something?"

"The man they brought out of Silver Cañon, Bud. That's the one."

There was a start and a gasp. "Lew, you are nutty. A hundred gents will swear I ain't never left Cayuse for ten days."

"You didn't hold the gun. You haven't got nerve enough for that. But you were behind it."

The fat coward was shaking from head to foot. "I swear . . . ," he began.

"Curse you." Lew recoiled with sudden horror. "You're a rotten skunk!"

A silence fell between them.

"You haven't left Cayuse for ten days," Lew said when he could speak again. "Where were you bound for now?"

"For Sliver Hennessey's place."

"Good," he said. "You lie well. But here's the end of your trail. You can see Sliver in hell later on."

The craven fear of the other cast a chill through Lew's own blood. He felt shamed for all men, seeing this shaken sample of it, tried and found wanting.

"Lew," said the other in a horrible whisper. "Lew, you and me . . . friends . . . other night when you was drunk . . . I . . ." He sank to his knees.

"You got the right attitude," Lew said. "Keep on talking. I'll wait till you say amen."

"You ain't goin' to do it, Lew . . . partner."

Lew Carney allowed his voice to weaken. "I ought to. You're as guilty as Judas, Bud."

"I was dragged into it. I swear I was dragged into it! Lew, name what you want, and I'll give it to you. If I ain't got it, I'll find it for you. Name what you want!"

"Where have Doyle and the girl gone?"

The other stumbled to his feet. His little eyes

under their fat lids began to twinkle at Lew with the remaining hope of life, but his face was still ashes.

"They're goin' to Miller's shack over to . . . to Dry Creek."

"Miller's shack?" echoed Lew, noting the faltering.

"Yes."

"On your honor?"

"So help me, God."

"One thing more . . . you told Glory to keep me inside the saloon even if he had to fill me full of lead to anchor me."

"He . . . he lied. He wanted to turn you ag'in' me, Lew!"

"You hound!" snarled Lew.

The other fell back a step. "You gave me your promise," he retorted shrilly, "if I told you where they was goin'!"

"I gave you no promise. And you lamed the roan for me, Bud, eh?"

There was a groan from the tortured man. "Lew, I was made to do it. I tell you straight . . . you'd've been deader than the gent you found in Silver Cañon if it wasn't for me. I headed 'em off. When they got a hunch you was after Doyle, they wanted to finish you. I saved you, son."

"Because you thought the job might be a bit tough, eh? I know you, Bud. But who are they?"

The big man blinked as though a powerful light

had been cast into his eyes. He began to speak. He stopped. Lew raised the forefinger of his right hand and pointed it like a gun at the breast of the other.

"Out with it," he commanded.

Once more the lips of Bud Lockhart stirred, but no words came. And a chill of surprise ran through Lew. Was it possible that this fellow valued that one secret more than his own life?

"Out with it!" Lew repeated harshly.

The knees of Bud Lockhart sagged. He closed his eyes. He clenched his hands. But still he did not speak. Lew Carney drew his gun slowly, raised it, leveled it, and then put the spurs to his horse. Swiftly down the cañon he galloped. For he had found the one thing Bud Lockhart feared more than death.

IX

It was this thought that made him go back more carefully over the words of the big saloonkeeper. For it was strange that if he would not name the men, he dared confess where they were to be found. Now he remembered how Bud had hesitated in mentioning the place. There had been a pause between "Miller's shack" and "Dry Creek," and the pause was the hesitation of a liar. No doubt it was Miller's shack but there were two such shacks in the hills—one at Dry Creek, and the other at Coyote Springs.

It needed only an instant of reflection to convince Lew Carney that the place he wanted was at Coyote Springs. In former days the spring had run full and free, and there had been a fine scattering of houses, almost a village, around it. But of late years the spring had fallen away to a wretched trickle of water, completely disappearing in certain seasons of the year. A fire had swept the village, and then old Miller had constructed his shanty out of the half-burned fragments. Once before Lew had been at the place, and he knew it and its approaches well.

Yet he did not swing directly toward this destination, but struck out down the valley toward Dry Creek. He kept steadily toward this goal until he was more than past the spring to his left. Having gone so far he turned again, and now rode hard straight upon Miller's place.

It was broad moonlight now and, topping the last ridge, he saw the big basin in which the village of Coyote Springs had once lain. To the west, a drift of narrow evergreens went up the slope, dark and slender points. The basin of the spring water was a spot of shining silver with the shack near it, and on the bank of the pool six men sat around a fire. Sometimes when the fire leaped, the long red tongue licked across the still surface of the water, and the murmur of men's voices went up the slope to Lew Carney.

Under these circumstances it was comparatively a simple matter to approach the shack without attracting the attention of the men about the fire. He took the roan to a point behind the ridge that lay on the line of projection through the fire and the shack, and tethered him to one of the young pines. Then he went again over the ridge and ran swiftly down to the rear of the shack.

There were eight men for whom he wished to account, if not for more, and only six were around the fire. It stood to reason that they must be in the cabin, and in the rear room, for that room alone was lit. The girl, too, would be where the light was. How he would be able to communicate with her, once he was beside the wall of the house, he had not guessed. That was a bridge to be crossed later on. But he had chosen the lit end of the shack because the light within would effectively darken the moon-lit night outside.

He was halfway down the slope when the boom of a man's laughter from the shack struck him. Someone of the eight watching him, perhaps, and mocking this futile attack by one man? But once started it was more dangerous to turn back than it was to keep straight on. He stooped closer to the ground and sped on, swerving a little from side to side, so as to disturb aim, if anyone were drawing a bead on him.

But he reached the cover of the side of the shack

without either a shot fired or a repetition of any human sound in the little house. But outside, from the fire by the pool, a chorus of mirth had risen. As though the six had heard of his coming and were in turn mocking his powers. He set his teeth at the mere thought, for now that he was actually under the wall of the house, the advantage, man for man, was really with him, and skirting down the wall, he came to a great crack from which he could reconnoiter. It was indeed one of those generous loopholes that occur where a board has loosened at the base, and bulged out. Through it Lew Carney could see the interior of the rear room of the shack as plainly as though he were looking at his ease through a window.

And the first thing on which his eyes fell was the face of the girl. She had apparently paused in her preparations for sleep. Her hair, formed into a great, loose braid, glided over her shoulder and slipped in a bright line of light down to her lap. She had taken off her boots and sat on the floor with her knees bunched high, one foot crosswise on top of the other. On her knees she supported a tattered magazine and, even as Lew glanced in, she began to read in a voice that was subdued to a murmur. The old, old pain that he had first felt when he looked at her was thrust home again in Lew's heart. For the first time he surmised what he might have guessed long before, that the reason she hoped for his interference, and yet dreaded it, was that one of the crew was her husband. Why not? Some gay young chap with a hidden wildness who she had married before he went wrong; he knew of stranger things than that in the mountain desert. There is a peculiar satisfaction in some forms of self-torture. Lew Carney crouched outside the house and suffered wretchedly for a time before he decided to lean farther to one side, to look at the person to whom she was reading. He saw a middle-aged man lying on a bed of boughs and blankets, a bald-headed man who now hitched himself with painful care a little to one side. It was plain that he was wounded. At the movement the girl turned from her reading and touched his forehead with her hand and murmured a few words of sympathy. What the rest of the words were Lew did not try to understand but he made out plainly the monosyllable—"Dad."—and a burden dropped from him.

Besides had she not spoken of "us" when she cried out to him for help in that first impulse that she had regretted? Two of them had needed help but what had kept her from continuing her appeal was a mystery to Lew Carney. Perhaps the gang had contemplated moving away and leaving this wounded member helpless behind them. In that case she would at once want help for her father, and dread the course that the law might take with him after his wound was healed. At any rate, Lew must speak with her at once. He stood up and went boldly to the window, and when his eyes fell on her, she looked up.

There was a moment when he thought that she would cry out, but she mastered herself and ran swiftly across the room to the window. Two small, strong hands closed on his hand that lay on the edge of the window. "You," whispered the girl. "You. Dad, he's come after me. He's found us."

"Thank God," murmured the wounded man. "How many men?"

"None," said Lew Carney.

There was a faint groan. Then: "Go back again. You're worse than useless. One man ag'in' this crew?"

"We'll talk that over when I'm inside," Lew said, and he was instantly through the window and on the rotten floor of the room.

"Mary . . . ," warned her father. "Get to the front of the shack and keep an eye on 'em. Now you, what's your name?"

"Lew Carney."

"All right, Carney, what's your plan? Where are your men? When are they coming? Are you going to try to four-flush half a dozen gunfighters? Talk sharp and act quick or they may find you here."

"I'll tell you the whole thing in a nutshell," Lew said calmly. "I followed a hunch and I'm here. And here I stay until we're all three cut loose of 'em or all three go under. Is that clear?"

"That's sand," said the older man, with a

grudging admiration. "But it don't get us very far."

Mary Hamilton appeared at the door. "No fear of them for a long time," she said. "They're busy."

"Whiskey?" asked Hamilton.

She nodded. Then to Lew Carney: "Oh, why, why, didn't you bring a dozen men?"

"Because I couldn't take 'em on a wild-goose chase, and because you hadn't told me what I could say. I could have taken fifty men with me but not without a reason to give them."

She admitted the truth of what he said with a miserable gesture. "I couldn't talk," she said. "I'd promised."

"Like a fool girl," groaned her father.

There was a flash of anger in her eyes but she said nothing. And turning to Lew Carney, she said: "You've done a fine thing and a clean thing to try to help us but it's no use."

"I can go back and bring help."

"It's too late. They intend to move on in the morning."

His head bent.

"Get clear before they know you're here," she added.

Lew Carney smiled, and she looked at him in wonder.

"Don't you see?" she explained. "I'm grateful for what you want to do. And when I first saw you, you brought my heart into my throat with hope."

She was so simple as she admitted it, so grave in her quiet despair, that Lew Carney felt like death. "But now there's nothing for you to do," she concluded, "except to leave us and see that you're not drawn into this yourself. Will you go?"

"Do you want me to go?" Lew Carney asked.

"What's all this?" broke in her father. "Carney, get out and ride like the devil. They may make things warm for you yet."

But he repeated, looking steadily into the girl's eyes: "Do *you* want me to go?"

"I like you," the girl said quietly. "I admire you and I know that you're clean and honest. But you can't help us. There's nothing for you to do. Please go."

"Then," Lew Carney said, "that settles it. I stay." He took off his hat to give point to his words, and hung it on a nail on the wall. Feeling their puzzled glances, he stiffened a bit and made his eyes, with trouble, meet the eyes of the girl. "I'll tell you why. I've been a drifter and a waster, Mary Hamilton. I'm not clean particularly, and if you ask a good many people, they'll laugh if you say I'm honest. No, I'm not a gambler, I'm a gold-digger. When you come right down to it, I don't take many chances. Cards are my business. Other fellows got their hands all hardened up with work and their brains all slowed up with making money. And after they've got their stake, they meet up with me. They play poker for fun . . . I play it for a living. What chance have they got? None. Well, that's what my business is. And all at once I'm most terrible, awful sick of it all. You understand? I'm tired of it. I want something new, and the first job that comes up sort of handy seems to be to do what I can for you and your dad. You want me to go. Well, if I'm good enough to be worth having my neck saved, I'm good enough to pull a gun in a pinch for you two." He paused. "Seems like I've made a sort of a speech, and now I feel mostly like a fool. But, there, I see that you're about to say something about gratitude. Don't say it. This is only another kind of a game and I enjoy taking chances. Here's our first chance and our big chance. If your father can stand it, I'll get him through that window and carry him up the hill to my horse, and . . ."

"Break off," cut in Hamilton. "Son, you mean well but I can't move a hand. I'm nailed here for a month."

And a second glance at his pain-worn face told Lew Carney that it was the truth. Once more the two pressed him generously to leave them, but, when he had refused, they sat beside the bunk of the father and talked of possibilities. But always in the midst of a scheme, the laughter from the men beside the pool where the riot was running high broke in upon them and mocked them. The helplessness of Hamilton was the thing that foiled every hope. No scheme could meet the great necessity.

Silence came over them, that grim silence when people wait together for a calamity. In the morning the band was moving on. They could not take the wounded man with them. They could not leave him behind to die slowly or else to be saved and to deliver an accusation that would imperil all their lives. The term of his life, then, was the dawn, and before the dawn came, John Hamilton told Lew the story of the ghost wagon. He told it swiftly in a monotonous voice. Now and again there was a moment of interruption—when Lew or Mary went to the front of the shack to make sure that the gang was thinking of nothing more than its whiskey—but on the whole the story of the phantom wagon went smoothly and swiftly to its dark conclusion.

X

Three short weeks ago John Hamilton had left his ranch for a prospecting tour. Though he had made far more out of cows than he had ever made out of gold and silver, the old lure of the rocks still held for him. From time to time he was in the habit of making a brief circuit through the hills, chipping rocks with an unfailing enthusiasm. Ten days of this each year kept him happy. He filled his house with samples and mining, as far as John Hamilton was concerned, stopped at that point.

On this season he had gone out with his burro to see the world, sighting between those two flapping, cumbersome ears. But it had been long since he had really taken his prospecting seriously, and now he chipped rock with more careless abandon than ever. What sincere and hopeful labor had never brought to him, he found by happy chance, or unhappy chance, as it was to prove. For drilling into a lead he had uncovered a pocket of pure gold!

He had run short of powder by this time and that pocket was a most difficult one to open. It was a deposit strongly guarded in quartzite, the hardest of rocks. Yet with the point of his pick, he had dug out five pounds of pure gold!

It was enough to set a more callous heart than that of John Hamilton on fire. When he saw that he could not work the deposit without more powder, he debated whether he should go to Cayuse for supplies and to file his claim or whether he should take the longer trip and return home to bring the supplies from there.

The temptation to convince the mockers in his own family, where his annual prospecting trips were an established joke, was too great.

"Mother was away, so I dumped the gold on the table before Mary and watched her eyes shine. Same light always comes in the eyes when you see gold. Can't help it. I've shown it to a baby, and they grab for it every time. It's in the blood."

Finally he had determined to return to the site of his mine with a heavy wagon and a span of strong horses, taking supplies in abundance, one tested ranch hand, Hugh Delaney, and his daughter Mary to run the domestic part of the camp. At the same time he sent to the nearest telegraph office a message to his son Bill. Bill, it appeared, was the scapegrace of the family. Three years ago, after a quarrel with his father, he had left home, but the finding of the gold unlocked all of John Hamilton's tenderness, for Bill had gone many a time on those annual trips. He had sent an unlucky telegram informing Bill of the find and inviting him to come to Cayuse and ride down Silver Cañon to the claim.

Without waiting for a reply, he started out in his wagon with Mary and Hugh Delaney, and they went straight to the pocket.

It had not been disturbed in the interim, and for five days of tremendous labor Hamilton and Delaney broke away the quartzite bit by bit and finally laid the pocket bare. It was a gloomy disappointment. Instead of proving a vein that opened out into the incredibly rich pocket that John Hamilton expected, it pinched away to nothing at the end of a few feet. In fact he had picked out a full two-thirds of the metal in his first attempt. Nevertheless, up to this point, the venture had been profitable enough in its small way, but when they were on the verge of abandoning the work, and only waiting for the arrival of Bill Hamilton from Cayuse, they were surprised late one afternoon by eight men who had left their horses at a distance, and crept upon the camp.

John Hamilton had thrown up his hands at the first summons and at the first sight of the odds. But Hugh Delaney, ignorant, stubborn, tenacious fighter that he was, had gone for his gun. Before he could reach it, he was shot down from behind, and then a volley followed that dropped John Hamilton himself, shot through the thigh.

The explanation was simple enough. A friend of Jack Doyle, long rider and bandit of parts, had seen the telegram that Hamilton sent to his son, and the outlaw was immediately informed. The surprise attack followed.

But when the first volley struck down the two men, Doyle himself remained behind to help bandage the wounds with the aid of Mary Hamilton until a cry from his men called him to them. They had found the niche in the quartzite and the gleaming particles of gold shining in it. And at the sight the whole crew had gone mad with the gold fever. They seized drills, picks, hammers, and flew at the hard rock, shouting as they hewed at it. There were practical miners among them but science was forgotten in the first frenzy. Jack Doyle himself was drawn into the mob. They threw off their belts in the fury of the labor. They discarded their weapons.

What were guns with one dying and one wounded man behind them, and the only sound enemy a young girl? But John Hamilton, lying on the sand, had conceived a plan for reprisal and whispered it to his daughter. She took it up with instant courage.

His scheme was both simple and bold. The girl was to come near the workers, get as many of the guns as she could, and at least all of the weapons that were closest to the frenzied miners, and then fall back to one side. In the meantime, John Hamilton was to squirm over to his rifle, train it on the bandits, and at his shout Mary also was to level one of the outlaws' own guns upon them.

It was a sufficiently bold plan to be successful. Rapt in the gold lust she could have picked the pockets of the gang as well as taken their weapons without drawing a word from them, and when the shout of John Hamilton came, the eight bold men and bad whirled, and found themselves helpless, unarmed, and looking down the muzzles of three guns. For the dying Delaney had dragged out a revolver, and now twisted over on one side, trained on a target.

Eight to three, when one of the three was a girl, seemed liberal odds but a repeating rifle in the hands of a good shot will go a long ways toward convincing the largest crowd. The gang might have attempted to rush even the leveled rifle of John Hamilton, to say nothing of the girl and Delaney, but a few terse words from their leader convinced them that they were helpless, and that the wise part was to attempt no resistance.

They obeyed grudgingly. John Hamilton issued curt orders. Delaney lay where he had fallen, his gun clenched in both hands, his dying face grim with determination. And the outlaws obediently stepped forward, one by one, obediently turned their backs, kneeled, and folded their hands behind them, and each was bound securely by Mary Hamilton. They threatened wild vengeance during that time of humiliation. Only Jack Doyle himself had remained cool and unperturbed, and had whipped his followers into silence and obedience with his tongue.

Accordingly he was the last to be bound, and, before the rope was fastened about his wrists, he was ordered to help Mary with the burden of Delaney. Together, under the gun of Hamilton, they lifted the wounded man into the wagon, Doyle making no attempt to escape to cover. And later, under the cover of Mary's revolver, Doyle, unaided, carried Hamilton to the wagon and laid him tenderly on a bed of straw.

"For his muscles ain't muscles . . . they're India rubber," Hamilton said. "He handled me like I was no heavier than a girl. He did that for a fact."

But the problem was still a knotty one. They

could not remain in this camp with Delaney dying, Hamilton wounded and liable to become feverish at any time, and therefore helpless, and one girl to guard and tend ten men. For every reason they had to get to the nearest habitation, and the nearest place was Cayuse.

But here again it was easier to name the thing than to do it. If eight strong men were placed in the wagon, bound, who would guard them, and also drive the team of horses? And if they were placed in the wagon—an additional burden of fifteen hundred pounds and more—would not the two horses be taxed to the limit of their strength?

There was only one young girl to handle eight men, bound indeed, but each of them desperate, and each willing to risk his life for freedom. For if they arrived in Cayuse, the mob would not wait for the law to take its course. It was the dying Delaney who suggested the only possible course that would start them toward Cayuse, and at the same time keep all the eight men under the eye of the girl. It was Delaney who proposed that they harness the eight men to the chain of the wagon and let the horses be led behind.

They discussed the plan urgently and briefly, for whatever they did, they had to do with speed. At length they decided that though the progress toward Cayuse by man power would be slow, yet the labor would serve to wear down the strength of the eight until they would shortly be past the point of offering any dangerous and concerted move. And above all it was necessary to keep them from an outbreak. Besides, though they might not pick up anyone during the night, it was more than probable that early the next morning some freighter up Silver Cañon would overtake them, and then their troubles would end.

In this discussion Delaney took the weightiest part, for his words had the force of one about to die, and the selfless, kindly Irishman had the pleasure of seeing his murderers harnessed to the wagon that was to draw him to Cayuse and draw them into the power of the law. Altogether, the plan was not without a neatly ironic side.

The outlaws at least felt that side of it. At first, though they could not refuse the urge of the girl's revolver prodding their ribs, they would not take a step forward. Even the voice of Doyle, trembling with passion but submitting to the inevitable, could not stir them. Until Mary Hamilton took out the long whip and sent the lash singing and cracking above their heads. She did not touch them with it, but the horror of the lash was sufficient. Under its flying shade they winced and then buckled to their work with a venomous lurch that shot the wagon forward.

The load was light for the broad wheels ate very slightly into the sand, rather packing it like the hoofs of a camel than cutting it like the hoofs of a horse, and the eight men found their labor easy enough. For the first hour they expended their spare breath in wild threats and volleys of curses. They cursed the girl who tormented them in the driver's seat of the wagon. They cursed themselves. They cursed their luck. They cursed gold. They cursed even the leader who had brought them to this pass.

Eventually the work grew keener, and the burden, which they had hardly noticed at first, now began to tell on them. They took shorter and shorter steps and began to move with a rhythm, leaning forward and swaying like a team of horses. And the spare breath was now gone. The dragging of the wagon burned out their throats and kept them silent. Once, in a futile outburst of rage, they turned and rushed about the wagon, gibbering at the girl, but their hands were still tied behind them, and the compelling point of the revolver sent them back to their places. They went, groaning at their impotence.

Night fell on the wagon moving forward by fits and starts in a dreadful silence far more terrible than the air of blasphemy through which it had moved at first. Sitting on her seat, Mary heard the death rattle of Delaney and ran back to him too late to hear his last words.

And later still, she was horrified by the voice of her father speaking to the dead man beside him. She lit a lantern and spoke to him, but he turned on her glassy, blank eyes. The fever had reached his head, and he was mad with delirium. So she put out the lantern again and went back to her place. There she crouched, never daring to take her eyes off the swaying line of eight who struggled before her, the dead man behind her, the madman close at her side.

Finally her father no longer spoke aloud, but his voice was an insidious whisper hissing into the darkness. And all over Silver Cañon was the ghostly moon.

In this formation they had passed Lew Carney. The girl did not see him, for she was sitting far back in the wagon. No wonder that the eight harnessed men did not speak to him, for he would have been one more enemy to keep them in hand.

But they plodded on interminably until a haze grew up the valley, and then the sandstorm struck them. Against it there was no possibility of pulling the wagon. Huddled together, the eight were a miserable group whipped by the flying dust.

Here the great calamity happened, for her father, rolling a cigarette in his delirium, managed to light a match in spite of the wind, but only to have the sulphur head fall among the straw that littered and piled the floor of the wagon. The blaze darted up at once, and the wind tossed it the length of the wagon in a breathing space. Her father began laughing wildly at the blaze. Through the darkness it lit the dead face and the living eyes of Delaney, and outside in the storm the eight men yelled with joy for they knew that their time had come.

There was no other way. She could not handle the weight of her father, and therefore she went to Doyle, cut his bonds, and forced him at the point of her revolver to drag out the body of Delaney and the living form of her father. He obeyed without a word, but when he had done his work, in the rush of sand, he took her unguarded and mastered her weapon hand. A moment later all eight were loosed, and the victors were again the vanquished.

Meanwhile the wagon burned furiously. Some of the eight were for throwing Hamilton back into the blaze along with Delaney, to burn away all traces of their crimes. But when their leader assured them that there was not nearly enough of a conflagration to consume the bodies, they gave up that vengeance. They would have worked some harm to the girl, also. They would have driven her with whips as she had driven them, but here again the leader interfered. He had been singularly gentle with Mary from the first and now he stood staunchly by her.

A can of oil overturned in the body of the wagon and the work of the fire was now quickly completed. Literally under her eyes Mary Hamilton saw the vehicle melt away, while the outlaws piled what loot they had rescued on the two horses.

A sharp altercation followed. For the seven

insisted that John Hamilton be left to die in the storm where he lay, but once more the will of the leader prevailed. He made them take the wounded man in an improvised litter between the two animals. He himself rode one, and Mary rode the other, and so this strange procession started away toward the southern hills.

Behind them they left the iron skeleton of the wagon, already covered by the blowing sand. And so the mystery of the ghost wagon was explained. As for the revolver in the hand of Delaney, it had been placed there on impulse by the ironically chivalrous Jack Doyle—a tribute from one fighting man to another, as he had said afterward.

They found the shack by Coyote Springs after a march that brought terrible suffering to John Hamilton. Once there the gang insisted on an immediate return to loot the mine and recover their horses. To secure the horses back at the mine, one of the men was dispatched immediately. Another went to Cayuse to buy a second wagon and mules. Jack Doyle, giving way to another of his singularly kindly impulses, agreed to ride into Cayuse with the girl, while she met her brother and warned him away from the useless and dangerous trip into the desert. Doyle had risked his own life and the danger of public recognition to escort her. It was partly for the sake of seeing his financial backer, Bud Lockhart, and partly no doubt for the sake of winning the girl. He had only extracted from her a promise that, while in the town, she would not attempt to enlist any sympathizers, and that she would not speak a word or in any way cast them under a suspicion.

When she met Lew Carney, the whole truth had come tumbling up to her lips, only to be driven back again by a remorseless conscience. One word to him, then, and she and her father could have been easily saved, and the outlaw apprehended by force of numbers. But she stayed with her promise, and, when Doyle found her after his fruitless trip back to Bud Lockhart, she had felt bound in honor to repeat to him every word of her interview with Lew Carney. But Doyle felt assured that Lockhart would take care of the fellow, though, to make matters safe, he made her run her horse with his for the first few miles to outdistance any pursuit among the hills.

Such was the story of the ghost wagon in all its details as Lew Carney gathered it, partly from the girl, mostly from her father.

"And there," John Hamilton said calmly at the conclusion, "is the end of it."

He pointed as he spoke, and Lew Carney saw the gray of the dawn overcoming the moonlight and changing the black mountains to blue.

XI

The three watched in silence.

"There's one thing I can't understand," Lew Carney said at last, "and that's how a man of the caliber of Jack Doyle can stand by and see a helpless man murdered. Why is it? He's played square the rest of the way."

The answer was both terrible and simple. The father raised his arm and pointed to the girl.

"He was pleasant to her as long as he could be," explained John Hamilton. "But on the way back from Cayuse he figured that he'd done enough for her. He asked her then if there was any chance for him to be her friend, as much her friend as she'd let him be. She told him that she could never regard him as anything other than a black murderer. And she threw in a word about Delaney. And since then he's changed. He sees there's no chance with her by fair play, and I think he's ready for foul. And there she stands, free to leave if she will . . . and there she stays, doing me no good . . . an anchor around my neck dragging me down, knowing that I'll suffer double because she stayed with me to the finish. After they finish me . . . Mary . . ."

He choked as he looked at her, and she laid her finger warningly upon her white lips. She was wonderfully steady, and there was no quiver in her voice as she said: "It'll never come to that. Never!" And the two men glanced at each other, for they knew what she meant.

The revel outside rose to a yell of laughter and song. Lew Carney, his heart too full for endurance, went to the front door and looked out. There sat the six. Five of them were doing a veritable Indian war dance around the blaze, and their faces were the faces of madmen. But one man sat with a coat drawn like a cloak around his shoulders. He did not move. He did not glance at the others once. He sat with his knees bunched before him and his hands clasped around them, and Lew Carney knew that his position had not changed for hours. He felt, also, that there was a greater distance between that calm man sitting beside the fire and the wild men who danced around it, than there was between himself, Lew Carney, and the outlaws. While Jack Doyle was one of the band he led, at the same time he was apart from it. A touch of understanding and pity came to Lew Carney: the outlaw had sat there through the night looking on at the debauch with a stony face, never touching the liquor, but eating his heart out with the acid thought of the girl. He was not with the rest no matter if they rubbed his shoulders. And in that quiet, sitting figure there was strength greater than the strength of all the others combined, a controlling strength, no matter how they raved.

It was this last conclusion that gave the idea to Lew Carney. He turned and went hastily back to the room.

"Go to the front of the shack," he said to Mary Hamilton, "and call in Doyle. Don't ask any questions. This is the last chance for all of us, and I'm going to take it."

Instead of immediately obeying, she stood for a moment looking at him, her head held high. He would have thought that she was smiling if her eyes had not been bright with tears. But that look stayed with him to the day of his death.

Then she went to the front of the house, and they heard her calling.

"What is it?" asked John Hamilton. "Are you going to try to do for Jack Doyle alone? No use, Carney. There's too many of 'em. They'd only have to touch a match to the house, and . . . there's the end."

They heard the girl coming back and the tread of a man moving with a soft, long step behind her. In a moment she was back in the room, and Jack Doyle, entering with her, was met by a soft call from the side. He did not turn. He seemed to see through the side of his head the leveled gun of Lew Carney, but he kept his glance steadily on the girl, and his face was working. She had turned toward him with a faint cry and now she shrank away, frightened by his expression.

"But now that you have him," John Hamilton

said in a disgusted tone, "what are you going to do with him? Eat him?"

"I'm going to use him," Lew Carney advised, "to lick seven skunks into shape for us. That's what I'll do with him."

For the first time the outlaw turned toward Lew Carney, and Lew felt as though a pair of lights had focused on him. Once before he had felt fear. It was when the ghost wagon crawled up Silver Cañon. He felt it again looking straight into the eyes of Jack Doyle. For the fellow escaped classification. One could not say of him "good" or "bad". If the eyes of Lew Carney sometimes flamed with mirth or hate, these eyes of Jack Doyle had a property of phosphorus. They seemed self-luminous. He turned to the girl again.

"Is this your idea?" he asked.

She shook her head.

"Well?" he repeated to Lew Carney.

"Yes," nodded the other, "it's my idea. Now, watch yourself, Doyle. I've an eye on every move you make. I'm reading your mind. These folks didn't see any way of using you, but I do. There's only one way we can get loose from this shack, and that's by having you call off your pack of biting dogs. And you're going to do it, Doyle. Why? Because if you don't, I'll blow your head off. Is that all straight? Yes?"

"You want me to talk to 'em while you keep me covered with a gun?"

"No. Give us your word that you'll do what you can to make your men pull away, and you're free to turn around and leave the room."

The outlaw flushed and paled in quick succession. "I give you my word," he said without effort.

"Wait," murmured Lew Carney. "Don't give your word to me. Give it to Mary Hamilton. She'll be glad to hear you talk, I think."

"Curse you," whispered the leader through his teeth.

He turned slowly to the girl. Standing back against the far wall of the room, with the shadow across her face, she put her hand behind her to get support. She trembled when the look of Doyle fell on her, and Lew Carney saw her eyes shift and glow in the shadow. He knew then that the outlaw had once inspired something more than fear and horror in her. He could see Doyle standing on tiptoe like a leashed dog, straining with all the force of will and mind toward her, and Carney knew that the fellow had at least had grounds for hope, that he was fighting for the last time to regain that hope, and that he read in the whitening face of the girl the end of his chance.

At last—and it all happened in the gruesome silence—he looked across from her to Lew Carney, and the fingers of Lew Carney shuddered on the handles of his gun. He knew why this one man could tame the seven, wild as they might be.

Doyle looked back to the girl. "I give you my word," he said quietly, and he turned away.

"Wait!" called John Hamilton. "Are you going to trust to the bare word of a . . . ?"

But Lew Carney raised his hand and checked the father. He did more. He restored his revolver to its holster. And Doyle stepped close to him. He spoke softly and rapidly in such a guarded voice that no one else could hear the murmured words.

"You win," he said. "You've made a pretty play. You've got her. But as sure as there's a moon in the sky, I'll come back to you. I'll smash you as you've smashed me. You're free now. But count your days, Carney. Drink fast. You pay me the reckoning for everything."

He was gone through the door, and his soft, swift step crossed the outer room. They heard the voices of the seven raised beyond the house. They heard one calm voice giving answer. Before the dawn broke, the eight men were gone miraculously and all the danger passed with them.

When the last sounds died away, Lew Carney turned to the girl, and she let him take her hand. But her face was hidden in her other arm, and to the end of his life Lew Carney was never to know whether she wept for sheer relief and happiness or because of Jack Doyle.

And this was how Lew Carney came over to the side of the law and reached the end of the trail of the ghost wagon.

About the Author

Max Brand is the best-known pen name of Frederick Faust, creator of Dr. Kildare, Destry, and many other fictional characters popular with readers and viewers worldwide. Faust wrote for a variety of audiences in many genres. His enormous output, totaling approximately thirty million words or the equivalent of five hundred thirty ordinary books, covered nearly every field: crime, fantasy, historical romance, espionage, Westerns, science fiction, adventure, animal stories, love, war, and fashionable society, big business and big medicine. Eighty motion pictures have been based on his work along with many radio and television programs. For good measure he also published four volumes of poetry. Perhaps no other author has reached more people in more different ways.

Born in Seattle in 1892, orphaned early, Faust grew up in the rural San Joaquin Valley of California. At Berkeley he became a student rebel and one-man literary movement, contributing prodigiously to all campus publications. Denied a degree because of unconventional conduct, he embarked on a series of adventures culminating in New York City where, after a period of near starvation, he received simultaneous recognition as a serious poet and successful author of fiction.

Later, he traveled widely, making his home in New York, then in Florence, and finally in Los Angeles.

Once the United States entered the Second World War, Faust abandoned his lucrative writing career and his work as a screenwriter to serve as a war correspondent with the infantry in Italy, despite his fifty-one years and a bad heart. He was killed during a night attack on a hilltop village held by the German army. New books based on magazine serials or unpublished manuscripts or restored versions continue to appear so that, alive or dead, he has averaged a new book every four months for seventy-five years. Beyond this, some work by him is newly reprinted every week of every year in one or another format somewhere in the world. A great deal more about this author and his work can be found in *The Max Brand Companion* (Greenwood Press, 1997) edited by Jon Tuska and Vicki Piekarski. His Website is www.MaxBrandOnline.com.

Center Point Large Print
600 Brooks Road / PO Box 1
Thorndike, ME 04986-0001 USA

(207) 568-3717

US & Canada:
1 800 929-9108
www.centerpointlargeprint.com